GHOST HAWK

ALSO BY
SUSAN COOPER

The Dark Is Rising Sequence
Over Sea, Under Stone
The Dark Is Rising
Greenwitch
The Grey King
Silver on the Tree

Green Boy
Seaward
Victory
The Boggart
The Boggart and the Monster
King of Shadows
The Magician's Boy
The Silver Cow

GHOST HAWK

SUSAN COOPER

Margaret K. McElderry Books
New York London Toronto Sydney New Delhi

FOR BETTY LEVIN

MARGARET K. McELDERRY BOOKS † An imprint of Simon & Schuster Children's Publishing Division † 1230 Avenue of the Americas, New York, New York 10020 † This book is a work of fiction. Any references to historical events, real people, or real places are used fictitiously. Other names, characters, places, and events are products of the author's imagination, and any resemblance to actual places or persons, living or dead, is entirely coincidental. † Text copyright © 2013 by Susan Cooper † Cover illustration © 2013 by Alejandro Colucci † All rights reserved, including the right of reproduction in whole or in part in any form. † MARGARET K. McELDERRY BOOKS is a trademark of Simon & Schuster, Inc. † For information about special discounts for bulk purchases, please contact Simon & Schuster Special Sales at 1-866-506-1949 or business@simonandschuster.com. † The Simon & Schuster Speakers Bureau can bring authors to your live event. For more information or to book an event, contact the Simon & Schuster Speakers Bureau at 1-866-248-3049 or visit our website at www.simonspeakers.com. † Also available in a Margaret K. McElderry Books hardcover edition † The text for this book is set in Palatino LT. † Manufactured in the United States of America † 0715 OFF † 10 9 8 7 6 5 4 3 † First Margaret K. McElderry Books paperback edition August 2014 † The Library of Congress has cataloged the hardcover edition as follows: Cooper, Susan, 1935– † Ghost Hawk / Susan Cooper.—1st ed. † p. cm. † Summary: At the end of a winter-long journey into manhood, Little Hawk returns to find his village decimated by a white man's plague and soon, despite a fresh start, Little Hawk dies violently but his spirit remains trapped, seeing how his world changes. † ISBN 978-1-4424-8141-1 (hardcover) ISBN 978-1-4424-8143-5 (eBook) [1. Coming of age—Fiction. 2. Wampanoag Indians—Fiction. 3. Indians of North America—Massachusetts—Fiction. 4. Ghosts—Fiction. 5. Survival—Fiction. 6. Massachusetts—History—New Plymouth, 1620–1691—Fiction.] I. Title. † PZ7.C7878Gho 2013 † [Fic]—dc23 2012039892 † ISBN 978-1-4424-8142-8 (pbk)

New Hampshire

North Atlantic Ocean

NAUMKEAG

Salem °

Massachusetts

Boston °   *Massachusetts Bay*

MASSACHUSETT

Marshfield °

Plymouth °   *Cape Cod Bay*

NARRAGANSET

POKANOKET
(WAMPANOAG NATION)

Providence

Rhode Island

Sowams °

Mt. Hope °

NAUSET

Buzzards Bay

Nantucket Sound

Rhode Island Sound

MARTHA'S VINEYARD

NANTUCKET

N
W   E
S

Boston °	Important settlement
NAUSET	Native American tribe
Massachusetts	Present-day States
··········	Present-day boundaries

0 ___ 20 mi
0 ___ 20 km

Map copyright © 2013 Springer Cartographics LLC

Boast not proud English, of thy birth & blood
Thy brother Indian is by birth as Good.
Of one blood God made Him, and Thee and All.
As wise, as faire, as strong, as personall.

ROGER WILLIAMS, 1643

This land is your land, this land is my land
From California to the New York Island,
From the Redwood Forest to the Gulf Stream waters,
This land was made for you and me.

WOODY GUTHRIE, 1944

PART ONE

FREEZING MOON

O N E

He had left his canoe in the river, tied to a branch of a low-growing cherry tree. Now there was green marsh-land ahead of him, all round the river's last slow curve. He pushed his way through waist-high grass toward one of the three high places in the marshland, where trees grew. They were islands of trees, never visited; the duck hunters went only to the marsh. He had chosen this place months ago, and now was the day to come back.

In a squawking flurry two ducks erupted ahead of him, flying low, but his bow stayed on his back; he would not hunt till later, on the way home. He reached the trees— a tangle of pin oak and cherry, sumac and hickory, juniper and birch—and threaded his way through the grabbing branches to the two rocks that marked the tree he had chosen. There it still was, beside the rocks, still the proper shape: the small bitternut hickory tree with its twin leading stems growing in a slender V.

He gave the tree a respectful greeting, and explained what he was about to do.

The woven birch-bark pouch was heavy round his neck. He took out the stone blade, a long, notched rectangle of flint with one edge chipped to a fine sharpness. This blade had belonged to the tomahawk used by his father and his grandfather, until its handle broke; nobody knew where it had come from or when it was made. It was very precious to him.

Carefully he fitted the blade into the cleft between the tree's two slim branches, twisting them together above it. Then, with tough strands of deer sinew from his pouch, he bound the joined branches tightly above the stone—so tightly that they would grow together as the years went by, enclosing the blade.

To make a tomahawk for your son, you needed the stone blade, and the wooden shaft, and time.

In my father's day, there was still time.

When he'd finished his binding, he thanked the small tree, and gave it good wishes to grow straight and strong.

Then he went back across the marshland to his canoe. On the way he shot three ducks, for the feast celebrating the arrival of the baby son who had been born early that day.

I was that son. Because Flying Hawk was my father, the name they were giving me was Little Hawk.

T W O

Eleven winters later, my father Flying Hawk took me to the bitternut hickory tree on the marshland. It was a longer journey than it had been for him before, because a year later our village had moved on. All the goodness of the land where it stood had been used up, by our years of growing crops on the fields, and the time had come to give the land back to the trees who would replenish it. This is the way of things.

So the crops had been harvested and packed into baskets, corn and squash and beans, and one by one the houses of elm-bark shingles and woven birch-bark matting had been taken apart. Everyone had carried the shingles and mats a long way through the forest to the new land that the men had been burning and clearing since spring, and poles had been set in the ground to make new frames for the houses.

This was home—the only one I could remember. Though

hunting or fishing would take us away in their seasons, this was now the place to which we always returned—until, once more, the time would come for us all to move on.

From here the marsh had to be reached on foot, and that took my father and me three days. But when after all our walking we came out of the woods to the open marshland, I could hear the distant breathing of the sea. And across the waving grass—fading now from green to gold—I could see the three islands my father had described to me. They were three dark hummocks of woodland, in this flat bird-haunted elbow of almost-land that the river made on its winding way to the sea.

My father headed for the smallest island, zigzagging on clumps of grass so that our moccasins would stay dry.

"We were out here on a hunt, before you were born," he said. "I saw the small bitternut then. It was already a toma-hawk tree."

A tomahawk tree is a sapling with that double shoot, the two leading branches that can—with help—become one.

"If I wasn't born yet," I said, daring, "you didn't know I would be a boy. I might have been a girl."

He said quietly, "I knew."

And I saw the bitternut hickory, beside its two rocks. It was a tall tree now, twice the height of a man. The stone blade stuck out on both sides of the slender trunk, a little way below the branches; it was as deep in the wood as if it were a natural part of the tree. It had been there as long as I had been alive.

There was an odd feeling in my throat as I looked at it, like pain and happiness mixed together, and I did what my father had instructed me to do. I said to the tree, "Thank you, my brother."

My father's hand rested on my shoulder for a moment, and then he took some tobacco from the pouch at his belt and put it on the ground as a gift to the spirit of the tree. And he too thanked the hickory, and gave apologies for what we had to do.

Then he took out his own axe and cut down the tree. Because it was green wood, the trunk was tough, but before long he had trimmed it down to the first unfinished shape of the tomahawk that he and the tree had begun for me the day I was born. At home, by the time it was finished and perfect, winter would be here.

That was when I would be taken deep into the woods, blindfolded, for the three-month test of solitude that would turn me into a man. This tomahawk would be one of the very few things I could take with me, to help me stay alive.

THREE

When my proving time came, snow lay on the round roofs of all the homes in our village, and the ground and all the forest trees were white. You were truly a man if you could manage to survive alone, out in the forest, in the darkest part of the year, when most living things on the earth die or sleep, and the cold rules all.

This was also the sacred time when you would be given a vision of the spirit who would guide your life: your Manitou.

All through the summer and fall my father had been rehearsing me in the ways of trapping and hunting that I had watched since I was a very small boy. My mother had been teaching me to cook and to sew, skills that my sisters seemed to have by nature, and my grandmother had methodically made me show her all the plants, seeds, and roots in the woods that could be used or eaten. All our lives we had been learning these things from her, but this time one of them could decide whether I lived or died.

Four boys from our village would be taken out, this winter: Leaping Turtle, White Oak, Spring Frog, and me. We had been talking about it, planning for it, as far back as we could remember. Now that it was really going to happen, there was much less talk. I knew that although nobody would admit it, each of the others was feeling, like me, a coldness at the pit of his stomach when he thought about the moment of being left alone.

The sun went into the trees early, this short winter day. Inside our house in the warmth from the fire pit, I looked down at my sleeping mat, where my mother had set out a little row of things to go with me. There was a skein of sinew thread, and a special stone for making fire; a small skin pot for cooking; the bone awl that my grandfather had made, in its little case of bone. My bow, and the quiver with twelve arrows. And my tomahawk. Privately I thought that these last three were the only things I should be allowed to take, but I didn't argue.

My sister Quickbird came in from outside, carrying a pot packed full of ice and snow. She pulled off the skin draped over her head, and shook it near the entrance. Then she peered at my collection.

"Needles," she said. "For goodness' sake—you have thread and no needles. Boys have no sense."

My mother clicked her tongue reprovingly, bending to put the pot beside the fire. The baby was bound to her chest, fast asleep.

"Hah," said Quickbird.

"I have three needles for him," my mother said. "Show respect."

Quickbird had the sense to hold her tongue, but I heard the very small snorting sound she made. She was my younger sister, only a winter younger than me; we grew up together, and the older we grew, the more she wished to be a boy. Whenever she bragged about her skill at girl things—sewing, planting, cooking—I knew it was to hide her longing to learn instead to hunt and fish and track with our father, like me. She was totally unlike our older sister, Southern, who was as peaceful and gentle as our mother.

Southern wasn't there; she had gone to the women's house, because she had her moontime bleeding and that was when women stay separate. She had managed to give me a hug before she went.

"Come back safe," she said.

I knew she was remembering the time four winters ago, when the boys who had been her playmates had been sent out one by one for their lonely testing time. The boy who was her favorite never came back, and it was a long time before they found what was left of his body.

My mother reached into a bag hanging from the wall and put a small fold of doeskin on my mat. "There," she said.

Inside the fold, stuck into the skin, were three tiny strong bones from a bird or an animal, each with a hole bored in the blunter end.

"Beautiful," I said. "Thank you, Mother. But are you sure—"

"Don't lose them," Quickbird said. "Keep them all together. Like this." She picked up the doeskin fold and the loop of sinew thread, wound the thread round the doeskin, and tucked the tiny package into the top of my belt. She gave me her quick brilliant smile. Then it vanished.

"Moccasins!" she said. "You forgot the most important thing: spare moccasins! I know where they are."

She dived into the shadows behind her sleeping platform at the back of the house. I wondered if she was right. On hunting trips in winter, my father did indeed make sure always that we had extra foot coverings with us. Walking in snow without moccasins, your feet will freeze, and you will die.

A wave of cold air washed over us and my father came in, turning to make sure the entry mat was closed behind him. He straightened up, and shook snow from his head. The tiny flakes dropped in a shower, melting as they fell.

He looked down at the things set out on my sleeping mat, which was right in front of him, and he frowned. He was a tall, fine man, my father, with a brow and nose as strong as a cliff, and a frown on his face was an alarming thing to see.

"What is this?" he said.

Quickbird was back with the extra moccasins; she put them down beside the rest and smiled up at him. I sometimes felt she was the only person in the world who was never afraid of my father.

"For Little Hawk when he goes," she said.

My father ignored her; he was looking directly at our mother. It was a terrible look, and I felt suddenly cold.

"What can you be thinking?" he said. "Have you lost your senses? You know how it must be."

My mother was as strong as him, in her way, and she looked right back at him, chin up. Wrapped against her chest, our baby brother gave a little sleepy sigh.

"I have one grown son," my mother said.

"I too," said my father. "And he will go out into the winter as all sons do, with a bow, an axe, and a knife. Those things only. And he will come back a man."

They were staring at each other as if they were enemies. Quickbird had been standing still as a rock beside me, holding the forbidden moccasins, but I felt her shift very gently until her shoulder was touching my arm. I lifted my hand just enough to rest my palm briefly against her back, for comfort—and with the other hand I took out the little pack of needles and thread that she had tucked into my belt, and quietly gave it back to her.

My mother said nothing.

"Come, Little Hawk," my father said. "It is time to go to the sweat lodge."

He turned back to the entrance, and after a quick glance at my mother's rigid face, I followed him. There was nothing else I could do.

Outside, the houses were glimmering white shapes in the winter twilight; snow was drifting slowly down, and there was no moon. The snow had come early that year;

our elders said it would be a hard winter. Two dogs lying huddled against the wall of a longhouse stirred hopefully as we passed, but my father hissed at them and they lay still.

Smoke was billowing from the hole in the roof of the sweat lodge. The land sloped upward here, and the lodge had been built into the slope so that half of it was under the earth. Like our house, it was made of heavy bark shingles and reed mats on a sapling frame, but it was much bigger. The lodge was not a house but a center for cleansing and special rituals—like this one, the final sweat for the boys who would go out the next morning on their quest for manhood. We would sit naked in the hot steam. We often did this, whole families together, but this time we would sweat out not only the dirt on our bodies but also the fears in our minds.

And tonight the sweat lodge was only for the men. The women had special places of their own too, like the house where my sister would stay until she stopped menstruating that moon, and where she would be if she were having a baby. It is the way things are.

At the entry to the sweat lodge my father and I dropped our clothes, then we went in. The air was thick with heat and steam and smoke, from the fire pit where water had been poured onto heated rocks; it was like walking into a barrier, except that the barrier was the air you breathed. Through the steam I saw a blur of naked bodies shining with sweat, and I heard deep voices greet my father. Then a damp hand grabbed my arm.

"Hawk—here."

It was my friend Leaping Turtle; he pulled me down to sit beside him on the wooden bench with the other boys, White Oak and Spring Frog. We had grown up together, he and I—done all our learning together, from the day we strung our first small bows to the stretch of nine moons in which patient, wise old Running Deer led us through the transformation of a live growing birch tree into a small, light birch-bark canoe. That was a magical time, perhaps the best of my life. But neither of us would take our canoe on the solitary journey that waited for us the next day.

"Can't breathe!" I whispered to Leaping Turtle.

Complaints were strictly forbidden; our fathers would never say such a thing.

He hissed back, "You'll die out there anyway!"

Jokes about serious things were even more unthinkable; if anybody had heard that, we'd both have been banished from the sweat lodge and maybe the whole solemn ritual.

We grinned nervously at each other for a private moment—and then we heard a great hissing and we were choking in new clouds of steam, as an elder poured more water on the hot stones. Sweat was running down my forehead and dripping off my eyebrows; it stung my eyes; it made little rivers down my back and chest.

One of the deep voices rose, booming through the steam-filled room, and the ritual of chant and prayers for the departing boys began.

By the time it was all done, my brain was spinning from the noise and the heat and the sense of mystery. They sent us out through the entryway, the four of us boys who in a few hours would be gone from the village, and we dived into the thin layer of snow on the ground and rolled our sweaty bodies in its wonderful crunching cold.

Above us the sky was clear of cloud now, and the stars blazed down, countless chips of Manitou fire in the darkness, each star with a human being somewhere in his care. I wondered which one was looking out for me, and hoped he would be paying attention in the morning.

By dawn I was up from my sleeping mat, dressing in my belt and breechclout, tunic and leggings, with my body underneath them already covered in grease like an extra skin, to keep out the winter cold. When I put my moccasins on my feet I could tell that my mother had fitted an extra layer of rabbit fur inside—something she must have done the night before, a secret, defiant gesture, when only Quickbird was there to see.

I took no food or drink that morning, nor would I have any until I could find it for myself. Out there, alone.

This was what we had been taught: that you must go out fasting, and that this first fast couldn't be broken until you were given the vision of your Manitou, the spirit who would go with you all your life. Only then might you hunt for food, to start the long lone survival ordeal. My father said that too long a fast would bring not just a vision but weakness and death, so my Manitou would wisely decide the time when he revealed himself. So did my grandmother, who was the wisest person I knew. I hoped they were right.

Everyone was awake—except my baby brother, tucked into his cradleboard, fast asleep. My mother set a log on what was left of the fire. Her face was stern and unhappy, as it had been the day before. Quickbird came and gave me a silent hug, and I could feel that her cheek was wet.

My father was dressed for our journey. He set my bow beside the door, and put my quiver of arrows across my shoulder and my tomahawk in my belt. I reached for my sharp stone knife in its deerskin casing, but he gripped my wrist to stop me.

He said, "I have a better knife for you to take. It cost me many skins, so you must take care of it. And take care of your fingers, too. It is very sharp."

And he gave me something I'd seen only twice before in my life, in the hands of those who had traveled north to trade with the white men from across the sea. It was a knife made of metal, in a holder of thick hide, moose skin perhaps. The handle was covered in skin too, and the blade was shiny, flat, thin: like the leaf of a bulrush but a thousand times more strong. It was a treasure. I couldn't imagine where he got it.

I was amazed and delighted. And from the look on my mother's face, I could tell not just that she too had never seen this knife before, but that she felt sure it would help me survive.

I said, "Thank you, Flying Hawk. I will keep it as safe as my tomahawk. And I will bring it back to you."

I put the knife in my belt. I was ready. I went to the baby's cradle and touched his smooth round cheek in fare-well. He gave a small sigh but he did not wake. Someday, I thought, all this would be happening to him, too.

We went out into the cold grey morning. My father and I strapped on our snowshoes and put our long bows over our shoulders. My mother kissed me on the forehead and handed my father a scarf of soft doeskin and a long deer-skin strap. I smiled at her, and at Quickbird's anxious face, and they were the last things I saw before my father bound the scarf across my eyes, tying it securely behind my head. Then he put one end of the strap into my hand; this was how he would lead me into the forest.

"You will come back a man," he said.

My mother and Quickbird said together, one voice strong and one small and sad, "You will come back a man."

The strap tightened round my hand, and in my new darkness I followed my father away from home.

We walked, I suppose, for half the short winter day. It was fairly easy at first, once I made myself stride out in confidence that my father wouldn't let me run into any-thing. Because our people had been burning and clearing and farming this land for ten years, there was good space between the trees, free of vines and scrub. Though I was walking in darkness, I could feel the breeze on my face, and hear the chickadees calling and the soft crunch of our feet through the snow.

After a long time branches began to catch in the criss-cross sinews of my snowshoes and in the top of my bow, and gradually my father slowed our pace. We must have reached the wild woods, where men had never yet cleared the land and the new trees grew up through a tangle of old ones that had died and fallen down. The only paths here were those of the deer and the raccoon, the possum and the fox—though even here, now and then, you would find one of the long-distance trails made by the feet of runners taking news of our people from one village to the next.

I could see nothing at all, of course. Splatters of snow fell cold on my face sometimes, from the unseen trees above. My father was holding my arm now, no longer using the strap as a leash. We walked more and more slowly, until finally he stopped. I felt his fingers at the back of my head, and he untied the doeskin scarf covering my eyes.

I blinked in the sudden daylight. There was no sunshine; the woodland was grey and white under the snow.

My father grasped my shoulders with his two hands and looked me in the eyes, his face grave and strong. He said formally, once more, "Come back a man, Little Hawk."

Then he gave me a quick fierce hug and he turned and went away, disappearing into the trees and scrub. I could hear the sound of his snowshoes only for a very short time. Then there was silence, and I was alone.

When I was a little boy, I had always liked being alone in the woods. My father enjoyed telling a story about a spring morning when I was about two winters old; he said I had slipped away from my mother and was not found for the whole of that day. Just before nightfall a search party found me sitting peacefully under a tapped maple tree, with my mouth open to catch the sweet sap dripping from the little hollow sumac stem fitted into a slash in the bark. The birch-bark bucket that had hung under the stem to collect the sap was empty at my side. For some time after that I was called Little Maple, because—they said, making my poor mother cross—I had chosen to be suckled by a tree instead of a woman.

But this time I would be alone for a quarter of the year, and nobody would come looking for me.

Leaping Turtle and I had often discussed the best plan for our first solitary days. We would recite our list to each other. *Before dark comes, find a safe place for the first night. Make fire. Travel. Be ready for your Manitou to find you. Then you must eat, and hunt. Make sure you have made yourself a real camp before the hard snow comes. And look for the sun and the stars when you can, so that you can find your way back home at the end.*

There was no sun in this grey, cold day. I thought about what I would need soon for making fire, and looked round at the bare trees for a slim, straight branch the thickness of my thumb. That was easy; there was a thicket of small maples right next to me.

I chose a tree, asked its pardon for cutting its lowest branch, and for the first time I took out my father's knife. The thin metal blade went through the wood so fast that it flicked out at my wrist as well, and the blood welled up in a neat line on my skin. I sucked at my wrist, amazed. A knife so sharp was going to have to be treated with very great respect.

I trimmed the branch into a stick, dropped it into my quiver to join the arrows, and began picking my way slowly through the trees. All our lives we had been taught to run races with each other, to run fast, fast—but to move always in the woodland as quietly as fox or deer. There were no sounds of life anywhere, and no animal tracks on the snow.

After a while the land rose and became rocky, and it was harder to find spaces for my snowshoes. I took a long, awkward step forward—and fell headlong over a steep ledge, down through a mass of vines masked by snow.

For a moment I lay there, dazed. This was the worst thing that could happen—an accident at the very start. There was pain in my leg, bent by a trapped snowshoe. Was it broken? The other snowshoe was gone. Something hard was digging into my ribs. When I moved my head, long vicious spines dug into my cheek, and I could feel the blood trickling down.

So I knew I must have fallen into a great tangle of greenbrier, the toughest, prickliest vine in the woods. Nothing can kill greenbrier; it will climb a tall tree in a single season, and a small animal that runs into a really thick tangle can find itself held so fast by the spines that it never gets out. My sister Quickbird had found a little skeleton once, caught in a greenbrier patch near the village, with shreds of grey fur still attached; it might have been a baby rabbit. Even though Quickbird, like all of us, set traps for the rabbits that came after our crops, she had touched the little bones with one finger, and cried.

But I was not a rabbit, and I made myself roll over out of the briers in spite of the sharp spines and the screaming pain in my leg. I took off the snowshoe. Its ash-wood edge was crushed at one side but not broken. Nor was my ankle, I decided when I felt it up and down. I held a handful of snow against it for the pain, and tried not to think about how I might have banged my head against a rock, or caught a greenbrier spine in my eye. My knife had flown out of my belt but was caught in the vines, still in its leather case, and out on the snow I could see my bow and its quiver, the arrows spilling out of it from the force of the fall. My other snowshoe lay there too, its binding still attached.

The hard thing that had been digging into my ribs was my tomahawk. It lay there as if it were waiting for me, and it felt like an old friend in my hand.

I hacked at the greenbrier stems to rescue my knife. Looking up now at the rocky ledge over which I'd fallen, I could see that the vine grew over it like a great snowy curtain—and that against the rock, behind the cascading vine, there seemed to be a dry space. If it was deep enough, perhaps I could shelter there for the night and rest my hurt leg.

Moving faster, I cut away enough of the vines to make

myself a space free of their grabbing prickles, under the overhanging rock. The ground there was soft with dead pine needles, and I could see bits of scat from some small animal—but the scat was old, and there was no sign of a nest. This really could be my first night's shelter, in spite of the greenbrier.

I strapped a snowshoe on my good leg, and tried to keep my weight off my bruised ankle by clutching at trees. Hobbling, I rescued my bow and arrows and set them under the overhang. Then I went scouting round the cluster of pine trees growing on this slope, until I found a big fallen branch that had clearly been there for a long time. I chopped out a piece of it and brought it back, with an armful of dry twigs. Twice more I hobbled out to collect bigger pieces of dry wood, and after that I cut two live branches from the nearest pine tree, shaking the snow from the needles, thanking the tree.

My ankle was hurting so much after all this that I had to drop the branches and sit on a rock, bent over like an old man. But only for a moment. The air was very cold; the grey light was beginning to fade. It was time to make fire.

For now, there was only one way I could do that. I took out the stick I cut from the maple tree, and with the tip of my knife I cut a shallow hole in the piece of old pine wood and set the stick upright in it. Then I crushed some dry pine needles round the stick, held it between the palms of my hands and began rubbing my palms together, to and fro. They had grown very sore before I saw the first curl of smoke, but a flame jumped in the pine dust when I blew on it, and I fed my crackling little fire with small branches, and started to feel warm for the first time since I came out of our house. I also felt very hungry, but I knew there was no chance of finding food here.

Then I remembered the greenbrier that had half-killed me.

In my mind I was a small boy again, back in the spring fields, perched with Leaping Turtle on the rickety wooden platform where we were posted to scare the birds away from the new-planted seeds. And my grandmother Suncatcher came out into the field with a basket and her digging stick, and called to us.

"Come down, little ones! Time for learning!"

Having been trusted with work by our fathers, we didn't take kindly to being called little.

"We have duties, Grandmother!" we shouted importantly. "We have to keep the birds off!"

Suncatcher snorted. "And do you see a single bird in this field while I am here? *Come down!*"

And she led us to the enormous stand of spiny greenbrier that was kept at bay around a big dead elm tree near our planting, and showed us two things: how to pick its new shoots as a sweet green vegetable, and how to dig its roots.

But now, just as the water came into my mouth from thinking about roasting greenbrier roots in my fire, I remembered the rules. I was fasting. I couldn't eat, not until my Manitou showed himself to me. It was almost as hard a disappointment as falling off the ledge.

All the same, in winter food must be taken when you see it, even if it is kept for later days. The ground was not quite frozen yet here under the trees, so with my tomahawk I dug up some small greenbrier roots, the size of my finger, and dropped them into my quiver with the arrows. There were a lot of pine tree roots too; they were very thin but tough, and I should need them to make snares. I teased them carefully out with the axe head and tucked them inside my tunic in a long bunch, to keep them from drying out.

My fire was a dwindling glimmer in the black night. High up, through a narrow gap in the trees, I could see one bright star. There was no breeze, and the thin line of smoke from my fire rose straight up toward the star. Since I had no water to drink, I sucked some snow. I went a little way off to relieve myself; I came back and banked up my fire with wood and dirt. Then I curled up on my pine branches under the rock overhang and I went to sleep.

I had been so busy thinking about how to stay alive that it hadn't yet occurred to me to feel lonely, or afraid.

FOUR

I woke just after dawn, out of a dream about my grandmother Suncatcher. In the dream I must have been very
small, because she was singing to me, though the song
drifted away before I could trap it. Lying there half awake,
I tried to send my thoughts to her. My grandmother is a
strong, special person, a member of the tribal council and
the center of our family. I wished she had been there on my
last day, but she had gone to the women's house with my
sister Southern. Before she left, she gave me her blessing
and she kissed me on the forehead, and she said, "You will
see me first when you return, Little Hawk."

Though it had seemed an odd thing to say, since she
knew how much I would be longing to see my parents and
my sisters, I had said yes, of course I would do that.

But return was a long way off: three moons from now.
I stretched, on my bumpy pine-bough bed. I was cold and

very stiff, and my fire was dead, but I beat myself with my arms for warmth. The strands of pine root fell out of my tunic, so I braided them into a long string and tied it round my waist, to keep it safe.

It was a grey day again; the sky above the treetops was full of cloud. I kicked away the ashes of my fire and strapped on my snowshoes. My ankle ached, but it was much less painful than the night before.

Blindly I set off through the trees and snow, with nothing to tell me which direction to take. All the world around me was cold and silent and empty, as if it would never change. A few flakes of snow began to drift down through the branches. I found myself longing suddenly for the warmth of our firelit house, with my mother grinding corn, singing a soft rhythmic song to match each thump as the pestle came down on the mortar. I made pictures in my head of my sisters separating deer sinew into threads, my father carving a burl from an oak tree into a bowl. I could smell a stew simmering in a pot on the rocks beside the fire, with deer meat in it and groundnuts and corn and beans. . . .

I tripped over a tree root and fell headfirst into the snow. When I got up, brushing off snow and leaves, my eye caught a movement somewhere ahead through the trees, and I froze. Was it a deer? As my hand tensed to reach for my bow, I remembered regretfully that I couldn't yet hunt.

But it wasn't a deer—it was my friend Leaping Turtle, walking purposefully, carrying a large branch. My heart leapt at the sight of him, and I shouted in delight. Happiness washed over me in a great wave—and then in the same moment vanished.

The rules said that we were not allowed to speak.

Leaping Turtle stopped as he saw me. Our eyes met, and on his face I could see the same quick anguished mix of feelings. We could not greet each other or even make any sign, let alone share our ordeal. The road to manhood had to be taken alone. We had to live as our fathers and our ancestors lived; we had to obey the law.

So each of us went past the other, on through the trees, alone, away. It was the hardest thing I have ever done. The drifting snowflakes were cold on my face. I could hear the soft sound of my snowshoes moving through the snow. I stopped for a moment and strained for the sound of Leaping Turtle's feet moving away too, but I could hear nothing.

Sorrow made a great lump in my throat, but I walked on. On and on, up slopes and down slippery rocks. All that day I walked, until the light began to die. No birds sang. The snow had stopped falling; the air was colder than before. Before night fell, I found a low-hanging tree and made a nest for myself as I had done before.

Day after day I walked on through the trees in the grey light, with no idea where I was going. I was cold all the time. It was so long since I had eaten that I was hardly aware of hunger, but I could feel myself growing weaker. I sucked handfuls of snow often, because water was allowed. Over and over again I thought about Leaping Turtle and wondered what he was doing, and whether we should ever see each other again.

Each night I found myself a place to sleep and made a fire to keep myself from freezing. And I would sit by the fire for a long time, staring at the small flames, trying to empty my mind so that the Great Spirit could send me my Manitou. But nothing came.

Then there was a day when snow began to fall again, slow but persistent. My heart sank. I had hoped to reach a place where I could build myself some kind of real shelter before the big snows came, but I had found nowhere yet. The day was perhaps half done.

The snow kept falling. I reached a place where two big trees leaned together, and began yet again the long process of collecting firewood and green cedar branches. I cut bigger branches as well this time, to fit between the tree trunks like a kind of roof. Far away, very faint, I could hear wolves howling; it was like a warning. By the time I had a fire, darkness was all around my little flame-lit space.

By now the snowflakes were coming very thick and very fast. They hissed as they fell on the flames. Reluctantly I pushed dirt over the fire and pulled more branches around my little space. The air was so still that they stayed where they were, and in no time at all the snow had covered them, fat white flakes falling silently, softly, relentlessly, on and on. There was no sound anywhere.

This would be a big snow, and it would take a long time.

I curled up beside my bow and my quiver of arrows, and because I was dog tired, I fell asleep.

When I woke, after what must have been a long time, there was a faint whiteness outside the branches covering me, and they were closer to my face than they had been before. Something told me not to move. Nothing was wrong with my curled-up body, warm with its own heat, and for once the air was not icy as I breathed it into my chest. But fear crept through me. What had happened outside?

Moving just one arm as I lay there, I pulled an arrow from my quiver and pushed it out in front of me. It disappeared into thick, thick snow. I churned it round a little, to make a small hole so that I could see out. I was inside a snowbank, and the snow was still falling out there, in big silent flakes. If I were to break out of this tiny oppressive space, new snow would cover me before I walked even a few steps.

I fought with myself to lie still. I tried to guess what my father or my grandmother Suncatcher would say to me, but thinking of them only made me lonelier. I was afraid.

The thoughts ran around my mind like ants. I was totally alone, trapped in this cold snow-buried winter. I had failed to find my Manitou. Perhaps I was not worthy even to have a Manitou. I couldn't go home. I should die like Southern's friend who never came back from the woods, whose body was found many moons later half-eaten by animals. I should never see my family again.

A great snorting sob came out of me, though a man does

not cry and a man does not show weakness, ever. For a few moments I pressed my face into the cedar branches and I howled like a coyote. Outside, the snow came silently down and down, burying me deeper, and I drove myself into a kind of trance of despair.

I had never known how my Manitou would come to me, but I never expected it to come as a comfort for shame. They had taught me that you can earn your revelation only by fasting or by bravery, by heroism. They were wrong.

He came as a great osprey—a fish hawk, the bird we see only in summer—and he swooped over me with the spread feathers of his broad wing brushing my face, in my mind. He called to me, and his voice sang like the throb of a drum.

"Stop this," he said. "Stop this at once. You are Little Hawk, given life on this earth. You will keep yourself alive."

"I can't," I said wretchedly. "I can't. I've failed."

"I will show you your strength," said my Manitou. "Come. Come."

And I was flying with him, up into the grey-white sky, swooping down over the snow-mounded treetops. The snow was no longer falling, the clouds had taken shape—towering, churning clouds full of winter, with a break in the eastern sky where the sun was beginning to glimmer through.

My arms were wings; I lay on the wind. I followed my Manitou as he banked and turned. Far below us I could see the sea.

He said many things to me, that I may not tell to you. Nobody may share the heart of a man's vision of his Manitou. He spoke to me for a long time, high up over the winter world, and then he showed me that my vision was, for now, at an end.

"Remember," he said. "You are Little Hawk, and with my help there is nothing you cannot do. Say it."

"There is nothing I cannot do," I said. "With your help."

I knew it was true. I was smiling. I could feel the air all around me as if I were swimming in the sea, held up by the water and the waves.

"Go now," said my Manitou. "Go as one with earth and water and air. Find your way."

His broad wings swept by me, with a noise like the wind in the trees.

Then I was wide awake in my hole in the snowbank, in the cold air, and I was no longer the same person that I had been before.

This was how my Manitou the great fish hawk came, and is still coming. Now and forever, I believe.

The white glow inside my burrow was brighter than before. My arrow was still there, just visible in the wall of snow that had closed over it. I grabbed it, pushing up with my other hand at the pine branch above my head; snow came cascading down, and all at once I was blinking in a white blaze of sunlight. Through the gap, I saw that the wall of snow enclosing me was as wide as my forearm was long.

I shook the snow off my face and hair. Above my head

I heard a short harsh cry, and as I looked up, a red-tailed hawk flew up from a pine tree branch into the blue sky, crying out twice more as he went. I knew at once that my Manitou had sent him, and that I should follow.

He was wheeling slowly overhead, in the way of hawks. I scrambled up, strapped on my snowshoes, and took my knife and my tomahawk, my bow and my quiver. When I stepped out into the feathery snow I sank into it, in spite of the snowshoes.

The hawk flapped away to the west, and was lost behind the tall pine trees. I flurried after him through the deep snow; it was very slow going, and I stumbled and fell often and was soon very wet. Nothing mattered, though, except that I should follow the hawk. I caught another glimpse of him high in the blue sky and I heard the brief faint call.

Then all at once there was more light and sky ahead, and I was out in the sunshine at the edge of a large pond, its frozen surface glaring white with unmarked snow.

Then I saw one mark on the snow. At the far edge of the pond there was a long gash that could only be the new trail of a deer.

F I V E

It was the first moment in my winter journey when I knew in my bones that I should survive. Through the will of the Great Spirit, my Manitou had found me. And though the deer who left that trail might be long gone by now, sooner or later there would be another. I knew that in the end I should return alive to my home, as a man.

I also knew that all of this would be very hard.

The red-tailed hawk had disappeared. The winter sun was halfway up the sky, so there was not much time before cold night would come again. I looked out across the pond. The deer's track vanished over a low, snow-mounded part of the shore, too far away to investigate today. The nearer bank was steep, with big rocks and tall pines. Each rock was twice the height of a man; there was a great pile of them, as if some huge god had tossed down a handful.

I took off my snowshoes and scrambled to the top. I

could see neat rows of small footprints in the snow, the tracks of squirrels lured out of their winter nests by the sunshine, and I could hardly wait to set my traps.

This was a place where I could live. I wished I could show Leaping Turtle.

In the tumble of rocks facing the woods, I found two great slabs leaning together in a way that made a natural shelter. It was like a little cave, with its back to the pond and the wind. There was a musty smell inside, and I wondered nervously whether it was the smell of bear. But a bear would be tucked away somewhere much deeper in the woods at this time of the year, lost in his winter sleep. Perhaps he had paused in here last spring, heading for the coastal rivers and the herring run, when bears and men alike can catch more fish than they can eat.

Excited, I strapped my snowshoes back on and went into the trees, and cut some big pine branches for a roof and a bed. I cut out sections of the thin inside bark of the pine tree too, giving the tree my thanks, and stuffed some in my mouth to chew. Pine bark is not filling, but my empty stomach was comforted. Then I cleared out piles of twigs and stones from the cave-house and I found a treasure. Buried in a corner were a few acorns, saved for the winter by a chipmunk or a squirrel—the perfect bait for a trap.

I grabbed the braided root-strings that were still wrapped round my waist, and with the acorns as bait I set three snares on twigs near the squirrel tracks in the undergrowth.

The light was dying. I was so tired I could hardly move, but my stomach was reminding me of the greenbrier roots in my quiver. So I picked up wood and made a fire, setting the roots in the earth underneath it to cook, and sat there for a while chewing my pine bark. The stars were blazing above the trees, and I could see the line of three stars that my father called the canoe, crossing the river of the sky. Near them, the big star that is a fish in that river was very bright. I wondered if it was the star of my Manitou. I gave thanks to him for coming to me, and I thanked my brothers the trees who were standing above me like a guardian family.

Then I burned my fingers pulling out the charred little roots, and peeled them with my wonderful sharp knife. I ate them very slowly, chewing carefully, eating bites of snow in between, as we had been taught to do when the fast ended. I think the slowness took more willpower than everything else put together. It helped me to pretend that I had food, even though I felt hungrier when I finished than when I began.

When I woke the next morning, sunlight was filtering through the branches, and from somewhere in the trees I could hear the angry chittering of a squirrel. I jumped up and headed for my snares. Two of them were broken, but a squirrel was struggling in the third. He would soon have gnawed himself free, so I smashed him on the head with my tomahawk, fast. He was a fine fat squirrel, with sleek grey fur, after his months of autumn eating to prepare himself for winter. Perhaps I had caught him with one of his own acorns, but he would save me from starving. This is the way of things.

I gathered wood and made a fire right away. Then I thanked the squirrel for becoming my food, and gutted and skinned him with my sharp knife, careful to keep the skin in one piece. While the meat was cooking beside the fire, I scraped the skin as clean as I could and rubbed it with snow—and then burned my fingers again eating roasted squirrel meat. Nothing had ever tasted better in my whole life.

It was a cold day; the surface of the snow had frozen hard overnight. I knew I had to make this cave into the winter nest that would help me survive, so I packed branches into the gaps between the two slabs of its roof, and stamped down the snow outside—making a dance of the stamping, to cheer up my legs as well as my mind. It was a short dance, because the leg I had bruised was not grateful. I dug a proper fire pit, lined with stones that would hold the heat, and I kept up the endless hunt for firewood, dragging a small dead tree toward my home so I could burn it by degrees.

As I reached the rocks, my eye caught a flicker of movement out in the trees. When I looked, it was gone. Then it came again—and I saw a wolf heading toward me. I caught my breath and stood very still.

Perhaps he had smelled my squirrel. He was walking carefully across the frozen surface of the snow. He was a big wolf, but his shaggy grey-white winter coat looked somehow patchy. And he was alone, which was strange; wolves are pack animals.

One of the pine branches in the roof of my cave chose that moment to fall down; it made only a small sound, but that was enough. The wolf jumped, startled, his head up, his ears high. The jump broke the icy crust beneath his hind feet, and he dropped, floundering. In a flurry of glittering snow-mist he turned and ran, high-stepping awkwardly through the deep snow.

I was sorry to see him go. We were always taught to respect the wolves, who never troubled us if we didn't trouble them; all of us shared the same land, and though we were all hunters, there was more than enough food for everyone. But the strange solitary wolf didn't come back.

Before I slept that night, I ate the last few scraps of squirrel meat, nibbling the little bones clean and saving them. I sharpened the end of a leg bone against a rock, so it could be an awl, and then I did something my father might have thought foolish: I took the squirrel skin and with my new awl I made holes along opposite sides of the skin, folded the bottom edge halfway up the rest, and pushed my last piece of braided tree root in and out of the matched holes, joining the sides. Now the skin was a little bag, and I tucked it behind me when I went to sleep. Inside was the squirrel's bushy tail, saved as a toy for my baby brother.

After the squirrel, I caught nothing. Every day my traps were empty or broken, and soon I was back to chewing the bark of the pine tree. I had to find a deer. Old Running Deer, who taught my friends and me to make a canoe, had reminded us always that this great test we went through, as boys becoming men, was really a test of the hunter. At home there were our stores of plants and seeds and fruit to keep us alive through the winter, when the meat and fish ran out. But we boys on the quest for our Manitou, we had no such supplies.

"Out there alone," said Running Deer, "your best chance of staying alive is to kill a deer. For its skin above all. You can feed yourself with a turkey or a rabbit, but when the teeth of winter bite really cold, only the deerskin will be sure to save you from death. Only your arrow, finding a deer."

And he would make us take time every day to practice shooting arrows into a ball of vines that he tossed along the ground, or threw into the air. Then he would set up a stick the height of a deer's shoulder and a finger's breadth wide, and make us shoot at it from all angles.

So every morning now I went to wait on the rocks, where the wind wouldn't take my scent across the ice, and I watched for the deer to come back. The stand of small trees behind the mounded snow across the pond were almost certainly oaks, and that was where the deer tracks I saw had been heading. It had been a good year for acorns; I had helped my sisters collect baskets of them for our mother to boil and wash and grind into flour. Sooner or later the deer would come back to nose about in the snow to find the last lurking acorn. Or so I hoped.

And one day, when I had gone so long without food that I had to force myself to stand, two deer came. I could only just see them, picking their way along the far shore of the pond toward the oak trees.

I waited until they went out of sight, and then I followed them, quick and quiet. From the look of the land, they would come back along the same path.

It was very early morning; the sky was light blue and the air was very cold. I could hear a chickadee calling, but no other bird. I squinted through the sunlight that glared up from the white snow.

And I saw the deer among the oaks, nosing in the snow, two of them, moving slowly. The bigger one was stripping the bark off a sapling, which would die as a result, though the deer of course neither knew that nor cared. The other was only a little smaller, perhaps a grown fawn; if the first was his mother, he was with her for company, not out of need. And he was a better size for me to manage, so he was the one I must kill.

I strung my bow and took out my best arrow, with a very sharp point. I had made all my own arrows, and I knew each of them like a friend. Two more were high in the quiver in case I had to shoot again very fast, though the first shot was the one that mattered. Then I stood at the side of a rock face, silent, downwind of the deer, and I waited.

And waited.

Waiting was a part of the hunt. For years our fathers had taught us how to shift the weight from one foot to the other, how to flex and loosen the sinews in your arms, how to blink regularly so that you can see with clear sight, how to be invisible and still. So I did these things by second nature, even though it was so cold.

It was the doe who came back first along the trail. She walked across the pond below me, and paused. As she stood broadside to me there her whole flank was exposed, and I was aching to let the arrow fly, but still I waited.

The younger one came running down the bank toward her in that leaping way deer have, though he was hindered by the deep snow. My heart sank because he was so difficult a target, but as he came level with me I shot my arrow, aiming ahead of him and a little high in case I caught him in a leap—and there was a flurry of snow and they were both gone, away down their trail, white tails up and flashing.

I had lost him.

I scrambled down through the snow to look for my arrow.

But when I came to the trampled patch where they had rushed away, there were speckles of blood on the snow, and no sign of the arrow anywhere. The sun had come up, bringing color into the world, and the blood was bright red; it was easy to follow the trail. I was sorry I had only wounded the deer and so brought him pain, but I was very glad to have hit him.

I began the long struggle through the snow, following the footsteps and the splashes of red. They were there every step of the way, so I knew I should find him in the end, though because he was young and strong it might take a long time. By the time I reached him, the sun was at its highest winter point in the sky and I was soaking wet from hours of pushing through the snow. I paused in relief as I saw the brown body lying under a tree.

But the big wolf had found it too. He had ripped open the deer's belly and was tearing at it ravenously, and as he saw me he lifted his head and snarled, teeth shining out of his bloodied muzzle. *Mine*, said the snarl, *mine! Keep away!*

I was so angry that it stopped me from being afraid. I yelled at him, and grabbed for my bow. It was *my* deer, and I was just as hungry as the wolf.

"Get away from there!" I yelled.

The wolf snarled again. He gave a kind of half jump so that he was facing me, challenging, forelegs tense and apart, yellow slit eyes blazing over the dripping teeth. I was screaming at him now, dancing about like a mad thing, reaching for an arrow.

He paused; I don't think he'd ever seen anything like this before. He let out a long low growl, and then made a jerky move toward me, snarling.

So I shot at him. The arrow hit him in the leg, and the snarl became a yelp; he leapt sideways and faced me again, teeth still bared. I could see the arrow sticking out of his foreleg, but it fell away as he moved; it must have hit the bone. I was still shouting at him, angry shrieks with no words, desperate now because fear was kicking in over the rage.

And for a terrible moment I thought he would leap, because it would be so easy for a wolf to kill a boy—but instead he turned away. As I went on yelling and waving my arms, he loped off over the snow, limping a little, and disappeared into the trees.

So there I was, alone in the forest with the carcass of my deer. There was no sign of the doe his mother, of course. The broken shaft of my arrow was sticking out of his side. For a moment I felt remorse for having driven away the wolf; there was more than enough deer meat here for both of us, and like me, he was alone. And now I had wounded him. But there was no time to feel sorry, because I had so much to do before dark.

I did everything I remembered from our teaching, every stage, one by one. I gave thanks to the Great Spirit and my Manitou for giving me this kill, and I thanked the spirit of the deer. Then I shifted the deer so that he was tilted downward on a snowbank and I cut his neck in the proper place to bring the blood out. He was still warm. I pulled out my broken arrow, to save the sharp point. I would have slit his belly and taken out everything inside, perhaps cutting off a piece of his liver and eating it warm and raw, as I had seen my father do. But the wolf had done all those things, and the liver was gone.

Instead I did something harder: using a big rock and my axe, I broke the deer's skull to take out the brain. This was the rule for curing deerskins, that you must rub the skin with the brain, to keep it from drying as hard as oak tree bark.

Then I pulled the deer by his hind legs to lie in a clean patch of snow, away from the bloody mess the wolf and I had made, and I skinned him. It took a long time, and I could never have done it alone without the white man's knife my father gave me. I couldn't hang the deer by his forefeet in the proper way, but I managed fairly well to take off his skin in one piece. When I had finished, I cut out the long sinew next to the backbone, because deer sinew is one of the most useful things there are.

I was listening and watching all the time for the wolf to come back, but there was no sign of him.

The skin was heavy. I cut off one of the deer's legs and made my way back down the trail with the leg and sinew and brain bundled up in the skin. I pulled a big flat rock on top of them, and reckoned there was just enough of the day left for one more trip, so I went back to the deer, very cautiously. One wolf would be bad enough, but if he had summoned a hungry pack, that could be the end of me.

The carcass was just as I had left it. Hastily I hacked off as much more meat as I could carry. As I turned to go, I saw a movement among the trees.

I called to the wolf, "The rest is for you, brother."

And I was gone, and nobody followed me.

By the end of my second stumbling journey the sun had gone down and it was almost dark. I was very tired and very dirty and I thought longingly of the sweat lodge. But of course all I could do was clean my hands and my clothes with snow, and make a fire.

While strips of the deer meat were cooking I buried the rest deep in a snowbank beside the cave, along with the skin, and then I gorged myself on the meat while it was still half red. It tasted wonderful. My stomach felt as tight as a drumskin. And I was asleep so fast that when I woke the next morning I couldn't remember the careful way I must have covered the fire, and put my tools and leftover food inside the cave. Perhaps my Manitou made sure I did all those things.

The weather stayed kind, though wintry; for days, the air was still and the sky was blue. There was no sound or sign of the wolf, nor of any more deer. The moon rose very small and late, and the night sky was black and cold but blazing with stars.

And I was part of it all. Since that day when my Manitou came, I had stopped thinking of myself as a lonely boy separated from his family. Like the trees and the rocks and the pond, I was here, part of the pattern, doing what I had to do to survive. Each of us had our own part in a long harmony of things, a balance. The dead deer and the dead squirrel were part of it too. Without ever thinking it out, I had discovered why my people sent their boys out on this solitary voyage of learning.

I was burning my fire almost continuously now, and not just for warmth. I cut the raw deer meat into long strips and hung them on sticks around the fire so that they slowly dried. At the same time I did my best to cure the skin, though it was a poor copy of the proper way I had been taught. I scraped and scraped the inside of the skin with the blade of my tomahawk and cleaned it with snow. At night it generally froze, but this didn't seem to do it any harm. In the mornings I rubbed ashes into it, then scraped and cleaned it again. The only thing wrong with it was the small hole my arrow had made.

I used the deer's brain, too, when I'd thawed it out. At home, my mother would have made it into a kind of soup and soaked the hide in that, but all I could do was mash it up with snow, using my patient tomahawk, and rub the mixture into my deerskin. After a day and a night of this I did more rubbing, more scraping, more cleaning—and in the end the skin was clean enough for me to wrap it around myself, like a kind of cloak. The brain treatment was supposed to have softened it, but it was very stiff, and it smelled really bad. Still, I probably smelled bad myself, by then.

One day I went back to the place where I had skinned the deer. Nothing was left but the bones, picked almost clean by other creatures as hungry as I was. One of them was the wolf. I could see his big pawprints among the jumble of smaller ones, with the pad and the four toes, and in one frozen print the faint marks of his claws as well. So he was still alive, and he was still alone; there were no other wolf tracks. It must have been his strong jaws that had cracked a few of the biggest bones lying on the snow.

The prints looked about two days old. He was still nearby. At least he, like me, had a full belly for now.

I went back along the trail and turned off to look at the patch of trampled snow where the deer had rooted for acorns. There were the tracks of squirrels, but no new signs of deer. I went on through the small trees, where the snow was thinner than in my pine forest above the rocks—and then suddenly I came out to a great open sweep of sky and snow-patched land, and saw that without knowing it, I had come very close to the coast. Out on the horizon I could see the line of the sea, a dull blue-grey, with white lines of surf moving very slowly as the big waves rolled in. Closer, the land was flat except for three white hillocks where there must be trees, holding more snow than the land around them.

I stared out, and then I realized where I was.

This was the coastal marshland to which my father had brought me six months earlier, and those hillocks were the islands in the salt marsh—on one of which the stone head of my axe had grown into a tomahawk, in the embrace of a bitternut hickory tree.

I was so pleased with this discovery that it was a few moments before I noticed something else. Though the sun was still shining and the sky blue, the northern horizon was dark with a mounded line of clouds. They were massive thunderclouds, taller than I had ever seen, and they were coming closer very fast, growing to fill the sky. I felt the first stirring of a breeze against my cheek as the air began to move. Very soon I should be overtaken by a very big storm.

Instantly I forgot the salt marsh islands and I went back as fast as I could, through the woodland to the pond, and round its shore to my cave. The wind picked up behind me as I went. It was coming from the northeast, and a big northeasterly storm was always the most dangerous part of winter for my people. The only comfort I had was that the cave faced away from the pond, so that the rocks would be some protection.

For a wild moment I thought of trying to outrun the storm by fleeing into the woods—but only for a moment. Where could I go? The wind would catch me and I'd freeze to death very fast. Instead I must tuck myself into my rocky cleft as a wild animal would, and hope I could outlive the storm.

Nobody had invaded the cave, and my food was still there. Hastily I made a fire, to have its warmth for at least a little while. I folded my stiff, shapeless deerskin around myself, and I waited.

And the storm came.

SIX

The most frightening thing of all was the noise. It grew and grew, as if the Great Spirit were angry with his people, shouting in a rising fury. Overhead, the big trees began to creak and groan. The wind howled into my fire, bringing icy snow with it. Hastily I put the fire out, and I clutched my deerskin round my body and pressed myself into a corner of the cave. Everything I owned in the world was there with me, like a tiny family: axe, knife, bow and arrows, the strips of dried deer meat tied in bundles, the squirrel-skin bag. I could hear thunder rumbling as the wind rose.

The storm raged on. For hours and days I lay there, curled up under the deerskin, sometimes sleeping, some-times half-dreaming. If I was hungry, I nibbled deer meat. If I was thirsty, I sucked on snow. There was so little light that it was hard to tell night from day. I had become an animal like a winter squirrel: sleeping away the bad weather in its nest, emerging again when the sun shone.

And in the end, on the fourth day, the storm blew itself out. The constant high howl of the wind dropped to muttering gusts. I stretched out my cramped arms and legs and pushed aside the icy branches that had been protecting me, and suddenly I saw sunlight.

I stood up, with the deerskin round me like a cape, and stared out at the snow. The storm had left such beauty behind it; the trees glittered in the sunlight and above their white branches the sky was blue as a robin's egg. Nothing moved but occasional hunks of snow falling to the ground here and there, as the sun warmed the branches where they lay.

I could hear in the distance a long low rumble, going on and on without a pause. It took me a moment to realize that this was no longer the wind, but the roar of the waves breaking on the shore, way out beyond the pond and the marshland. It was the voice of the sea, whose anger would last much longer than the storm that had stirred it into life.

I spent the rest of my day clearing the snow away from the cave and digging out my fire pit. When night came, the star-scattered sky was clear of cloud, and through the trees I saw a full white moon rise, banishing the stars and casting black shadows over the gleaming snow. So I knew I had been away from my home and my village for a whole month. It was a long time, and in it I had become a different person.

Every day I went scouting through the snow, and I saw

no other living thing except the small birds who hopped and foraged through the branches above me. Once, in a rotting hollow tree near the pond, I came across a pile of lily roots, a wonderful discovery; it was probably the winter hoard of a muskrat. I took away only half of it and left the rest for him and his family, and I set no trap to catch him.

I was setting traps in other places, though, and one lucky day I caught a turkey.

Perhaps it was the smell of the roasting bird that brought back the wolf next day. He came close enough to snatch up the turkey's entrails, which I had buried in the snow among the trees. He was clearly very hungry indeed, to go after such worthless stuff, and he didn't behave as most wolves do. When I shouted at him, he crouched down and snarled, baring his teeth as if in challenge.

I threw a rock at him, and he moved to one side but still stood there, poised, belligerent. For a long moment he stared at me, and then he turned and loped away, still with a slight limp in his foreleg. I climbed on the rock and watched until he was out of sight.

I was uneasy that night, knowing that he was close again. Though the wolves are our brothers, he was a strange lone wolf, surviving on his own, and I didn't trust him. I took care that my food was always at the back of the cave, hidden behind a rock, and at night I banked up my fire so that it would burn for a long time. The moon was growing thin again, and a wolf's eyes could see better in the dark than the eyes of a boy. Fear made me sleep lightly, and whenever the fire died, I brought it back to life, to burn till the dawn came.

The turkey was small, and lasted only for two days. Nothing came to my traps, and there was no sign any-where of the tracks of deer. I was staying alive now only on a few lily roots and the brittle strips of deer meat that I had dried, and I ate very little at a time so that they would last. And perhaps they would have lasted, if it hadn't been for the wolf.

It took a lot of wood to keep the fire burning all night, and much of my day now was spent hunting and cutting dry branches and trees. The forest floor was full of dead wood, but I had to go further and further away to find more, digging for it in the snow. One day before the light began to die, I came back out of the trees dragging a big oak branch, and I saw something that made my heart stop for an instant.

The wolf was in my cave, crouching, eating.

I shouted at him angrily, and grabbed up the branch as a weapon. For that moment I was an animal just as he was, defending the food that would keep only one of us alive. But this time, I had no arrow to shoot at him.

He crouched in the cave, facing me, snarling. He looked huge, all gleaming teeth and yellow eyes, and in the same moment that I swung the big branch at him, he leapt at me.

The branch knocked him off balance, so that he missed me, but I lost my own balance too, rolling over, banging against rocks. I scrambled up, pulling my knife out of my belt, still yelling, half out of my mind with rage and fear. With both hands I held out the knife in front of me, wheeling, facing him.

The air was full of flying snow and splintered branches, and the noise of our voices, screaming boy and snarling wolf. And the wolf spun round and leapt at me again.

I don't know why I didn't die then. For that one moment, I knew my life was over. The wolf was leaping at my throat, mouth open, teeth bared, because that is the way wolves kill their prey always, aiming to rip out the throat and bleed the animal to death. But in the flurry as he crashed into me, instead his claws carved a gash down the side of my face, and he ran his own throat onto the knife held out at arm's length in both my hands.

As I fell sideways the sharp knife ripped across his neck and blood came spurting everywhere. We were rolling in a whirl of bodies and blood, dirt and snow, terrible noises coming from both of us. I found myself stumbling backward into the cave, blinking through the blood that coursed down my face, still holding out my knife in front of me with two rigid arms.

But even though he was so big, and far stronger than me, the wolf was no longer attacking. He rolled to and fro, as if he were trying to stop the bleeding. He got to his feet and began to lope away, but he was staggering, and when he was almost hidden by the trees I saw him fall down.

My heart was still beating so fast it was like a drum in my ears. I stood there gasping, and the side of my face was beginning to hurt furiously. My cheek was wet, and hurt too much for me to want to touch it.

I came slowly out of the cave onto the trampled snow. Our battle had turned it bright red, and there was no difference to be seen between the blood of the wolf and the blood of the boy.

From a snowbank I took handfuls of clean white snow and pressed them carefully against my cheek, so that soon the wound was cold enough to numb the hurting and I could try to dab more snow against it. My hands were shaking, I couldn't make them stop, but I kept reaching for the snow. All I could think of was that my grandmother Suncatcher said any cut had first of all to be washed clean if it was to heal.

My fingers told me that the gash ran down past my ear to my chin, and that there was a flap of skin torn loose on my cheek. I tried to press the skin down and was glad I couldn't see what it looked like.

After a while the bleeding seemed to stop. My tunic was wet with blood, but there was nothing I could do about that. My body was aching all over, and suddenly I felt desperately tired. But supposing the wolf were still alive, and came back? I was almost certain he must be dead, but I knew I had to go and make sure.

So, very cautiously, I took my knife in one hand and my tomahawk in the other, and in the dying light I went through the trees to the place where I had seen him fall down. There was blood on the snow all the way, and more when I found him. He had dragged himself along the ground a little way, but he was lying there dead.

He had died in just the way that he would have killed me, and I was glad that I was safe from him now. But I was not glad he had died.

I stood there, and in my mind I looked for my Manitou.

I said, "He was hungry and he wanted to live. He was like me. I'm ashamed I killed him. I am ashamed."

And in my mind, the great fish hawk coasted over the trees, over the pond, down toward me. His voice was like the wind.

He said, "All creatures must die, in the end. It is possible that he in turn has killed you. Now you yourself must fight to stay alive. But honor your brother—honor him in his end. . . ."

And the voice faded as the wind fades, and he flew out of my mind. Snow was beginning to fall, and the daylight was nearly gone. Suddenly I felt terribly cold.

Trying to ignore my throbbing cheek, I went back to my cave and made a fire. In its flickering light, I saw what my Manitou had meant.

It is possible that he in turn has killed you. The wolf had eaten all my precious stock of dried meat. There were only a few tiny scraps of it scattered on the ground. He had been so desperate for food that to get to it, he had pushed aside a rock as big as himself, which I had been able to move only inch by inch. And now he had left me desperate.

I slept very little that night. The snow went on falling,

lightly but steadily. Hunched inside my deerskin, I could hear the hissing of the snowflakes as they dropped on the fire. I was warm enough, but the gash on my face throbbed and ached, and I could feel that my cheek was swollen. I kept putting snow to melt near the fire, in a piece of a branch that I had hollowed into a kind of cup, and I drank the water, and tried to guess what Suncatcher would have had me do.

She had a medicine for everything. When we skinned our knees and elbows, she would use the bark of a particular kind of elm tree to help us heal. She taught us how to collect it, so I remembered how the tree looked—and I thought now that I had seen a little copse of them beside the pond. I kept hoping for dawn to come, so that I could go and look.

But first I remembered the other thing that my Manitou had said.

Honor your brother.

The wolves are our brothers, even though this lone wolf had been my enemy. All living creatures are our brothers, even those we must kill for food, and we are taught to pay them respect. So the first thing I did when the morning came was to go out with my tomahawk and a flat digging stone, and look for the body of the wolf.

He was covered in snow now, but I brushed it off his shaggy coat. The thought of skinning him jumped into my mind, but I pushed it out. Though his fur would have been warmer than my deerskin, that would have been no way to honor a dead enemy.

The ground was so cold and hard that I couldn't dig a hole deep enough to bury him properly. But he was lying near a big rock among the trees, where the leaf mold was not frozen as hard as the dirt nearer the pond, so I scraped out a shallow space beside the rock and pushed his stiff body into it. This was hard work and took a long time.

I covered the wolf with snow again, and pulled some big stones over the top. It wasn't a proper grave, but it was the best I could do.

Blood was running down the side of my head again; I should have been resting, not digging. But I couldn't rest, not yet. I went to the pond, stepping through the new snow and blessing my mother for the thickness of my moccasins. After much stumbling along the banks, at last I found the clump of young trees I had remembered, and with my father's beautiful, deadly sharp knife I cut out wide strips of the inside bark—asking the trees to forgive me, because in winter this would quite probably cause them to die.

"My wound will thank you," I said to them, with the pain from my gashed face telling me that indeed it would, in a while.

And as I looked down at the frozen pond, a picture came into my mind. Perhaps it came from the Great Spirit, perhaps from my Manitou—or perhaps from the pond itself. We are all one. Suddenly I had a memory of the day my father first took me out to a frozen pond where the men were fishing. He had showed me that through a hole in the ice you could catch a pike big enough to feed the whole family, even in dark winter, even in water whose bitter cold would kill you if you fell into it.

If I could make a fishing line, I could fish for food, in this icy world that offered no food anywhere.

Back in my cave, I made fire again, and for the sake of mending my torn head, I sacrificed the gift I had been saving for my baby brother. I took out the little squirrel-skin bag I had made and threw away the dried-up squirrel's tail, and with my knife I slit the bag so that it became once more a flat skin. Onto the skin I shredded the bark from the healing tree, drizzling a little water on it to hold it together. Then I lay down so that the wound on my face was against the bark and the skin, and with strips of deerskin I tied the skin to my head.

I slept that night lying so, and in the morning I tightened the strips so that the squirrel-skin stayed tied to my head as I moved about. It was a good thing there was nobody to see me; I must have looked ridiculous. But the bleeding stopped, and gradually the throbbing went away. I rested in the cave for a day and another night, and made sure the bark was close against the wound all the time.

Winter was deep enough now that the ice covering the pond below my cave was as strong as rock. I went down there with a flat stone in each hand and cleared away the snow, so that I could chop a hole in the ice with my axe. It took two days, and I had to hold my head carefully still all the time, but at last I had a hole big enough for fishing—though every morning there was a new layer of ice to break through.

For a fishing line I used my bowstring. I hated to risk losing it, and it was too short, but it was all I had. I'd made some line from my saved deer sinew that was strong, but it would have fallen apart in water. So with a hook made from a turkey bone, and one of my last lily roots for bait, I dropped my short line into the water and waited. And waited. After a long time I felt a faint nibble, but then nothing.

And then there was a jerk on the line so fierce that it almost pulled me into the fishing hole. I tugged back as hard as I could, and only just managed to yank the fish clear of the water before the line whipped out of my hands, and he went flying across the ice.

It wasn't a fish at all—it was a big eel. He wriggled all over the place, and nearly got back into the hole before I managed to whack him on the head with my axe.

But as I hit him, my knife, loosened by all this flurry, flew out of its leather case on my belt and across the ice—and slid into the fishing hole. Without even a splash, it vanished.

I heard myself shout in horror, and dropped on to my hands and knees to stare into the hole. There was nothing I could do. It would have taken half a day to chop the hole any bigger, and just a few moments in that cold dark water would have frozen me to death. The knife was gone forever: my most valuable tool, which had done so much to keep me alive. The knife that my father gave me, and that I promised to bring back to him.

Kneeling there on the ice, I wondered if the knife had brought death to me, through the killing of the wolf.

I knelt there for a long time, trying to find my Manitou, to ask what I should do. But there was no feel of him in my mind, and he did not come.

I said to myself, trying to believe it, *There is nothing you cannot do. With his help, there is nothing you cannot do.*

So I got to my feet and reached for the eel, the cause of all the trouble. My line was sticking out of his mouth; he had swallowed the hook. That was a good thing, because it meant I could drag him home by the line instead of carrying him; his slippery skin was covered with a thick layer of slime and mud, from where he had been lying at the bottom of the pond.

I took him home and skinned him with the blade of my axe. It was far, far more difficult than it would have been with the knife.

But eels are good to eat, and I made his meat last for a long time. I felt myself growing stronger, and within a few days the wound on my face began to have the itchy feeling that showed it had begun to heal. But I still kept the squirrel-skin tightly covering it, with the shredded bark against the skin. There would be an ugly scar, but I wasn't going to disturb anything until I was sure it had healed.

After a long time searching among the stones on the shore of the pond, eventually I found two stones to help me make a new knife. One had a shape friendly to my hand, one side rounded, one side straight. The other became my chipping tool, made of harder rock, to chip the first to a sharp edge. So in a while I had a knife again, though it was a hundred times less good than the white man's knife at the bottom of the pond.

Three times in those days, I heard a thin harsh call from the sky, and looked up to see the red-tailed hawk coasting in a long arc above the pond. Each time he disappeared behind the trees. He was probably hunting, but I wondered whether he was also a sign from my Manitou—a sign of warning, or instruction, or change.

Then one night I woke up in the dark, though not because I was cold. I could still see a glow in my fire pit, a small red light in the darkness. Suddenly something above it caught my eye, in the piece of sky up there behind the trees, and I saw a wonderful thing that my father first woke me to see when I was a very little boy.

The stars were dancing.

It was a slow dance, like a game. They took turns. Every so often, one of them rushed across the sky and then hid himself. Then another. Then another. All in the same part of the sky, the northeast. They were like sparks blown out of a fire by the wind.

"Look," my father had said that first time, holding me in his arms and pointing upward. "They are your ancestors, Little Hawk. Every year at this time they leap, they dance. It is Manitou. They are saying to us, 'Look, we are still here. We are watching over you. We dance for you, in our beautiful home.'"

Then he had taken me back into the house and put me back on my sleeping platform, and pulled the doeskin blanket over me.

"Remember them," he had said.

So looking out from my lonely cave, this starlit night, I remembered them, though then it had been summer and now it was cold midwinter.

And I knew this was my second sign, and that it was time to plan my journey home.

That night the moon was not in the sky. Soon it would start to grow and we should be halfway to the Cold Moon, which would be the second of my three moons away. If I began to travel then, I should arrive back at the proper time. I knew the way to go, because I had been watching the star of the north, to which the Big Bear pointed, ever since I left. And I knew the land around our village so well that I should recognize it long before I reached home.

It was wonderful to think about this. Once I had begun, I found I thought of little else. I thought myself through it, minute by minute. First I should begin to hear the sounds, far off: the barking of dogs, the chopping of firewood, the calls of children playing. Soon after that I should smell the smoke rising from the roofs of the houses. And at last, across the cleared land, through the wide-spaced trees, I should see my own home.

I kept trying to decide what would be the best time to arrive. After one last night sleeping out in the cold, I could come in through the door flap in the early morning. My mother would just be up, feeding wood to the fire, starting to cook the first and biggest meal of the day. I could see her in my mind, in the warm house hung with mats and baskets, and lined with the sleeping platforms where the rest of the family still lay snug under furs and skins.

I thought of choosing a moment when she was turned away from me, and then slipping into the house and putting my hands over her eyes. Perhaps I should say "Mother" softly first, so as not to frighten her. Or better still, perhaps I should simply walk in and let her catch sight of me, so I could see the look on her face.

This was a game I played with myself often in the cold days and the long nights that followed. I rehearsed my first words to my father, my apologies for losing his knife. He would be regretful, but not angry. I invented my first meetings with my sisters, my grandmother, my uncles and aunts—and with my friend Leaping Turtle and the two other boys who left the same day that we did, on the journey to become men.

I wondered how they had survived the big storm. I wondered how they had changed—because I had certainly changed. Whether or not the elders would count me as a man, as a warrior, in some way I had grown up.

I also knew I was exceedingly dirty and I stank, and I longed to be able to strip off in the sweat lodge and get clean again. I was thinner than when I left; my mother would be horrified and want to fatten me up. But of course I had learned to eat less now, and I was tougher and quicker, I thought, because I also worked harder than I ever did before.

The thing that would most distress my mother would be the great scar on the side of my face. The wound had healed itself; one morning I had woken up and found the squirrel-skin fallen away, and there was no pain when I reached up and felt my cheek and my chin. But the skin was lumpy, and here and there I could feel points where a fragment of bark had embedded itself in the long scar. All my life now, people would look at this ugly scar before they looked at the rest of me.

But that wasn't much to pay for being still alive.

There was one thing I wanted to do before I left. I made my way to the edge of the salt marsh, all white now, with little icebergs in its creeks. Straining my eyes in the white glare, I gazed all around until I found the white hummock that was the island where my tomahawk was born.

I sent the little island a farewell, and wondered whether I would ever see it again.

Early the next morning I buried my fire pit under dirt and snow and cleaned out my cave so that it looked as it did before I came. It had given me shelter in a hard time, and I was grateful. I thanked the place, and I left.

The journey home was hard and slow. Each morning I set off early, but each day before dark I had to make a nest for the night so that I shouldn't freeze. Each time, all over again I had to find a sheltered place between trees or rocks; all over again I had to cut pine branches to keep me from lying on icy ground. It was hard to be on the move in winter. My deerskin was a stiff, clumsy garment that caught on the trees. I chewed bark to cheat my stomach as I trudged through the snow.

On bright days the sun told me which way to go; at night, the gleaming stars told me whether he was right. If I was so cold at night that I could hardly breathe, I made a fire. Sometimes I heard wolves howling, but they weren't close. I wondered why the solitary wolf had never joined them; I hoped I was forgiven for killing him.

The journey seemed endless, but gradually excitement began to grow in me as I thought of food and warmth and comfort—and most of all, the people I loved. I swore to myself that I'd never say a bad word to any of them again, not to my mother or father or even Quickbird.

And I stopped trying to decide on the best time to arrive at home. The moment I caught sight of my house, nothing would stop me from running toward it and in through the door.

The trees were more widely spaced now, with no scrub between. This was land that had been burned over for farming; I was near the village. I gave a shout across the snow, but heard no answering voice or barking dog, not yet. Then I saw ahead of me a collapsed structure of branches that I recognized: it was the remains of a tower from which we watched over the corn the summer before, to keep away the animals.

I started to run.

I was in a field of dead cornstalks beaten down by the snow, and in the distance, through the trees, I saw a roof. My bow and arrows jumped against my back as I ran.

It was a bright sunny day; the sky was clear blue. The roof that I could see was the sweat lodge—I knew its shape. I ran past it into the center of the village, breathless, feeling a huge smile on my face. I was home.

S E V E N

But as I passed the sweat lodge, something made me slow down. Though it was broad daylight, I could see nobody anywhere in the village. No smoke was rising from any of the houses. And the snow around them, mounded in drifts where the wind took it, lay smooth and unbroken, with no sign of footprints.

I tried to tell myself that everyone was away on a hunt, even though it was winter. Then I caught a faint smell in the air. I sniffed harder, casting my head round like a dog. It was the smell of rotting, the smell of death. Something was terribly wrong.

I headed for my own house, stamping through the crusted snow that lay knee-high everywhere, and I stumbled over something. As I scrambled up, I found it was a man's foot, heel upward.

I stood there, staring. A dead man, unburied, under

old snow. I wasn't brave enough to dig and find out who he was.

Feeling sick with fear, I went slowly to my own house. Snow lay in a drift against our entrance. A little had been dug away, but there were no footprints.

I kicked aside the rest of the snow and said a wordless prayer to the Great Spirit, and I went in through the hanging flaps of deerskin.

A beam of sunlight slanted down from the open hole in the roof. The baskets still hung from the walls, the pots stood beside the fire. There were ashes in the fire pit, but the house was cold and empty.

A great shout came out of my throat, all my fear turning itself into noise.

"Mother! Father!"

At the far end of the house there was a tiny movement in the shadows, and a small whisper of a voice.

"Little Hawk? Is that you?"

My grandmother Suncatcher was lying wrapped in furs on the furthest sleeping platform. I rushed over to her and knelt beside her, holding her.

"Grandmother, where are they? What's happened?"

She seemed very small, and her face was thin, hollow-cheeked. She looked up at me without any expression.

"They are dead," she said.

I stared at her.

"They all died," she said in that breathy whisper. "There was a terrible sickness. All died."

"Mother? And Father? The girls, and my brother?"

"All died," she said. "All the village."

I felt I was in the middle of a nightmare, and that although I knew nothing was real, I couldn't wake up.

But it was real.

"Everyone died?"

Suncatcher tried to speak, and failed. Her throat was too dry.

I scrambled up and looked round wildly. There was a bark bucket on the floor near the fire pit, half full of icy water, with a wooden ladle hooked to its edge. I knew that ladle—I had watched my father carve it from the burl of an oak. I dipped it into the water through the crust of ice and took it to my grandmother, helping her to lift her head, and she drank from it in little sips.

When she had enough, she raised her hand. It was a tiny hand now, its bones like the bones of a bird; she was dreadfully thin. So I drank the water myself; I drank three ladles full, like a man dying of thirst. I could feel Suncatcher's big eyes on me.

"Be strong, Little Hawk," she whispered.

There was nothing to say to this.

But now she was staring at me. At the side of my face, at the long puckered scar I had never yet seen myself.

Don't look, Grandmother. Not now. Not yet.

I jumped up. The house was so cold, I had to make it warmer or my grandmother would die. Kindling and logs were piled by the door as they had always been; the bag of milkweed fluff and dried moss was hanging beside the fire bow, just as always. I seized everything in a kind of frenzy, and made a fire.

Suncatcher watched the flames catch.

She said, in a whisper, "Your father had the sickness first of anyone. He died in two days. Then the baby. Then your mother. I sent your sisters to the women's house and I nursed your mother, but she died and so did they." She paused, waiting for breath. "White Eagle and Quick Fox had died by then too, and their families after them. And all. And all."

"Running Deer?"

"Everyone."

"Did something poison them?" I said. "What had they eaten?"

"No," Suncatcher said. "It was nothing that they ate."

"Then what?"

She lay there quiet for a long time, looking at nothing, and then she took a long breath and let it out again.

"I have heard of it before but never seen it," she said. Her voice was very weak and tired. "It is a disease from the white men who come here from the sea. It jumps to you in the air and burns you up, and then it jumps to the next person, and the next, and the next. A terrible disease, a plague. We have no medicine for it. The medicine man did his best, but he died too."

I reached out and touched her face. "You didn't die, Grandmother."

"No," she said with great bitterness. "The Great Spirit allowed one useless old woman to live, amongst all this death."

There was nothing to say to that either.

She looked so weary and old, and her words came out so painfully, but I had to understand what had happened.

"Where did this plague come from? There are no white men here."

"Trading," Suncatcher said. "Our people trade."

"But not with white men. My uncle White Eagle has seen them, but that was in the north. He said they come in big boats to catch fish, and go away again."

"They come closer now. They trade for furs."

A picture flashed into my head, of a pile of furs in our house and my father holding up a bearskin in front of him so that his head was sticking up over it where the bear's head would have been. He was laughing, happy. I did not often see him laugh.

"But they don't come *here*, Grandmother. I don't understand."

Suncatcher closed her eyes and lay there silent, her mouth a thin unhappy line. Then her eyes opened again and looked straight into mine.

She said, "Four moons ago, your father and White Eagle and Quick Fox went away to trade."

"To the villages up on the river, yes."

"Not just to the villages. Your father had heard of a white man hungry for furs who was leaving to sail back across the sea for the winter. The weather was kind so they took canoes down the river and found him. And they made a good trade; they were very happy with it."

She stopped to rest, to capture more breath. A cold place began to grow in my heart as I thought about what she was saying.

"But when they came back with their trade, the white man's plague came with them," Suncatcher said. "I think it is like a snake that grows slowly and quietly and then strikes. It waits its time. I think it does not kill white men. It kills us."

I said, "My father gave me a beautiful knife to take with me. A white man's knife. That must be why he went to trade, to get me the knife."

"It was one part of his trade," Suncatcher said. "One part only."

"If he hadn't gone to trade for my knife—"

"Stop that!" my grandmother said sharply. For a moment her voice was strong, like my Manitou in my vision. "Little Hawk, it is not for us to tell how great and terrible things come about. Only the Great Spirit can see all. Your father and your uncles went to trade for whatever things the white man had to offer, not for one little knife. This load is not for your back, nor for any man's."

All I could think of was my father's pleasure in giving me his knife, and the glow in my mother's face when she saw it.

"I couldn't even bring the knife back to him. It saved my

life, and I couldn't bring it back. It fell to the bottom of a pond."

"A good place for it," Suncatcher said.

She lay back, exhausted, and her eyes closed again. Light from the fire flickered on her lined old face, with its strong straight nose. My mother had that same nose.

My mother is dead. I shall never see her again. My father is dead, and my two sisters are dead. My baby brother is dead. I shall never see any of them again.

I had to find something to do. I fetched more logs from the woodpile inside the door and built up the fire. The flames leapt up, warming the house.

I poured water into my mother's biggest clay pot and set its pointed base into the hole at the side of the fire pit. Into the water I dropped a handful from each of the baskets hanging on the wall: onions, garlic, lily roots, dried cranberries. I had watched my mother do this so often that I hardly needed to think. I wanted to ask my grandmother a hundred questions, but first I needed to feed her, or she would die too. I wondered how long it was since she had eaten.

I could see now that although furs and skins were mounded on my own sleeping platform, there were none on those where my parents and my sisters used to sleep. Each wooden frame was covered only with a woven bark mat. While Suncatcher slept, very slowly I went all round the inside of our house, looking.

All the familiar tools were in their places, and everything for cooking. There was enough food for a month or more—

I knew that the rest of the winter supply for the village was buried deep in the cold ground, wrapped in baskets and mats. But there was no sign of my parents' clothes, or those of my sisters, nor of any of their personal possessions.

There was a sick feeling in my throat as I faced the fact that they were indeed dead. When we die and are buried in the ground, our friends and family put with us all the things that were most precious to us, or that we might need in an afterlife that resembles the one here on earth. My father would certainly have been buried with his bow, and his tomahawk.

The only hunter in this family now was me.

On a shelf above my sleeping platform, with my own clothes and belongings, I found my sharp stone knife that I had before my father gave me the one he got from the white man. It was an old and trusted friend, and I was very glad to have it in my hand again.

So, using it, I shredded two handfuls of dried meat and added them to the pot beside the fire, which was beginning to steam and smell good. There was no more light from the smoke hole in the roof now, but in the dark circle up there I could see one bright star.

When I went outside, night had swallowed the village, and all the stars in their moving patterns were blazing out of the black sky. Their light glimmered on the snow, but the only sign of life in the world around me was the little glow of the entrance to our house, and an echo of firelight in the smoke rising from the roof.

Oh my Manitou, I thought, *please watch over me and tell me what to do.*

Then I went back indoors and gently woke my grandmother, so I could give her some hot soup. I helped her to sit up, very carefully. I was almost afraid she might break.

She sat propped up by the furs of her sleeping nest and slowly spooned up a bowlful of soup while I wolfed down three. Gradually some color began to filter back into her bony grey face.

"D'you remember when you last had anything to eat, Grandmother?"

"No," Suncatcher said. Then she shook her head, as if she were exasperated with herself. "I am ashamed," she said.

"Ashamed?"

"We are put here to live out the time the Great Spirit wills to us, but I had given up my joy in the earth. I lay down in this bed to die, Little Hawk. It is not so hard to die, at my age, if you no longer eat or drink. The body is already tired."

My throat closed up, and I could feel tears filling my eyes. I stood there holding the bowl very tightly and not looking at her. *I am a man now. We are strong; we do not weep.*

Suncatcher could sense this. She tried to speak without emotion.

"I had lost track of the days and nights," she said. "I thought you would not be back for a long time. And you are young and strong—I knew you would survive. You were not part of my thinking. Forgive me."

I made some sort of noise, and I nodded.

"I was the last person alive in this village and I did not want to live," Suncatcher said. "I had seen my sons die, and my daughter, and my grandchildren, and all my friends."

She stopped.

Looking at the grief in her small fierce face, I loved her very much. She too was strong. She did not weep.

"I don't want you to die, Grandmother."

"No. Now there are two of us."

She held out her arms to me and I knelt down and hugged her, but we did not cry. At least, only a very little.

Suncatcher said, "You have seen your Manitou, have you not?"

"Yes. I have."

She knew better than to ask more than that.

She said, "And the scar on your face says that you have come through danger."

"It was a wolf. I killed him."

I found I couldn't say anything more than that. And again, Suncatcher did not ask.

"We will make a plan," she said.

Under her instruction, I took several kinds of dried herbs from small woven pouches hanging on the wall near her bed, and heated them in water. She was making a drink that she said would strengthen us both; she said we should drink it every day. She had me help her walk around the house, though not yet outside, so that her legs would get used to moving again.

She told me a little more about what happened when the plague came. It was a dreadful disease; it filled the body with pain and made it very hot. Then the heat would go down for a little but come back worse, and soon the person would die. Often the skin would have a yellowish color at the end. None of our traditional medicines made any difference, nor the sweat lodge, nor any of the prayers and sacred rituals that our medicine man desperately tried. One after another, families died: most often, Suncatcher said, the small children died first, and the very old, and then the rest. All the women in the women's house died, including my sisters.

"Day after day," she said, "those of us who were still alive buried those who had died. They were poor burials, because the ground is so hard. And fewer and fewer of us were left. Toward the end, the dead had to be left in their homes. If they are still there, perhaps they should not be disturbed."

"There is a man lying dead out in the village. Under the snow. I must give him rest somehow."

"You cannot dig frozen ground," Suncatcher said. "Even though I think that is the body of my brother Morning Star."

Morning Star was our medicine man, the wisest person in the whole village. She told me that he had ordered her to go home to rest, one day when she and the few who were left had been working without sleep for days. She was so tired that she could hardly walk, and he took her back to our house to sleep and brought her food. The next morning she heard only his voice, from outside the house.

"He said, 'The others are dying, Suncatcher. I am the last, and now I have the sickness too. You can do nothing for me, you must stay where you are. And the Great Spirit be with you.'"

Suncatcher sat looking into the fire.

"I called out as loud as I could, 'I love you, brother.' But there was no answer. I don't know if he heard me. So since there no longer seemed any reason to go on living, I decided I would simply lie here until I too died."

She looked up at me. "And then you came back."

For seven days Suncatcher and I took care of each other, until she looked stronger and more confident—and so perhaps did I. More snow fell, a long soft snow, mounding itself against the houses until they half-vanished into it. Now they were a little range of round white hills. I went out and dug a path away from our own house to the pile of firewood my father had had us gather before the winter came. Every house had such a pile. Every day I brought wood back for our fire pit, but Suncatcher made me swear not to investigate any other house.

"We have food enough," she said, "and there is danger in those houses. The plague is still there, eating the bodies of the dead until it can be driven away. And I do not have the skill for that. Keep away from them, Little Hawk. Swear."

So I did.

And then came the morning when I had brought in wood

79

and was feeding the fire, and Suncatcher was pounding dried corn in the oak-tree mortar that our grandfather hollowed out for her. We had heard no footsteps, but suddenly the house brightened as the door flap was pulled open. We stared.

Leaping Turtle was standing in the doorway. He was wrapped in a rabbit-skin blanket and covered in snow. His face was thinner, his eyes huge with horror.

He said, *"What has happened?"*

EIGHT

For many days in the long winter, Suncatcher, Leaping Turtle, and I lived together in this house. She cooked for us; we hunted and trapped for her, and collected firewood. The three of us kept one another alive. We were all that was left of the old village. Suncatcher prayed with us and even sang for us, in her voice that was scratchy now but still found its note. She said that now she had two grandsons.

When Leaping Turtle had come back, he had found his home buried in unbroken snow. He dug his way through to the door; inside, the house was empty and cold. Staring around the deserted village, he caught sight of a thread of smoke rising from just one snow-mounded roof at the far end; it was us, of course. Like me, he knew something terrible had happened before he even asked.

Suncatcher told us that Leaping Turtle's family had died early in the plague: his mother and father, his two brothers and his sister. They had been buried in a place not far from the village that was easy to reach: an outcropping of rocks where enough of the frozen soil could be dug away to put bodies to rest and cover them with slabs of rock too heavy for digging animals to move. We both knew the place; we had played there often when we were small boys, jumping to and fro. Jumping perhaps from the same rocks that now covered our dead.

We went there through the snow, Leaping Turtle and I, to say farewell to our families and to pray to our ancestors to receive them, and the Great Spirit to bless them. We stayed there a long time, without talking. We both knew that we were no longer boys; sometimes I felt I had lived through as much as an old man.

Before we went back, we looked hard at the rocks in that place and tried to decide which of them might be moved, and where we might still dig some soil. Although my grandmother wanted us to keep away from the houses that might hold bodies killed by the plague—she thought there were two—we knew that sooner or later we had to put these people to rest with proper ceremony. Especially our medicine man, Morning Star, still lying frozen out there somewhere under the snow.

"Suncatcher says that the plague will jump to us from their bodies," Leaping Turtle said.

"But we can't leave them unburied. I buried the wolf who fought me—and these are our brothers and sisters."

"Yes. They are."

We stood there unhappily on the high rock, looking out over the trees.

Suddenly Leaping Turtle grabbed my arm, pointing. It was a clear, freezing cold day, bright with sunshine, but out in the blue sky a pillar of grey-white smoke was rising. As we watched, there was a break in the smoke—and then a new puff of it rose, darker this time. Another break, another puff. Then a third.

Then the smoke rose again, in its unbroken pillar.

"To the west," Leaping Turtle said. "It's the village on the river."

"Are they talking to us?"

"Three smokes—remember? It's the greeting for anyone who sees it. Three just means 'I am here.'"

I was suddenly overwhelmed by the thought of other living people. "We have to answer!"

We scrambled down into the snow and hunted for sticks, leaves, anything that would burn. Soon our moccasins were soaked, our fingers frozen. It was a long time before we had enough kindling, and the sun was beginning to drop down the sky.

The pillar of smoke had gone. But Leaping Turtle had a firestone and some moss at his belt, and we managed to make a fire on the tall rock. The wood was so damp that it smoked well.

I pulled off my tunic to cover and uncover the smoke.

"What are the answers? One puff means danger."

"Two says come. Four says, I am coming."

"Best to send three, like them. So we are saying, 'Look, we are here too.'"

So we sent our signal, to tell that there was life still in our village. But there was no answer, and I pulled my tunic back on in a hurry.

We checked our traps on the way home, and we had a big rabbit for Suncatcher. She was pleased by the meat, but even more by our sight of the smoke in the sky.

"If there were still sickness in the village, they would not signal," she said. "You boys must go there. You should not be in this unhappy place."

"Not without you," I said.

Leaping Turtle said, "We go nowhere without our sachem."

She looked at us and shook her head, but she smiled a little. I knew she could never go on a journey, though. The cold had done something bad to her feet, in those last days before I came back, and she could hardly walk. Though she would never show me her feet, I had glimpsed her ankles, and the skin was very dark and tight over the thin bones.

Leaping Turtle and I had grown up together. Our lives had been like two brier vines twining round each other. We had followed all Running Deer's hunting rules together, learned to sing and pray and stamp the ceremonial dances together; we had swum and trapped and played games together for as long as I could remember. But now we were truly brothers; we had known it since that hard testing moment when we had to ignore each other on our solitary quests. In spite of everything that had happened since, I think we both felt that our life together now was like a reward from the Great Spirit for our obedience then.

Leaping Turtle's time alone was as hard as mine, though he went inland instead of seaward, so the blast of the northeast storm toward the end was not quite so fierce. Fierce enough, though. He saw no deer but he trapped rabbits, often enough to have many skins that he stitched together— with pine-root thread and a rabbit-bone needle—into a blanket. It was his cloak by day and his coverlet at night, and it kept him alive, though my grandmother clicked her tongue over the hard, half-cured skins. As for my deerskin, she had taken one look at it and made me throw it away.

I never asked Leaping Turtle how long he had to fast before he found his Manitou. The vision of your Manitou is a private thing, not to be revealed even to your brother until the proper time.

In the next days Suncatcher tried often to persuade us to leave her and go to the village by the river. She felt strongly that our village was no longer a place for us; that no living creature should have a home there until the spirits had been set to rest. Leaping Turtle and I talked and talked, whenever we were away from the house, and we decided to do two things.

One, we would not leave her alone. Instead we would build a kind of litter, in which we could carry her with us to the village on the river. It might be a journey of seven or eight days, but we thought she could survive it.

Two, before we went, we would find the body of Morning Star and lay him to rest near our families and friends.

So we did these things. We dug in the snow to find Morning Star, and we wrapped our largest mat round his body and sewed it closed. It was the first time I had touched a dead man. The sewing was not very good but we did our best. He was not as big as I remembered—he seemed almost the size of a child.

We scraped out a shallow grave in the burying place and dragged him there, and when we had put earth over him, we pulled as big a stone over the top as we could manage. Then we said prayers for him to the Great Spirit, and told him we were sorry we didn't know the words for a proper ceremony. He was a medicine man famous through all our nation, and should have had a big solemn funeral.

Suncatcher was not pleased when we told her we had done this without her, but she knew she would not have been able to walk to the burying place. She said some prayers of her own for Morning Star, and at dawn the next day she sang for him, and we listened.

Then we cut down small trees to make a litter, and trimmed off their branches. On the trodden snow outside the house we lay down two hazel saplings, each of them twice the height of a man, and in between them we lashed two shorter pieces and interwove them with strips of deerskin. So this made a kind of bed where Suncatcher could lie, with two handles at each end for us to carry her.

Telling this takes a very little time; doing it took much longer. Suncatcher was anxious for us all to leave the village now that we had convinced her to come with us. She still forbade us to enter the other houses, for fear the plague would jump to us from any dead still inside.

"But we touched Morning Star, we buried him, and we are still here, Grandmother."

"Risks may be taken for a great man," Suncatcher said. "But I will not put two young lives in danger again. It will be forgiven."

And she came to the entryway of the house and stood outside, to watch our litter-building.

It was while she was standing there, leaning on a walking stick we had cut for her, that we heard a shout from the edge of the village, and saw a group of figures coming toward us. We all stood there staring. They were the first living men we had seen for a long time.

There were three of them, and they came from the village by the river. Two of them Leaping Turtle and I recognized instantly, because they had been so good in the games played at a gathering of the villages last summer. The gap since then seemed like a lifetime.

Suncatcher knew all of them.

"Hunting Dog," she said as they came hurrying toward us. "Wolfchaser. One Who Waits."

This last one was an older man in a deerskin cloak, with

ceremonial red stripes on his cheek and forehead. He took Suncatcher's hands.

"I give thanks that you live, my sister," he said. Then he looked at us, and to my surprise he knew our names. "And Little Hawk, and Leaping Turtle."

"We give thanks too," said Suncatcher. She had discarded her stick and was standing as straight as she could, her voice strong. "We are all that is left of our village. All else is eaten by the white man's plague."

Now that I looked at One Who Waits, I remembered his face. My father knew him; he had eaten in our house. He was still gazing at us with an odd, haunted look. He shook his head, and there was a silence. Then he said, very low, "Too many of our young have died."

The plague came to their village as to ours, they told us. It ran fast through the youngest boys and girls, and killed many others too. The elders decided that the surviving families should move away from what had become a place of death—even though this was their winter home, even though the building of new dwellings would be much more difficult in the cold and snow.

So they had done that, and were still resettling themselves in a valley not far away. And they had been trying to find out how far this dreadful plague had spread through the nation. Of the five villages who would have been able to see the signals they sent into the sky, only two had sent an answer.

Leaping Turtle said, "We didn't know whether you had seen our signal. We were afraid it was too late."

Wolfchaser said, "We saw, and we came. And there is one person from your village who is now in ours, and will be very glad to see you."

"Who? Who is it?"

He smiled a little. "Soon you will see," he said.

And although they had come a long day's journey, they set to work to help us finish the litter for Suncatcher—which, they said diplomatically, was an excellent piece of design but could perhaps be a little stronger. Suncatcher went into the house to make food for us all, One Who Waits went with her to exchange more news, and the two younger men pulled out their tomahawks and went in search of more saplings. By the time night fell, we had a litter sturdy enough to carry a large bear.

There were not really enough skins and blankets for six people on the sleeping platforms that night, but the fire burned warm and I kept it fed. And Suncatcher fed all of us with stew and cornpone as if she were welcoming a normal visit from neighbors, in normal times. I remembered that night for long afterwards, as if it were a glowing bright star in a very dark sky.

At daybreak, we left our village forever. We were so busy packing bundles of anything that could be useful, and making the litter comfortable for Suncatcher, that we had no time to say a proper good-bye. But as we walked away through the trodden snow in our small procession, Wolfchaser and Hunting Dog carrying the litter, Leaping Turtle, One Who Waits, and I laden with bundles and baskets, I heard my grandmother's brave voice in the cold morning air. She was singing a chant of mourning, for the people and the place that we were leaving behind.

We walked all day, with one pause only, and just as the light began to fade we came to the new village that these valiant people had built, and were still building. There were perhaps twenty houses, and more partly finished, made in the usual way, with saplings set in a circle or oval and their heads lashed together in arches. The shingles that covered them had been brought from the old village. No new snow had fallen here since their building started, so the houses were dark hummocks in the white world, with strands of smoke rising from their roofs.

One Who Waits called out, loudly, and one by one people began to emerge from the houses, happy that their trackers had come back again. Some of them shouted a glad greeting as they recognized Suncatcher. I trudged over the snow with my bundles in a daze of fatigue and relief, and at first I didn't notice the figure of a girl running from one of the houses toward us. She ran fast, faster than all the others, heading straight for me, and I broke my stride and dropped my bundles just in time to catch her as she ran into my arms, laughing and weeping both at the same time.

It was my little sister, Quickbird.

N I N E

We were sitting round the fire in the biggest house of the village, which was long and had two fire pits. It had been the first one to be put up when they moved, to give shelter to as many as possible during the rebuilding. Quickbird was sitting between our grandmother and me, very close; I think she would have been sitting on Suncatcher's lap if it had been sturdier. They had each thought the other one was dead.

"I don't understand why Morning Star let you believe that," Quickbird said to her.

Suncatcher said, "Morning Star was a wise man." But she didn't explain precisely what she meant by this.

My sister, like me, had had to grow up very fast. First she had watched our parents and the baby die, helpless to do anything to save them. Then, when Suncatcher sent her to join our sister Southern in the women's house, hoping this might keep her from the disease, the plague went there too. And Southern too had died, with Quickbird in anguish at not being able to help her.

But the Great Spirit had not let the plague touch Quickbird. Though she nursed others in the women's house, she never fell ill. In the panic that overtook the village as more and more people died, she had been able to help Morning Star in his desperate attempts to aid the sick. Soon she had become too busy to run back to Suncatcher for herbs and advice, as she had often at first—and then there had come the day when Morning Star told Quickbird that her grandmother had died.

"And he said, 'This is enough. If you stay here you too will die, and I will not permit that. You must go at once to the village on the river. Your uncle Strong Bear will take you. The gods are angry with our people here, but not with all our nation. You are young and you must live for the rest of us, for your family and for the future.'"

Quickbird's voice faded for a moment, and she swallowed and tried again.

"So I said, 'What about my brother?' And he said, 'When Little Hawk returns from his journey, I will send him to you.' And then our uncle took me out on the trail, and Morning Star told grandmother that I had died."

Suncatcher said gently, "It was half a lie. He said he was the last one left, when he told me he was dying. His only full untruth was to you, and that was done to save your life—because you would not have left if you thought I was alive."

Quickbird nodded. For the moment, she couldn't talk anymore.

I said, "What happened to Strong Bear?"

One Who Waits was sitting on the other side of the fire. The lines on his face were darker in the light from the dancing flames.

He said, "Strong Bear was strong indeed. He knew we were making a new village free of plague, and he brought your sister here. He gave her into my care, and then he told her he had to go and do one more thing—'I may be some time,' he said. We found his body in the woods ten days later. I think he could feel the plague beginning in him, and he would not bring it here."

Our uncle Strong Bear was our mother's brother, the son of Suncatcher. She must have been very proud of him. She said nothing, but nodded her head slowly.

Wolfchaser nodded his head too, but differently. He was a strong young warrior with a tall scalp lock, one of the sons of One Who Waits. He said, "The gods were angry with Strong Bear, as with some of our people and so many of yours. Now let us pray that their anger is satisfied."

"In all the time of our people there has been no such great anger shown," Suncatcher said. She was a strong person, my grandmother; here as at home, people listened to her. "No. I believe this is a plague brought to us by the white men. It comes only when they have been near—and it brings death only to us, not to them."

Wolfchaser hesitated. He was reluctant to contradict an

elder, but he said, "Perhaps the gods are not angry with the white man."

"Hah!" said One Who Waits. "Not angry with the white man who comes in a ship and kills our people?"

I had heard this story, before I went on my solitary winter journey. South of here, not far from the Pokanoket village of Sowams, where our great sachem Yellow Feather lived, a trader from across the sea had invited a number of our people aboard his ship and suddenly, for no reason, had killed them all.

Wolfchaser hesitated again, because this was his father. "You yourself have traded with a white man," he said mildly.

One Who Waits said, "I will buy his knife for ten beaver skins, but I will not therefore trust him."

I wished I were older and could have joined this talk; he was describing exactly what my father had done. But my father had never said anything to me about his opinion of white men, and I had never seen one. All I knew was that after my father had taken that knife, he also took the plague, and died.

We heard more talk about the white men in the weeks and months after this. But it was a busy time, full of hard work. The village elders, who all knew Suncatcher well, had already taken in Quickbird as if she were one of their own. They had also embraced our friend Spring Frog, who, luckily for him, had ended his winter ordeal at their village instead of ours. We had hoped for word of White Oak, but there was none.

Now the village had adopted Leaping Turtle and me in the same way. We helped with the long hard business of rebuilding more than thirty houses in the new place, half a day's distance from the old village that their medicine man felt had been cursed by the plague. We set traps, too, to bring extra food to the house of One Who Waits, where we were living—though we were careful beforehand to find out which places were not already trapped. The land and all that it supports belong to all men equally, but this was a matter of good manners.

Wolfchaser approved of us, I thought, and the others respected his opinion. I also thought he might have warm feelings for Quickbird, since although he was a tough young man, he was oddly awkward when he was talking to her. Quickbird didn't seem to notice this; after all, she was still very young. In spite of everything that had happened she was often the same bright cheeky person she always had been, making fun of Leaping Turtle and me if she thought we were behaving too much like know-it-all big brothers. Wolfchaser too had a big brother, Swift Deer, but Swift Deer lived in his own house with his wife and two daughters. He was a fierce person, and I sometimes wondered how he had behaved to Wolfchaser when they were boys.

The outside shingles of all the houses in the new village that had been brought from the old houses were great heavy sections of bark from elm or oak or chestnut trees. In winter, the bark on all the trees is too hard to be taken, so we leave our brothers the trees in their cold sleep. But by the second moon of the year, the Snow Moon, even though the air is still cold and the snow still covering the ground, the trees are beginning to wake, and the sap is starting its long journey up from the roots into the branches and the twigs.

So when the big beautiful white moon shone full over the village, Leaping Turtle and I carefully sharpened our axes. We took turns, stroking each blade against a precious sharpener flint we had borrowed from One Who Waits.

Quickbird gazed at my axe, and at the rippled wooden shaft that enclosed it.

"Tell the story," she said.

I looked at Suncatcher, and she nodded her head.

So I told One Who Waits about my father binding his grandfather's axe head into the cleft of a young tree, so that it would grow for ten years and create an axe for Little Hawk. Fortunate Little Hawk.

One Who Waits took the axe and touched its shaft gently, reverently, with the tips of his fingers.

"There is time in this axe," he said. "It is like our people. Whatever may happen, it will carry the past into the future. Some day, Little Hawk, your Manitou will bring you peace by returning your axe to one of the trees from which it came."

"But not yet," I said, rather nervously.

"Oh no," said One Who Waits. "For now, it is your father's gift to your life." He touched the edge of the blade. "Aiee! And sharp!"

So we gave him back his sharpener stone, with our thanks, and the next day, with help from Wolfchaser and his friends, we set off into the woods to cut bark shingles for a brand new house in which Quickbird, Suncatcher, Leaping Turtle, and I would live. Spring Frog was living with the family who had taken him in when he first came; he was as close to them as if he were a son of their own.

We had already made the frame that would be the bones of our new house, by setting a circle of tall young saplings into the thawing ground and lashing all their tops together for a strong curved roof. Now we would give it its outside shell, to protect us from the weather as a clamshell protects a clam.

And when that house was finished, one week later, it marked the start of a new part of our lives. Suncatcher, Quickbird, Leaping Turtle, and I were a part of this village now, one family among thirty-two others, all of us linked by suffering and survival. Though we didn't share the blood ties of most of the others, we had been drawn into the community not only by One Who Waits, who was their sachem, but by everyone.

Even fierce Swift Deer, who by nature mistrusted all strangers, had accepted us. When he came by one day to thank Leaping Turtle for mending a toy for his younger daughter, he was even heard calling him "little brother."

In all parts of our nation that had been hit by the plague, these same changes must have been happening.

The days were growing longer; we had passed the Snow Moon, and though the snow still lay on the ground, it was softer. It had gone altogether from most of the trees, who were waking slowly from their winter sleep. Soon the sap would be rising in their woody veins, and Suncatcher had already sent us out for twigs—slippery elm and sumac—that she would hollow into pipes for tapping the maple trees.

Whenever I could hardly bear the ache of missing my mother and father and all the rest, the ways of this new village were a comfort because they were just the same as the old. As the snow began to melt, all the men left for a deer drive, since the long winter had used up nearly all the food put into store in the autumn. Two other villages—the only two near us to have survived the plague—sent hunters too. The older men said sorrowfully that this year's hunt would be very small compared to the past, when more than a hundred would take part, but Leaping Turtle and I were excited. This was a ritual for men, not boys, and for the first time in our lives we were to go too.

Small or large, a deer drive was a complicated matter, and took a long time. Out in the woods, we dug holes and planted a long line of logs as if they were trees, weaving brush between them so that they were like a fence. Then a long way away, perhaps five hundred paces, another line was planted to come very gradually closer to the first, so that they formed an enormous arrowhead shape with a gap at the tip. Then it was time for more than half the men to go and hunt down a herd of deer, and drive them into the arrowhead, where they would be an easy target for the waiting bows.

The hunters had been gone overnight; it was almost dawn, the favorite feeding time for deer. Leaping Turtle and I were told to wait by the fence, with Wolfchaser, Swift Deer, and a dozen others. We were as tense as our bowstrings, straining for a sound of running feet.

"Aim for the neck, remember," Wolfchaser said. "And don't waste your time following a wounded deer, sooner or later he will lie down. Track, not chase."

We were waiting beside the gap in the arrowhead fence, clutching our bows. For the third time, Leaping Turtle reached round to loosen the arrows in his quiver. Watching him, Wolfchaser smiled.

"At my first deer run I kept doing that," he said, "and my father reached over and took all my arrows away. He gave me back three of them, and he said, 'If you aim well, this is all you need.'"

Leaping Turtle looked embarrassed, and I tried to rescue him.

"Your father is not here?" I said to Wolfchaser.

Wolfchaser's smile faded.

"He has gone to Sowams," he said. "Yellow Feather has called together all the sachems, because many white men have come in a big boat—not just traders, but whole families. Yellow Feather is not happy, he would like them to go away."

"Whole families?"

"Men, women, children," Wolfchaser said.

I had never thought of the white man, the sailing trader from far away, as having a family—let alone bringing them to our land to live.

Leaping Turtle said, "Where are they?"

Swift Deer had heard our talk; he turned to join it, and his face was grim. He said, "They landed on Nauset territory, where the plague has struck the villages even harder than here. They dug up the winter corn store in an empty village and they stole it. Then they trod through a sacred burying ground, and they dug up a grave and stole the grave offerings. The Nausets shot arrows at them, so they went back to their boat—and now they have moved to our land."

Wolfchaser said, "They do not belong here. Yellow Feather wants all the medicine men to ask the gods to send them away."

"And if not," Swift Deer said fiercely, "we shall shoot our own arrows!"

Wolfchaser looked unhappy at this—but suddenly a deer came leaping toward us and we heard the sounds of the drive, and we were all shooting arrows not at the white man but at deer.

I did not forget those two faces, though: the determination of Swift Deer and the unhappiness of Wolfchaser.

We killed twenty-three deer; the share for our village

was fourteen. Swift Deer was in charge, fittingly. We all gathered in silence as he cut off the tongue and the left hind foot of each animal, for an offering, and called out a prayer of thanks to Mother Earth and the deer spirit. His voice echoed through the trees and the blue sky above, and there was a silence—and into it came the high harsh call of a red-tailed hawk.

My eyes stung, and I sent a silent greeting to my father, and to my Manitou.

We gutted the deer, and tied their forelegs together and then their hind legs, and we carried them home, each one hanging by the legs from a pole carried by two strong men. It took all night and half the next day, but it was a triumphal procession, and our return was greeted with cries of praise and delight. In the crowd I saw Suncatcher's dark, lined face brightened by one of her rare smiles, and Quickbird was shrilling like a happy child.

That night, after the skinning and cutting up of the deer, the village had its traditional celebration of the hunt, thanking the Great Spirit for the defeat of winter by spring. We sang, we danced, we ate till our stomachs were so tight that they hurt. For the first time this collection of rebuilt houses, a broken community trying to make a new life, felt happy and whole.

But One Who Waits, who came back from Yellow Feather's council just before we arrived, was restless and uneasy. He greeted the hunters warmly, and led the triumphant Deer Dance, but whenever I caught sight of his face afterward it seemed to be looking at something a long way away.

One morning I came bursting into our house with a raccoon I had trapped, so big that I could hardly carry him, and I found One Who Waits sitting beside Suncatcher, talking. Their heads came up, they broke off. They both looked so grave that I knew I had interrupted something serious.

I dropped my raccoon on the floor and stood there, confused.

Suncatcher said, "Little Hawk, perhaps—"

"Let him hear," said One Who Waits. "It will be common knowledge soon enough."

He waved at me to sit down, and turned back to Suncatcher.

"It is true," he said. "I think our father Yellow Feather will have us offer help and friendship to the white men, now that our pleas to the spirits have not sent them away. For one thing, he is a man who does not enjoy war, and for another, the plague has so weakened us that, as you know, we have been paying tribute to the Narragansetts for many moons now."

"Perhaps indeed the white men will be strong friends," Suncatcher said. "Though they seem more like reeds than trees, if the winter has killed half of them."

I said tentatively, "Grandmother?" I was asking permission to say something, and because I was now a man they both respected that, and looked at me.

"Yes?" said Suncatcher.

"The things that they make are strong," I said. "The metal things, like my knife, and the weapons called guns."

One Who Waits sighed. "What have you heard about guns?" he said.

"That they are sticks that make a loud noise and shoot at you, not an arrow but a fast ball of metal."

"Which can kill more surely than an arrow," he said. "Yes."

"My father," I said, very formal because I was asking a serious question of an elder, "what do the white men want, besides our furs?"

One Who Waits said, "I think our father Yellow Feather fears that they want the land."

TEN

But the white men were still a long way from our village, and as spring began, life was so busy that nobody had much time to worry about them. We tapped the maple trees, collected the sap in buckets, and carried it back to the older women, who boiled it down gradually over slow fires.

When the sap was thick, it was poured into wooden molds to harden into cakes of sugar. Quickbird and her friends would splash dribbles of it into the remaining snowbanks, to harden into little sweets for the children. So many children had been killed by the plague that there were only five left in the whole village, three girls and two boys, and everyone spoiled them. Suncatcher said they were the rulers of the village, and she spoiled them as much as anyone. Often I found all five sitting in our house while she tried to teach them to rub hemp stalks into fiber, and told them the old stories.

When the maple sap was all boiled down into those hard cakes, to last through next winter, it was time to burn the underbrush from the land that would soon be planted. That was a job for everyone, even the children, armed with little brooms for beating back the flames, because the fire had to be kept from eating up all the trees.

One day, when the powdery black ash lay smoking in the fields, and the medicine man had just finished making the prayers for rain to wash it into the soil, Wolfchaser came running into the village. His voice rang out before we even saw him.

"The fish are running!" he was shouting. "The fish are running!"

Each day one of us had been sent on a long journey to the river to watch for the start of the spring run, when the herring and shad and bass come rushing up from the sea to the higher parts of the river where they will spawn. They are one of our many spring gifts from the gods. I loved being on watch, staring into the stream, hoping to be the first to see the flashing silver bodies and to run with the news, but it was Wolfchaser who was the lucky one.

And soon everyone from our village, and the other surviving settlements too, was camped in rough shelters by the river. The men were scooping up fish with nets and spears, the women splitting the slippery gleaming bodies and hanging them on racks beside rows of fires, to smoke and preserve them for the rest of the year. Fish soup steamed in pots beside their fires, and we ate it every day, along with fish grilled on sticks.

The dogs stole fish from the fishermen and for once nobody minded, because there were so many. One Who Waits's favorite dog ate so many that he threw them up— whole fish, because he had bolted them so fast—and then to our astonishment he ate them again.

Quickbird saw what he was doing, as she came to us on the riverbank to collect another basket of fish. She made a loud noise of disgust.

"How can you *do* that!" she said to the dog.

The dog grabbed his last thrown-up fish and ran away with it.

Leaping Turtle laughed at the expression on Quickbird's face. "Animals waste nothing," he said.

Quickbird picked up the basket we had just filled with small twitching silver bodies. She sighed.

"Everything smells of fish," she says. "Even the air, even the trees. You, me, Suncatcher, we all smell of fish—I shall be so glad to get back to the sweat lodge!"

Leaping Turtle stopped laughing. He was looking past her, past the women and the smoking fires, toward the camp.

He said, "Who is *that*?"

One Who Waits and Hunting Dog were walking from the camp toward the river, and there were some strangers with them: an important-looking warrior wearing an ornate beaded headband with an eagle feather, and three others.

Leaping Turtle was suddenly very tense, staring.

"White men!" he said softly.

They were two men and a boy, the first white men I had ever seen. They were dressed very strangely, in thick dark clothes from their necks down to their feet, and one of them was wearing a hat like a kind of dark basket on his head. Their skin was not white like snow, but it was lighter than ours—though there was not much of it to see, because both men had a lot of hair on their faces.

The boy was dressed just like them, even though he was quite young, perhaps seven winters old. He gazed around at us with his eyes wide and his mouth open, smiling. He was a very unafraid boy; you could tell that if one of the men hadn't had a firm hand on his shoulder, he would have been running to join our own children—two of whom were already there, peering at him from either side of Quickbird's deerskin leggings.

All the men beside and in the river had paused. They stood still, looking. Swift Deer and Wolfchaser came forward to join us; Swift Deer was very wet, and shook himself like a dog. The drops of water prickled against my skin like cold rain.

One Who Waits called out, "My sons! You remember the one they call Squanto?"

"Greetings!" said Swift Deer.

Wolfchaser said, "We greet you!"

Their voices were dutifully warm, but there was a thread of uncertainty in them that made me feel they had no idea who this man was.

The important man nodded his head to them.

One Who Waits raised his voice so that everyone could hear. The fishermen had come clustering round now, and the white man in the hat looked a little nervous.

"Yellow Feather wishes us to be helpful to these white men," he said. "He tells us they are friends of our people. They are in care of Squanto, because he speaks their language."

Squanto looked round at us all. He clearly knew he was somebody special.

"They are called Thomas Evans and Benjamin Wakeley," he said. "They are Englishmen. We are here only a very short time. Yellow Feather wishes us to show them the way we take the fish. I have taught them how to catch eels and how to plant, but this they can only learn by watching."

"Perhaps they would like to join us?" said Swift Deer, dripping.

There was a ripple of laughter, and Squanto frowned.

"You may continue with what you are doing," he said loftily, "and that will do very well."

Suncatcher stepped forward from the cluster of women beside the smoking fires. She had a small bowl in each hand, and so did two of the others. "May I?" she said to One Who Waits.

"Please," said One Who Waits, extending his hand.

Suncatcher said to Squanto, "We should like to offer them some fish soup. You too, of course. You must all be hungry after your travels."

Squanto eyed the soup hungrily, but he spoke to the Englishmen in their own language. They too looked at the bowls, but without enthusiasm; they bobbed their heads politely to Suncatcher but they shook them to Squanto, and talked. They were clearly saying no thank you.

"They give you thanks, but they say they would like to watch the fishing," Squanto said. He added, with a hint of scorn, "The white man is not good at eating our food."

Swift Deer said briskly, "Come then!"

Beckoning to the white men, he loped back toward the river, and the others with him. Soon the fishing began again, and Wolfchaser was in the water demonstrating with wide sweeps of his arms the way that our fish weirs worked. These are woven reed mats in the water that make the fish go in a certain direction to be speared or scooped up; it is much like the way we caught the deer on the deer drive. Squanto, translating when he had to, was taking breaks to swallow a bowl of soup.

The white men were watching Wolfchaser so closely that they didn't notice when the boy left them and came toward Quickbird and the boy and girl sheltering behind her. He smiled at them. They were Little Fox and Turtledove, and they looked at him solemnly. Then suddenly Turtledove beamed, and she showed him the toy she was holding.

The boy's father looked up, saw where the boy was, and called in alarm. Squanto patted his arm soothingly; they talked.

Squanto called, "Be careful not to frighten the child! Keep him in his father's sight!"

Quickbird waved. Turtledove and Little Fox and the boy were playing cup and ball. He seemed to know it already; perhaps all children everywhere play the same games.

Quickbird looked down at them. "Look how different they are!" she said. "The same, but so different!"

Little Fox and Turtledove were wearing deerskin shirts and moccasins, because it was still cold even though the spring was coming. If it had been warmer they would have been wearing nothing at all. The white boy was all wrapped up in heavy woven cloths and leggings, and his moccasins were made of some very stiff uncomfortable-looking leather. He was saying something to Turtledove, but of course she couldn't understand him.

"Tell him your names," Quickbird said. "Like this."

She took the boy's hand to get his attention, and pointed to herself. "Quick bird," she said slowly. "Quick bird."

Turtledove grabbed his hand in turn. "Turtle dove," she said, poking herself in the chest.

The boy said with some difficulty, "Turtle dove." He pointed at her. "Turtle dove," he said again, grinning in triumph.

Then he pointed at Quickbird.

"Bird," he said.

We went through this with Little Fox, and then the white boy tapped his own chest. "John," he said.

We all repeated it. Pleased, he looked round at all our faces—and stopped at mine.

I was next to him, but much taller, and he hadn't looked closely at me before. His eyes widened as he saw the ugly scar on my face. They were blue eyes, as blue as the sky.

He put up his hand and touched my scar very gently.

"Oh," he said softly. His voice was full of sympathy, like a woman's.

Then he said again, "John," tapping his chest, and he raised his eyebrows to me in a way that clearly meant, *What's your name?*

"Little Hawk," I said. I pointed to myself.

"Hawk," said John. He smiled at me. "Hawk."

Suncatcher came to us with a handful of the very smallest pellets made from boiled-down maple sap, that were kept as treats for children. Little Fox and Turtledove beamed and stretched out their hands, and John watched them.

I took a few of the pellets from Suncatcher's hand, and squatted down and held them out to the boy. He came closer, looking at me solemnly with those wide blue eyes, and helped himself from my outstretched palm. We saw the eyes widen as he tasted the sweet maple, and we all laughed.

So did he. He laughed, and patted my arm.

"Hawk," he said.

Soon the white men came back, satisfied with their fishing lesson, and the boy's father came to find him. Seen close, he was a man not much older than Swift Deer, in spite of all the hair on his face. He wore the hair on his head long, like a woman. I sensed a faintly sour, unwashed smell about him, though the smell of fish masked almost everything around.

He put his hand on John's shoulder, and nodded to us in a friendly way.

John pointed at me. "Hawk," he said to his father helpfully. He added something in their language.

"Ah," said the man, and he caught my eye and smiled, nodding again. I saw his eyes go to the scar on my face.

Then Squanto came and took them away. Our people insisted on giving them two baskets of fish, since there were so many, sent by the Great Spirit not just for us but for all people. One Who Waits sent two of the younger men to go with them, carrying the baskets, and I wished I were one of them. I had found an odd, warm excitement in me at having looked into the eyes of a white man for the first time. They were blue eyes, like his son's.

Small John turned as they left, and waved to me.

Squanto, said One Who Waits a few days later, had learned the language of the white men by living in their country. He and some others were carried there in a boat to become slaves, and he was there for some years before a white man from a different tribe brought him back again. Nobody seemed to know exactly what happened to him in the white man's land.

"When he came back, like Little Hawk and Leaping

Turtle, like so many, he found the plague had taken most of his village," One Who Waits said. "So his life was twice changed. He is useful to Yellow Feather, because without him we could not talk to the white men. But—"

He stopped talking then, and took a thoughtful pull at the pipe we were all sharing. We were in the sweat lodge, back from the fish and the fishing; it was wonderful to feel the sweat washing the dirt and the stink out of our skin.

Wolfchaser said, "I think you do not like this Squanto, my father."

"It is hard to know what is in his mind," said One Who Waits. "But he has done me no wrong."

"He was foolish to let the white men take so many fresh fish from here," Wolfchaser said. "They surely spoiled before they could eat them."

Swift Deer said, "You forget what he said—he is teaching the white men to plant. Those fish were not for eating."

And I remembered the pattern that Suncatcher and my mother used to have my sisters recite: *fire before hoes, fish before seeds, corn before beans, beans before squash.* Here in the village the women were into the second part of the pattern already. Now that the rain had washed the ashes of the burning into the cleared ground, they had dug the soil into little hills with their hoes, made of big clamshells lashed to sticks. Each hill was a big stride away from the next, and in each they had buried several fish, deep enough to keep their smell from the searching nose of Brother Raccoon, who would certainly have dug them up again.

The fish would rot and feed the soil, and when the leaves on the white oak were the size of a mouse's ears, the women would plant four kernels of corn in each hill. Some days later they would plant a bean near each seed of corn, so that the bean vine would climb up the cornstalk, and when the leaves on the oak trees were full out and dancing, they would plant squash seeds between the hills. Then the squash vines would cover all the rest of the ground and keep weeds from growing. I always liked to see this pattern; it was a harmony.

Swift Deer said, "So Squanto will help the white men plant the fish we gave them—and then the corn they stole from the Nausets."

Wolfchaser said mildly, "I heard that the corn they took was the buried store in a village where all the Nausets had died of the plague."

Swift Deer made a snorting sound. "Did you hear that they left anything in return?"

"No," Wolfchaser said.

And then One Who Waits announced that it was time for us to leave the sweat lodge so that others might use it, and I was glad, even though my skin was happy to be cleansed. The tobacco in the ceremonial pipe was sacred to the gods, but I had never smoked any before and it was making me feel sick to my stomach.

ELEVEN

That spring was a good time in the village. More families had joined us, after long discussions at the fish-gathering. They had moved from another village closer to the river, where they too had lost many to the plague, including their sachem and their two wisest elders. There, they were at the far edge of our territory, close to the land where the Massachusetts people farm and hunt; now that they were so few, perhaps they wanted to feel closer to their own tribe.

So fifteen more families had come to join this new village of ours, which was already two villages joined together. When their houses were all finished we had a great ceremony of greeting, over which One Who Waits presided as sachem of us all. His council now was made up of elders from all the three original settlements, and Suncatcher was one of its most respected members.

Leaping Turtle, Spring Frog, and I had hoped that we might find our friend White Oak among these people, but he wasn't there. Though nobody ever found his body, we knew he must somehow have died, during the winter ordeal that we'd been lucky enough to survive.

There were young children among the newcomers, which made everyone happy—not least Leaping Turtle and me. We had been in charge of building the little wooden watchtowers in the cornfields, just like those from which we ourselves had scared away thieving birds and animals from the fields when we were young. With only five children available to sit up there with noisemakers and blunt arrows, we had begun to think we might have to join them, which would have been very undignified. But now there were enough extra children who would be delighted to chase away the raccoons and the woodchucks, the jays and the crows. And they would be instructed, just as we had been, that Brother Crow may be scared away but never killed, because it was his ancestor who brought mankind the corn and bean seeds in the first place, one seed in each of his ears.

So the cornstalks grew tall, and in due course the beans climbed up, starring them with white blossoms, and the squash vines filled the ground below. Quickbird and all the women gathered the new greens as spring became summer. They were busy weeding, digging roots, cooking, weaving, sewing—at this time of the year I was always glad I was not a woman. But we men were just as busy, hunting birds and deer, trapping, and traveling to the river to fish.

Leaping Turtle and I were good fishermen. After the snow melted, the two of us made a private journey back to our old village, not to visit the deserted houses but to rescue from its hiding place the beautiful little birch-bark canoe we had made under the instruction of Running Deer. Mice had nested in it, but the birch-bark was still smooth, and all we had to do after we carried it home was reseal the joins with spruce resin.

We carved new paddles from ash wood in the evenings. Wolfchaser and Hunting Dog came with us when we took the canoe to the river, and hooted with praise when it floated light as a leaf. I think they were a little envious that we had been taught by Running Deer, who was famous in the whole tribe for his skill in shaping canoes. Leaping Turtle and I went out together one day to a high place near the river and gave thanks to his spirit.

Another day we did something Suncatcher had requested: taking digging sticks with us, we traveled back again to our old village, and beside the overgrown trail just outside it we dug a memory hole. It was in honor of Running Deer, Morning Star, our parents, and all those who lived in our village and were killed by the plague. It was a round hole about a foot deep, lined with stones, and now that it was there it would be kept open by generations of people to come. These memory holes were all over our land, on our trails; they were the record of the people who lived before us, and of what happened in their time.

Suncatcher was pleased when we had done this. At

sunset that day she chanted a prayer for the memory hole and for those it remembered.

As time went by, we visited the memory hole regularly, to keep it clear of brush and fallen leaves. Through harvest and another deer drive, through the dark of winter and the first glimmering of spring, we lived our first few years in the changed world that we had entered when plague killed so many that we loved. I suppose Leaping Turtle and Quickbird and I changed too, as time passed, but everyone was working so hard that such things were not noticed. Our one concern was to make this village as strong a community as those it had been forced to replace.

In the rest of our land, though, there was thought for the things that changed. One day in late autumn, when One Who Waits and Swift Deer were visiting our house, a runner came through the village on his way to deliver a report to Yellow Feather. He was one of those who kept regular watch on a new settlement of white men, on the coast at Wessagussett among the Massachusetts. Since he was a friend of Swift Deer, he came to our house to greet him before returning to the trail. It would be a very brief greeting. Runners do not sleep until they reach the end of the journey; they run day and night, with only their pouch of ground corn for food.

His name was Bearclaw. He raised his hand in polite refusal when Suncatcher offered him a bowl of stew. "I thank you, Grandmother," he said, "but with a full belly I cannot run."

"I understand," Suncatcher said. She handed him a ladle of water instead, and he drank.

Swift Deer leaned forward eagerly. "What did you find? Are the new white men still stealing corn?"

Bearclaw shook his head. "Even by thieving they couldn't feed themselves," he said. "The Massachusetts are using some of them as labor in return for food. These white men are not like the others, they have built a fort but they have no skills. The Massachusetts have no respect for them. I do not like the feel of things there."

He turned toward the door. "My thanks to you all— I must go."

One Who Waits said, "Carry my greetings to Yellow Feather. I hope he is in good health."

"I pray so," Bearclaw said. "He was not well when I left."

He raised a hand and he was gone, with Swift Deer following. I knew the two would run together for a while and talk. There had been much talk in the sweat lodge that year, about the treaty Yellow Feather had made to help the first English settlers, about disagreements with the Narragansett people south of us, and about bad things said and done by Squanto to set Yellow Feather and the English against each other. It seemed that others besides One Who Waits were now feeling uneasy about Squanto.

Swift Deer and Wolfchaser talked often with their father, and sometimes argued. Leaping Turtle listened and tried to learn; like Swift Deer, he had an instinctive mistrust of all white men. I listened sometimes, but it was the kind of talk that made me wish I was away alone in the woods again. People seemed to me to fill life with shadows that should not be there. The Great Spirit gave us so much, and we had all lived our separate lives on the land in harmony—the trees, the plants, the birds, the animals, the fish, and—most of the time—men. There was surely room for all to go on doing the same, even if white men had come here too.

Leaping Turtle and I were digging a pit when we had our first argument about this. The Harvest Moon was past, the corn had all been dried and the beans threshed, and the women and small children were trying to beat the squirrels to the last berries and nuts. In our old villages, the pits for winter food storage had been in the ground for years, but here we had had to dig new ones, and each year we needed more than the last.

We were standing so low down that our noses were level with the ground. The digging had taken all day, and now we were lining the sides of the hole with stones.

"Just think," I said, as the sweat ran into my eyes, "our children too will fill this pit with corn. Just like the old village, where we stored food in pits our grandfathers had dug."

"How do you know our people will still be here?" said Leaping Turtle.

"Of course they will."

"Swift Deer says more white men are coming, and their families, and they will take the land."

"There is plenty of land," I said. "Hand me that long skinny rock over there."

"Swift Deer says—"

"Swift Deer is cross with everyone. Our father Yellow Feather has agreements with the white men, you know that, and they will live their lives and we shall live ours. That's what One Who Waits believes."

"You talk like a child," Leaping Turtle said, and he dropped a rock on my foot—but not on purpose, and it was a small one.

He kept on telling me that he had heard this thing and he had heard that thing, and all of it meant that I was simple in my thinking, and that nothing would stay the same. That everything was becoming different, because of the coming of the white men.

And though I could not see it then, he was right.

Winter came, and the village was full of whispers. One Who Waits had received runners from two different directions, who had spoken to him privately and been in great haste. Nobody knew what they had said. One Who Waits did something that had never happened before in this, our new combined village: he called his council and all the men ceremonially into the biggest space we had, a long house that was the home for four families. It was morning. The women and children of the four families slipped away to other houses.

I felt small in this gathering. Leaping Turtle and I were

by far the youngest present; we were surrounded by men who were bigger, older, and more important, and by a few wise grandmothers. But we were there, listening.

One Who Waits stood up and spoke loudly and clearly, with no expression on his face. He reminded us that our father Yellow Feather had joined us in friendship with the Patuxet settlement of English white men, by an agreement that both groups would live peaceably and protect one another. He told us that Yellow Feather had been very sick, and that some medicine from a leader of the white men, called Winslow, had helped him to get better.

Then he paused, and you could tell that he was getting to something he did not like saying.

"It seems," he said, "that our father Yellow Feather and the English had word that the Massachusetts were planning to attack the English settlements, both the new one at Wessagussett and the first at Patuxet. It seems they believed this, even though many of the white men at Wessagussett were living with Massachusetts families. So a group of the English went to Wessagussett and they killed six of the Massachusetts."

There was a long low murmur among the men listening.

One Who Waits's voice became quieter and more full of emotion. He said, "It seems that the leader of the English group, a captain called Standish, invited the leading warriors Wituwamet and Pecksuot to eat with him, and then he and his men stabbed them to death in that house. He killed his guests. And outside the house his people hanged

Wituwamet's brother, and killed three other Massachusetts."

The murmur grew louder.

One Who Waits held up his hand and the voices died down. He said, "But we are joined to these people by our treaty that Yellow Feather made. Their anger is not against us but against the Massachusetts. Remember that. They have no quarrel with us, they are our friends."

The men in the house were not raising their voices now, but you could hear a restlessness, a shuffling of feet.

"I have told you what took place, my brothers," One Who Waits said. "We will discuss it. But our father Yellow Feather would have you remember that we have had troubles of our own with the Massachusetts, as with the Narragansetts. This thing that has happened shows that if we remain friends with the English, we can have peace in our land."

Swift Deer stepped forward into the central space and said clearly, "May I speak, my father?"

He was entitled to do this, as the eldest son of One Who Waits, but there was a little pause before his father answered.

"You may speak," said One Who Waits. He sounded weary.

"It seems," said Swift Deer, "that the Englishman Standish also cut off the head of Wituwamet. And that it is now stuck up on a pole over the fort of our friends at Patuxet, where the crows peck at it."

There was a sharp burst of angry sound at that, but

because One Who Waits stood there erect and unmoving, it died down again. Swift Deer was still standing too. They gazed at each other, and you could feel a tension between them like the strain in a tug-of-war rope.

One Who Waits said, "We have suffered much already. For the sake of our children, let us not seek war."

And into the silence after his words, Suncatcher suddenly began to sing. From where she was sitting at the back, on one of the sleeping platforms of the house, her voice rose over our heads, into the smoky air. And it was not a war chant but an old song that the women sang to soothe an unhappy child, much like a lullaby. Some of the words in the song always changed to fit the name of the child, and Suncatcher used the name of one of the men in her family.

My name.

"*Little Hawk*," she sang in her clear true voice.

"Little Hawk, fly above the trees.
Fly in freedom, fly in beauty,
Fly as the Great Spirit wills.
The sky is there for you, Little Hawk.
Little Hawk, fly in peace."

When she was done, and the echo of her voice hung in the house, One Who Waits made the sweeping gesture that says, *It is finished*, and quietly we all made our way outside and went to our homes.

TWELVE

Leaping Turtle and I loved to run, and we had always been the fastest in any running games. Even when we were small boys, before the plague, we had both taken pride in running faster than the others, and we would each try all the time to beat the other one. Everything was a race, and each of us made the other run faster, try harder.

So before long we were chosen as runners by One Who Waits. Yellow Feather and his sachems kept careful watch over our land. From every important sachem, messages were sent every few days to and from Yellow Feather's home in Sowams, to report in particular on any event involving other tribes or the white men. The runner had to be not just fast, but able to convey his message well. Leaping Turtle and I were as tall now as any grown man, but we were the youngest of them, so perhaps that's why we were sent as a pair. If one inexperienced memory were to lose a piece of a message, the other would fill the gap.

One Who Waits told us what he wished to say, and we repeated it back to him. He instructed us to take a trail that would need a day's more running than a direct way, so that we could visit a village nearer the white men's settlement and bring a report from the sachem there. We were both very excited at the thought of meeting the great sachem Yellow Feather.

It was spring, and though the nights would be cold, our running would keep us warm. We each wore only a breech-clout, leggings, and moccasins, and carried at our belts a knife, a tomahawk, and a small pack of food. Quickbird gave Leaping Turtle and me each a pouch filled with grain that she had ground herself, and patted my shoulder.

"This time, they would let me give you needles and thread," she said, smiling, "but you won't be gone long enough to need them."

"Safe travel," Suncatcher said. "Carry my respects to our father Yellow Feather."

And we ran. We ran through the grasses and big trees of the land that had been burned for hunting and farming for so many years; we ran at night, guided by the stars. We ran along old trails that had been beaten down by centuries of feet, but were being gradually overgrown now that our people were so much fewer. When we had to, we paused to eat a little food, or to drink from a stream.

For a day and a night we ran toward the east, away from the setting sun, knowing that within another day we should pause at a village close to the first English settlement. After pausing to talk to their sachem, we should turn south.

We ran.

We were running along a trail so little used that it was being overtaken by scrub, slowing us a little. All at once we heard somewhere ahead of us a great thump, with a crackle of breaking branches. There was only one thing it could be: a tree falling. The breeze that day was only light, but even a small wind can bring down a tree if it has finally reached the end of its long tall life. We paused for a moment, then ran on.

But then we heard the screams. And we stopped again, looked at one another, and ran toward them.

The voice was high—a child or a woman. They were the short quick screams of panic, growing louder as we crashed through the undergrowth. Then we were out in the sunlight on the edge of a clearing, and we saw that a big tree was indeed down—not fallen, but chopped down. And clearly the white men who cut it down had made the terrible mistake of not running clear in the proper direction as it fell, for one of them was lying crushed under its trunk, which had come down squarely on his back.

The other was trapped by his leg underneath a big branch, and beside him was a boy, screaming.

We ran to the trapped man, who did not move, and the boy stopped screaming and started to babble to us in English. His face was all wet with tears. He was about ten years old and he was clearly begging for help, terrified.

"We can cut him free!" I was peering at the branch. "Look—if we can cut it there, we can roll him out!"

"No!" Leaping Turtle said. He grabbed my arm. "Leave them! Whites will come—if there are two, there are more. It's too dangerous!"

"Too dangerous to help?"

"You are a runner, you mustn't stop—you have sworn to run to Yellow Feather!"

And at that I would have turned to go, but the boy was staring at my face. At the scar.

He said, "Hawk?"

I looked at him, and although he was taller and a little changed by the years, I recognized him.

"Hawk!" He was pleading now. "Hawk!"

It was the small boy John, who had come to see us fishing, and the man lying trapped under the branch must be his father, who had smiled at me that day.

So I pulled out my tomahawk.

"No!" said Leaping Turtle urgently.

I motioned the boy to stand clear, and I took a great swing to hack at the branch that had trapped the man's leg.

It all happened so fast. My tomahawk hitting the branch must have masked the sound of the first shot. As I swung my arm back again, with my axe high in the air, I heard John shouting in alarm, and I saw a puff of smoke, though I never heard the sound of the second shot that blasted a great hole in my chest and killed me.

PART TWO

PLANTING MOON

O N E

Leaping Turtle knew instantly that I was dead. My blood spurted over him as my body dropped at his feet. Instinct sent him diving into the undergrowth, where branches and twigs stabbed him so that he too began bleeding. He did not look back. Stumbling up again, he crashed through the bushes, on and on, until he found a trail. Then he ran southward, sobbing as he ran, mourning his dead brother, tears and sweat mixing on his face. He ran and he ran, toward Sowams.

And as spirit, I was not free to leave. I was held there by the horror in the mind of small John, and by the tomahawk with the blade of my ancestors.

I watched. I listened.

The boy stood shocked into silence, staring aghast at my shattered chest and the bright blood, and at my face with the wide open eyes that could no longer see.

Two Englishmen came running out of the trees. One was tall and young, the other a short man in soldier's clothes, carrying the long gun they call a musket. He was grinning down at my body.

"The Lord delivered us the murderous savage!" he cried, and clapped John on the shoulder. "You're safe, boy! God be praised we were in time to save you!"

John shrieked at him. "He was helping us, couldn't you see? I shouted! I told you!"

"Are you mad? We saw him attacking you!"

"He was trying to cut my father free!"

In a brief instant of uncertainty, they looked beyond my spread-eagled body, and the tomahawk fallen near my hand. They saw the boy's father lying trapped by the leg, and the other man's body crushed under the trunk of the tree, and they rushed forward, the small man tossing his musket aside. They clawed at the branches, trying to reach the white man's broken body, and then fell back as they saw there was no hope.

"Goodman Ford is dead," the small man said.

John was still gazing at the great wound in my chest, caught up in horror. His white shirt was spattered with my blood. "Why didn't you stop? You've killed him!"

The younger man was angling himself to where the boy's father was lying.

"He was trying to help!" John was sobbing. "Why did you kill him?" He was gasping with sobs, on and on.

The small man swung round and slapped his face. "Stop it, boy!"

John was suddenly silent. The younger man was kneeling, feeling the father's neck.

"Goodman Wakeley is alive," he said. "Hand me that axe, we must cut the branch away."

A long-handled axe with a metal head was lying on the ground near the base of the fallen tree. With strong practiced strokes the tall young man cut through the thick base of the branch that was pinning John's father's leg. It was a wonderful axe, far quicker than my tomahawk could have been.

The weight of the branch came off the man with the last stroke of the axe. They pulled him free, carefully. The small man felt the leg. "The bone is broken," he said.

"I will run for a litter," the other said. "But—Master Kelly—" He hesitated, looking at my body.

John said dully, once more, "He was trying to help. He was a friend."

"A friend!" said the small man. "Hah!"

"My father will tell you," John said.

"Enough, boy!" the man snapped at him. "You were mistaken! With our own eyes we saw him attacking you—did we not, Daniel?"

"We did!" said the other. He was still standing over my body, as if asking what to do.

And the small man made his decision.

"The savage requires no record," he said. "Some hearts in the colony are excessive tender, as we have seen. A threat has been removed, and one sinful heathen is no loss to the world."

So they picked up my body, one man at the head and one at the feet; they swung it like a bag of corn and tossed it as far as they could into the undergrowth.

Small John watched them. He was sitting beside his unconscious father, hunched on the ground, rocking to and fro. He made no sound.

The tall man hurried away. The other pulled a few branches over the ground to cover my spilled blood. Then he stood beside John, looking down at him.

"Get up, boy," he said, "and hearken to me. The Lord by his Almighty power brought us here because he loves Christians, not the Devil's spawn. The Indian is of no consequence. I killed him for good reason, though I shall not brag of it. As you may know, I am Walter Kelly, and my friend is Daniel Smith. If you slander those who have rescued your father, none will believe you. Do you understand?"

John said, very low, "Yes, master."

He was ten years old.

Men came hurrying soon with a litter, and none of them gave John much thought. He kept out of their way as they picked up his father, as gently as they could, and placed him on the litter to be carried to their settlement. Some other men had arrived with tools, to begin the long task of sawing through the felled tree to release the body of the man who lay dead beneath it.

Nobody paid any attention to John as he edged close to the undergrowth and picked up my tomahawk, which had been pushed aside by the litter and was lying hidden by grass. He slid it up under his jerkin, where it rested awkwardly against his shoulder but was hidden, and he followed the little procession as it moved slowly away.

TWO

On the day that I was killed, Leaping Turtle took his grief and his rage to our father Yellow Feather, but was not comforted. Instead he was persuaded, by our peacekeeping leader, that he should not seek vengeance. "Remember that there are good white men as well as bad," Yellow Feather told him, "and remember that there is strength and safety for us in living alongside these people in peace."

So the next day a group of our people went quietly with Leaping Turtle through the trees to find my body and to carry it home to our village, where my friend tamed his own sorrow to comfort my sister Quickbird and my grandmother Suncatcher. They grieved in the old ways, with the sounds and tears of mourning, blackening their faces with charcoal because the light of life was gone, and they buried my body with its head to the southwest, and my knife and my bow and arrows beside me. Leaping Turtle had found the knife still in my belt when they went to take my body home. But he had not been able to find my tomahawk.

None mentioned me by name after I was gone. It is our custom. One Who Waits took some of my clothes and hung them ceremonially in a tree near where my body was buried. There they hung until the wind and weather tore them apart, and birds took torn pieces to help make their nests, and the rest fell into dust.

As for me, I was free but not yet truly freed, and so am I still. I am spirit, outside time but still following its flow. I am held here by the disharmony caused by my violent death, which would change the whole course of life for the boy John.

And I am within boundaries. I can see past and present, though not future. I can hear speech and thought no matter what its language. I may not intervene. I may be seen, if I choose, and I may communicate, if I choose, but only in a certain place, and at certain times. Each of us who has lived on this earth knows the place to which he or she would choose to belong.

The Great Spirit in his wisdom holds me, like the bird I was named for, to wheel over all, to observe all, and to tell this story.

To tell the story of a boy and an axe, a tree and an island. And to wait until Little Hawk is freed to fly.

THREE

Four young men carried John's father on a litter made of linen cloth strung between two poles. It was a bumpy journey but he did not wake. They were following one of the old paths of my people, leading to what was once the village of Patuxet, before the plague killed everyone in this part of the land. Now the white men from England had their own big village there. They called it Plymouth. At its center was a fort built on a hill, and all round the settlement there was a wooden wall taller than a man, broken by a pair of great gates.

In through the open gates they went, and children ran up the center street, calling of their arrival.

The houses were shaped like boxes, with slanted roofs of reed thatch. A chimney of stones and dried mud rose from one end of each roof, to carry away the smoke from the fire inside, and beside each house there was a small garden, edged with boards so that the soil was higher than the ground all about. People stopped digging their gardens and came running as the litter bearing John's father arrived. So did others watching from the houses. The young woman who ran fastest, anxious, was John's mother, Margaret Wakeley.

The litter was taken into her house, and she followed it in, with two of the women and the tall young man who witnessed my death, Daniel Smith. He appeared to be full of concern. The women were both older; like Margaret and all these women, they were dressed in heavy clothes with long sleeves, and full skirts down to the ground, in spite of the spring sunshine.

Nobody noticed small John pause for a moment to drop my tomahawk behind the woodpile before he went into the house.

The men carrying the litter moved Benjamin Wakeley very carefully onto a bed. He was still unconscious. He lay there pale and motionless, even when one of the older women took hold of his broken leg. The other woman helped her, with a skillful touch. The two of them must have been the nearest thing these people had to a medicine man. They did the right thing, putting the broken bone in line and tying the leg with straps to two pieces of wood, which would have been so painful if Wakeley were awake that it was a good thing he was not.

More than anything, I could feel the fear and grief in John's mind as he watched.

This little room had boards as a floor and a bed at either side, without much space in between. The house was very crowded with all these people. From the other room two small girls were peeping wide-eyed; I guessed that they were John's younger sisters, with a neighbor woman holding their hands.

Daniel Smith said, "It was a large tree to be taken down by only two men. I fear he hit his head most grievous hard when he fell."

"His head hit a rock," John said. "The tree knocked him down." He gave a great sob, and his mother put out a hand to him.

"And killed poor Goodman Ford," said one of the two older women. "Goody Ford is in great grief, I must go to her. God bless you all." She gave Margaret a hug, squeezed John's shoulder, and went out.

The other woman was feeling all round Benjamin Wakeley's head with gentle fingers.

"A damp cloth on his forehead, my dear," she said to Margaret, "and the Lord willing, he will wake in good time. The sleep will help him heal."

But it didn't, and he did not wake. The religious leader of this colony, a white-bearded man they called William Brewster, came with his wife, and with them was the man who had killed me, Walter Kelly. They all prayed to their God over Benjamin Wakeley, and Daniel Smith and Master Kelly prayed as loudly as any.

"And the Lord be praised that you came upon this sad

accident in time to save him," Master Brewster said to them.

"Praise him too for preserving us from attack by Indians," said Master Kelly. "Who were close by, but went away when we fired our guns."

His eyes were on John, but John would not look at him.

"Amen," said everyone in the room.

With help from her neighbors, Margaret fed soup to her children and put them to bed. Then she sat on the bed where her husband lay propped against pillows, and held a cloth moistened with cool water against his head.

John stayed beside her, exchanging the cloth for a cool one when it grew warm.

She said softly, after a while, "Thy shirt is bloody. Give it to me tomorrow."

And the words came spilling out of John in an urgent whisper, because he had to tell her.

"Mother, there was one Indian, but he came to help, after the tree fell. He had his axe out, to cut Father free—and Master Kelly shot him. And it was Hawk, the Indian with the scar, that I told you of, who was good to me, at the fishing—"

He broke off, as the tears came into his voice.

"What?" said Margaret, bemused.

"That's Hawk's blood on my shirt," John said, trying to whisper, trying not to cry. "I tried to stop Master Kelly, but he killed him."

All this ran through Margaret's mind like water; she

could spare no thought for anything but her husband. She heard only John's distress, and she reached for his hand.

"I know you did all you could, my dear," she said.

"Father will tell them Hawk was our friend," John said. He choked on the words, and tried again. "Father will tell them, won't he?"

"Of course he will," said his mother. She kissed his forehead. "Hush now. You must rest. Try to sleep."

So together they said one more prayer for Benjamin Wakeley and then John curled up in the covers at the other end of the bed, and in a while fell asleep.

Margaret stayed awake, sitting wrapped in blankets beside her husband. Just before dawn her eyes closed out of sheer fatigue, and for a few minutes she too slept.

When she woke, Benjamin's breathing was very faint and slow, his closed eyes deep and shadowed.

"Ben!" she said in alarm.

John scrambled up and came to her. There was no time to call for help, nor could any help have been given. Each of them had a hand softly touching Benjamin Wakeley's face when he stopped breathing altogether and his spirit went away.

Now John had watched three men die in the space of a day and a night, and this third death was by far the most terrible, because he loved his father dearly.

Margaret's friends and neighbors came in and out of the house all day to give help and offer sympathy. One of them was Daniel Smith, and with him once more was Master

Kelly, who clearly had high rank in this community even though he was so small a man. They both said kind words to Margaret and her two little daughters, and on their way out of the dark house they came face-to-face with John, who was carrying in some logs from the woodpile.

He looked up at them with no expression on his face.

Daniel Smith said, "Your father has gone to the Lord, John. He is in a better place, and free from all pain."

Master Kelly said, "We mourn the passing of a God-fearing man, for only such are welcomed to the arms of the Almighty. As the psalmist says, 'the Lord is King forever and ever; the heathen are perished out of his land.'"

He looked very hard at John, as if he were challenging him.

"Yes, sir," John said. He was looking straight back at Master Kelly without respect, and his voice was cold. Kelly frowned, but others were coming, so he walked on. John went into the house with his firewood.

When he was sure the two men had gone, he went back out to get more wood. He looked carefully round to make sure nobody was watching, and he slipped behind the woodpile to the place where he had dropped my tomahawk, and used his father's wood-splitting axe to dig a shallow hole in the ground. Then he took my tomahawk and buried it there, putting a rock on top so he could find the spot again.

He looked quickly all around him, and he said unhappily to the air, in a voice hardly above a whisper, "I'm sorry, Hawk."

I sent him comfort silently, and perhaps my Manitou put a little of it into his mind.

The next day two graves were dug in a piece of land not far from the community's meetinghouse, where they gathered to worship their God, and with a few solemn words from Master Brewster, the people buried the bodies of Benjamin Wakeley and the other man who was killed by the tree, Goodman Ford. There were wooden markers set nearby to remember other people who had died—men, women, children, babies. Though the white man's plague didn't hurt the white men, they had had a hard time learning how to survive in this land.

In the weeks after that John's mother, Margaret, wept often, and had the two little girls and John kneel down with her as she called on God to help her feed and clothe them. She and John worked hard in their garden, digging and planting, and the little girls did their best to pull weeds in spite of their long sleeves and skirts. These people's stern religion seemed to demand that they cover as much of the body as possible, as if it were a shameful thing. The women were not even allowed to show their hair, and wore close little caps on their heads indoors and out, and even when they slept.

The man Daniel Smith came often to offer help, when he was not working with Master Kelly and Captain Standish on building fortifications. John tried to avoid him, and was not happy when his mother smiled gratefully at Daniel and began calling him by his Christian name as if they were friends. He couldn't look at Daniel Smith without being back in the bloodiest day of his life, when his world had changed.

And all the time he remembered me. Whenever his father's death came into his mind, he thought too of mine. *Hawk . . . If I hadn't called out . . . If I hadn't said his name . . . Hawk . . .* Hardly a day went by when he didn't glance to make sure that the place where he had buried my tomahawk was still undisturbed.

Daniel Smith was younger than John's father and mother. He was tall and broad-shouldered and did not often laugh. As a member of the colony's militia, he was often in uniform, and on Sundays he was part of the armed guard that marched down the aisle of the meetinghouse, three abreast, when the congregation was all gathered. Behind them came the governor, the preacher, and Captain Miles Standish, officer's cane in hand—and after that, the long service began.

The rest of the time Daniel worked as pitman for Goodman Webster, who was the community's sawyer; they made the wooden planks used for every house in this village. The trunk of a tree was set over a great pit with a man in it, and between him and another man above, a toothed metal saw was pushed up and down to cut the trunk into planks. So much sawdust got into Daniel's hair and clothes that he wore his hair very short, and always had the faint sweetish smell of maple wood. He felt his was a manly and useful occupation, and suggested to Margaret that John should help around the saw pit, but to John's great relief Goodman Webster—a very large, muscular man—said he was too small.

John spent his days doing the work his father had taught him—tending plants in the field and the garden and collecting shellfish on the seashore. One day he came home with a basket of clams to find Daniel Smith's heavy flintlock rifle propped against the wall inside the door, even though it was the afternoon of a working day. Daniel was coming out of the inner room, smiling. His face tightened into its usual stern lines when he saw John.

But to John's amazement, he nodded at the basket and said, with some effort, "Thou hast a good catch."

Then he took his rifle and marched out. Over his shoulder he said, "Thy mother has something to tell thee." Then he was gone.

John turned; his mother was behind him.

She reached for the basket. "Well done—this is a feast," she said warmly, but she was not looking at him.

John said, "What did he mean?"

"Daniel and I are to be married," said his mother. "Next week."

John couldn't believe what he was hearing. Out of the whirl of emotions in his head, only one found words.

"They killed Hawk!" he said.

"They did their best to save thy father, John," his mother said. "Put the Indian out of your mind. All death is hard. I have spoken to Daniel about that terrible day.

He and Master Kelly truly believed that you were being attacked."

"Hawk was trying to help," John said.

His mother said, "And they have spoken to Captain Standish about the matter, and he agreed that it was best forgotten." She put out her hand to him. "Come in and wash yourself, my dear."

John stood there for a moment, and in his mind I could hear the words he did not say.

My father scorned Miles Standish for his arrogance toward the Indians. And you are marrying another such, with my father just three months dead.

The day before the wedding Mistress Saxon, who lived nearby, came upon John collecting kindling. She saw the look on his face, and was wise enough to know what it meant.

"John," she said, "thy mother loves thee. And Daniel Smith is a good, devout man who will work hard for the family. In this place, it is sorely difficult for one person to raise children alone."

John said, "I work hard too."

"Th'art a good boy," said Mistress Saxon, "but th'art ten years old."

"I am near eleven," John said.

She patted him on the shoulder, and went on her way to check a woman who was about to have a baby.

After the wedding Daniel Smith moved into the house, and John, who before had slept at the end of his parents' bed, had to share one with his sisters. His stepfather was indeed a devout man; very soon they were all praying far more often than before. They prayed together every morning and every evening and before every meal, and Daniel Smith's prayers were very long and eloquent and full of quotations from the Bible.

John found this a burden, especially when he was very hungry. He felt that surely God must be satisfied with all the praying they did on Sundays, when everyone gathered to listen to the minister preach for at least two hours in the morning, and then another two hours in the afternoon.

His mother said gently to him one day, when he was clearing ashes from the fireplace, "I need thee to be a good example to the girls, and not fidget when Daniel is saying grace. We all need to show gratitude to the Lord for what we are given."

"I am very grateful," John said. "But my father used to say thank you much more quickly."

"Daniel is a very devout man," his mother said.

John said, "I miss my father."

"The Lord giveth and the Lord taketh away," said his mother, as if reciting a lesson, and she handed him a bucket for the ashes. But she ran her hand across his hair as she left.

John could read the Bible for himself; his mother had taught him how. It was a wonder for me to see language turned into signs called letters; my own language had never been written down. Sometimes John gave his sister Mercy lessons, drawing the letters in the dirt outside the house with a stick; she was an eager pupil, and loved to practice. If Daniel Smith caught them doing this he was angry, and instantly found work for them both to do. The third time he came across them writing, he even hit John across the head, though not very hard because Margaret was watching.

"This is vanity," said Daniel Smith. "Margaret, have you no useful occupation for your daughter? And John, you should be in the field, keeping the birds from the corn. Go!"

"Mercy is very good at her letters," John said.

"Hush," said his mother nervously.

"Do not argue with thine elders," Daniel Smith said, though John had not felt he was arguing. "Mercy is a girl, and should be learning to sew and to cook. After that she will have time to learn to read the Bible. Now do what I tell thee!"

John went off to their allotted acre of land beyond the houses, where corn and pumpkins were growing. He did not point out to Daniel Smith that the swelling ears of corn were at more risk from night-prowling raccoons than from daytime birds. He tried to think of work that he and Mercy could do together, so that he could teach her to write when Daniel Smith was not looking. He had noticed that though Daniel knew a great many pieces of the Bible by heart, he was very rarely to be seen reading it, and indeed tried to avoid opportunities to do so. Perhaps, thought John, Daniel didn't want a little girl to be good at something he couldn't do very well himself.

He knew this was an unworthy thought, so he said a small private prayer apologizing to his God. He found, however, that this didn't make the thought go away.

As time went by Daniel decided that John would be better occupied by helping him move the family privy. Like my people, these English did their business into a hole in the ground at a decent distance from the house, but they felt it necessary to build a little house over the hole. It was always a smelly little house full of flies, and John hated his job of carrying buckets of earth from the new hole Daniel was digging, and emptying them into the reeking old one.

Between carrying buckets, he had to dig shallow trenches beside the walls of the little house, so that beams could be slid underneath it for men to pick it up and move it, in due course, to sit on top of the new hole.

"Th'art a slow worker," said Daniel, watching John struggle to pick up a bucket of stones and earth.

Their neighbor Goodman Evans was passing by, with a big wooden spade in his hand. He paused, and considered John's efforts.

"Perhaps the man does not match the task, Daniel," he said. "This boy of yours is a good little gardener—I would trade you his time for my big strong Ethan, who has just destroyed a whole row of carrots as weeds."

John smiled at Goodman Evans, who often used to exchange seeds and plants with his father.

Daniel did not smile. He said, "John must follow the ordinance of our Lord in the Bible—whatsoever thy hand findeth to do, do it with all thy might. Thank you for your interest, Thomas Evans, but we have a family task to accomplish here."

"As you wish, neighbor," said Goodman Evans amiably, and he went on his way with his spade.

So John went on straining to lift heavy buckets—and at intervals, glancing across at the stone on the ground beside the woodpile, where my tomahawk was buried. It was as if all the opinions he had learned from his tolerant father were buried there with it.

He was learning secrecy. The image of my body tossed into the undergrowth haunted him so constantly that one day, when Daniel was away with the militia, he went back alone to the clearing where his father's friend and I had died. It was a hard journey for a boy to make, and he had no idea what he might do when he got there. When he found no sign of my body at all, he was glad, because he knew that my people must have come and taken it away.

He saw few of my people in Plymouth, then. The severed head of Wituwamet, now a blackened skull, had been set on a pole above the colony's fort ever since Miles Standish's ferocious attack on the Massachusetts. For a long time after that, not one of the Indians—as they called us, using one name for all the peoples of this land—would come near this town to trade.

For my own people, though, our father Yellow Feather's agreement with the white men still held, keeping friendship between them and our tribe. All the past was clear to me now, all that he had done. He had come to the wedding of their leader Bradford, bringing more than a hundred people with him to help celebrate. Since then he had been making more agreements, through which the English gave us their knives, tools, cloth, and other goods in exchange for the right to build houses and farms on our land.

There were white men in the colony, like John's father Benjamin Wakeley, who tried to respect the beliefs of my people, and to keep the peace, but there were also those like the captain Miles Standish, who thought of all Indians as ignorant savages. As the months went by, every day John heard words from Daniel Smith's mouth that were the opposite of everything he had heard before. He tried to say nothing in argument, because he knew he would cause a problem for his mother.

But one day it was all too much for him.

They were walking home from the meetinghouse on Sunday with their neighbors Robert and Abigail Turner, after a sermon devoted to the mission of converting the heathen to the Christian religion.

"In God's good time," said Robert Turner, "we shall spread the word and there will be whole villages of praying Indians."

"Amen," said Abigail and Margaret hopefully.

"It is a wishful thought," Daniel Smith said, "but they are a barbarous and savage people, and in their fury they not only kill but torment men in the most bloody manner. There are many reports. They even eat human flesh, they are the children of the Devil."

Walking silently in the rear with his sisters, John let out a small infuriated noise and clenched his fists. Only Mercy heard; she looked up at him nervously.

"The love of God can reach out even to convert savages, surely," Robert Turner said. He was a large man and it was a warm day; his red face was glistening under his tall black hat.

"I fear Satan reached them first, long since," said Daniel.

From behind, John said suddenly, very fast, and more loudly than he had intended, "When my father took me to see the Indians fishing, they were very kind to us, and they showed the grown-ups how to fish, and I played with their children."

There was a silence. They had reached the family house, and Robert and Abigail Turner did not pause. "Good day, neighbors," they both said politely, and walked hastily on.

Daniel Smith glared at John. "It is a sin to tell lies," he said. "A wicked sin. And on the Sabbath!"

Before John could open his mouth again, Margaret said quickly, "It's true, husband—Benjamin did take him. It was at the very beginning, when Squanto showed us ways to plant and farm this land."

"No proper child interrupts the conversation of his betters," Daniel said angrily.

"No, indeed," Margaret said, and she looked at John for his apology.

John looked up at Daniel Smith.

"One of the Indians was called Hawk," he said. "But now he is dead."

Daniel's face flushed with repressed rage. "Get to bed!" he said. "And be glad I do not whip thee!"

It was the moment, no doubt, at which he determined to remove John from his sight.

A week later Daniel informed the family that John had reached the age where he should learn a trade, and that he had found him a place as apprentice to a cooper, a maker of barrels, whom he had met through his work as a sawyer. The cooper's name was William Medlycott, and his home was not in Plymouth, but in a new settlement a day's journey to the north. The apprenticeship meant room and board and the learning of the craft, and it would last unbroken for seven years.

Margaret, who had already been told this news, heard it in silence with her eyes cast down. Mercy and Patience stared at Daniel Smith in horror, and began to cry.

John said nothing. He could think only of finding a moment to dig up my tomahawk, and take it with him when he left home.

F O U R

A few days later, John left Plymouth. Daniel had arranged for him to travel in a cart drawn by two large oxen and driven by Goodman Bates, who was taking a load of timber and vegetables to settlements thirty miles away, near the North River. John could have gone up the coast by sea, since boats had begun to ply regularly out of Plymouth Harbor, but by land the trip would cost nothing, because Goodman Bates owed Daniel a favor.

The little girls were crying again, and Margaret held John very close, her own eyes full of tears. He had grown to look so much like his father that she felt she was losing Benjamin all over again, as well as her son.

John's face was wet too. "I will send you messages when I can, Mother," he said.

Margaret could hardly speak. She said, "God bless you, my dear one."

John scrambled up into the back of the cart and Daniel handed him up his bundles, one large, one small. The smaller one held food packed by Margaret for the journey; the bigger held John's clothes, nightshirt, slippers, and winter coat—the only things he owned, besides the clothes on his back, the shoes on his feet, and the jackknife at his belt.

There was one other thing in the bundle, tucked inside his good shirt. Very early that morning, before anybody was awake, he had crept out to rescue my tomahawk from its hiding place under the woodpile.

Mercy had opened her eyes as he was tying up his bundle again. She was a grown girl now, nine years old.

She lay there looking at him very sadly, and she whispered, "Don't forget us."

John leaned over and kissed her forehead. He whispered back, "Never."

Now Goodman Bates called to his oxen and shook the reins. The cart creaked off. Margaret, Mercy, and Patience waved, and John waved back until the fence that enclosed New Plymouth cut them off from his sight. I could feel the mixture of sadness and excitement in his mind. He was eleven years old—the same age that I had been when my father took me into the winter woods and left me there.

Trees shaded the beaten dirt of the road, which like all their roads had been made from one of our old tracks. John soon pulled off his jerkin, though, because this was late August and the air was hot. He pulled off his hat, too, to fan himself and chase away the flies. Up there in the back of the cart, he was sitting on an enormous log; there were three of these, three sections of a tree trunk. They were wedged tight by other chunks of wood to keep them from rolling, but John watched them cautiously. If any one of them got loose, it could crush him flat in a moment.

Above him, at the front of the cart, the broad back of Goodman Bates swayed to the rhythm of the big, slow oxen—mild, patient beasts, in spite of their impressive horns. Sitting next to him was a small woman; John could see only the back of her brown doublet, and her neat linen cap.

When they stopped to eat, two hours later, and Goodman Bates went to fetch water for the oxen, John found that the other passenger was not a woman, but a girl about his own age. She had a pretty, pointed face, and she gave him a small nervous smile. Her name was Huldah Bates; she was Goodman Bates's niece and she too was being sent away, to live with a family who had farmland in a new settlement near where John was going. Like him, she had no idea what to expect.

"The work will be just like at home, I suppose," she said. "But at home there were six of us children and another on the way, so my mother said there was no help for it, my brother and I had to go. He's off to be a 'prentice, next week."

"So am I!" said John. "To a cooper, Master Medlycott. Where will your brother go?"

"To the smithy near the harbor," Huldah said.

"My father let me watch the sparks there sometimes, when I was a little lad."

Huldah sighed. "Edmund is lucky, he will be near home. But he has to live over the smithy. He says his first job of the day will be lighting the fire before anyone else is awake. What will you do?"

"I don't know," said John, and felt suddenly alarmed.

Goodman Bates loomed over him with a dripping bucket; he had been down to a stream to dip up water for the animals. "Tha'll make buckets like this," he said. "Or maybe tha'll just fetch and carry, for a few years." He gave a great bellowing laugh and went off to his oxen.

John and Huldah stared out at the trees and the stream, thinking about their uncertain futures. But hunger drove out anxiety, and soon they were both munching stale crusty bread, and discussing the people of Plymouth, not always with reverence. Each of them had found a friend.

Not for long, however. After another hour Goodman Bates headed the cart up a side track, through woodland and then cleared fields, and they came to a house with a wooden roof, as big as the grander houses in Plymouth. There were two outbuildings as well. Beside them was an enclosed field with four cows and two horses, and chickens were pecking the ground outside the house. None of these were creatures native to our land; like the oxen, they had been brought from across the sea in the white man's ships. There were more and more of them now.

A woman and two small children came out of the house

to greet Goodman Bates, and he helped Huldah down to her new home. Huldah just had time to look up at John for a moment, a silent farewell, before she had to turn and curtsy. The woman had a kind face, John thought hopefully—and then there was the sound of hooves behind him, and a man rode up on a horse and the children shrieked in excitement. It was clearly the father of the family. John was too busy handing down Huldah's bags to pay him any attention. After that he had to climb out of the back of the cart and get up to sit beside Goodman Bates, who liked company.

It was only as they left, and he looked back and saw the father dismount and hand his horse's reins to a servant, that John saw the man's face. He was a small man, but strong; he grabbed one of the children and hoisted him up onto his shoulders.

He was the man who killed me.

"Do you see? Yes, it's Master Kelly," said Goodman Bates with pride. "Our Huldah is a lucky girl to be coming to this household."

John said, "Where are we?"

"They are calling it Duxbury," Bates said. "Only an hour's ride from Plymouth. Captain Standish is building here too. The leaders among us deserve to have more land and some peace. Governor Winslow has the same, up beyond where you're going, in the place they call Marshfield."

He called to the patient oxen, and they lumbered off again.

I knew this land, but it was changed. If I had been living, I would not have been there. My people were no longer there. For thousands of years, we had hunted and lived and farmed on the land over which John was now passing. Already, after less than one man's lifetime, these invaders from across the ocean felt that it belonged to them.

Goodman Bates's cart took John some miles further north, to a house that had been built on flat fertile land in this wide river valley. He gazed at the house, the place where now he would live.

It was a good sturdy building, on land rising above the track, and it smelled like a farmyard. Unlike the Duxbury house, it had a thatched roof. Beside it was another building, about half as big. The track up to them was steep, and the oxen hesitated; Goodman Bates yelled at them and for the first time cracked his whip over their backs. They strained hard, their hoofs churning up the dirt. The cart creaked up toward the smaller building and finally stopped.

Three men came out into the sunshine, and John had his first sight of his new employer, William Medlycott. He was a big broad-shouldered man wearing leather britches and a dirty white shirt, and his beard was flecked with grey; he raised an arm to Goodman Bates and went round at once to the back of the cart. His first interest was clearly the three massive logs wedged in there.

"Ah, very nice, very pretty, Richard," he said. His voice had a deep burr of an accent; John had never heard anything like it before.

Goodman Bates heaved himself down and they both stood studying the logs. John scrambled off the cart and stood at a respectful distance. One of the oxen, less respectful, let loose a pile of steaming droppings.

"A good straight oak it was," Bates said. "Fifteen feet or more without a knot, likely. This one came down last fall, and there are more on that island, for when you want them. I thought it worth the carrying."

"Very well worth," said Medlycott. "And there's a shipbuilder up the river will be glad to hear of them. Let those poor beasts of thine loose and Ezra will take them. Then come tell Priscilla all the news from Plymouth." He looked across at John. "And this is my new apprentice?"

John ducked his head awkwardly. "John Wakeley, sir," he said.

Medlycott looked him up and down. "Eleven years old, they said?"

"Yes, sir."

"Th'art small for a cooper," said Medlycott, frowning. Then his mouth gave a merciful twitch. "But Priscilla will fatten thee up. Go with the boys, now. Come, Dick."

The younger of the other two was a boy a head taller than John, with a friendly grin, and dark hair so short that he looked as if his head had been shaved. He grabbed one end of John's bundle and they carried it together.

"I'm Thomas," he said. "And that's Ezra Clark, he's my father's journeyman." He jerked his head at the young man helping Goodman Bates unyoke the oxen, who seemed untroubled by the beasts' size and horns even though they towered over him. Ezra Clark had spiky yellow hair and a wispy beard, and did not smile.

"What's a journeyman, please?" said John.

"Served his apprenticeship, works as a cooper—tha don't know that much?"

It was not an unkind question, and John smiled.

"I know nothing," he said.

"Well, come on, Know-nothing," said Thomas cheerfully. "Let's get this to the back—we sleep in the lean-to."

This also baffled John, but he followed, and they had just dropped the bundle inside a small door at the back of the house when there was a yell from Ezra. It was a surprisingly deep voice.

"Thomas!"

They both ran. Ezra had led the oxen into an enclosed piece of the yard and was pulling a hurdle to shut them in. "Straw from the loft for the animals," he said. "And pump them some water."

"This is John, the new apprentice," Thomas said.

Ezra looked John over, from hooded eyes in a long, lugubrious face. "Well, John," he said, jerking his head, "over there is the manure pile, and that's where tha can take the beasts' leavings. We keep a tidy yard."

So John fetched the long-handled wooden shovel that was sticking out of the manure pile, and spent the first half hour of his seven-year coopering apprenticeship carrying mounds of fresh ox manure, of which there were now three. He found himself wondering if his life had changed after all.

But before long, after washing at the pump in the yard, he was inside the house, at the table that covered the length of one room. Though he was here to work, he found he would eat with the family. It seemed a pattern not very different from his life in Plymouth—and here he was free of Daniel Smith.

There were four other young Medlycotts, all of whom had the same bright eyes and dark hair as Thomas: in descending order they were Joseph, Sarah, William, and Matthew. Mistress Medlycott called William "Willie," to avoid confusion with his father. She was a buxom, welcoming lady who somehow seemed to give off as much warmth as the enormous hearth on which she cooked. To John's great astonishment she gave him a hug when they were introduced, and he liked her immediately. Master Medlycott and Goodman Bates teased her over the hug.

"What shall I tell them in Plymouth?" roared Goodman Bates merrily. "Thy wife makes free with the apprentice!"

"To the stocks with her!" said Master Medlycott.

John blushed, and looked at the floor.

"Stop thy nonsense, he's the size of Matthew," said Mistress Medlycott. "And missing his mother already, I'll be bound." Her deep voice had the same rounded accent as her husband's. She plunked a large loaf of bread in front of Medlycott, and he attacked it with his knife.

Ezra was not smiling. John wondered if he was as strict

as Daniel. But then he forgot everything except the food, which was plentiful at this long table. They had delayed their dinner until the arrival of Goodman Bates, who was an old friend and would stay the night, and the children were all ravenous. Like all the Plymouth children, they ate in silence unless spoken to, standing with Ezra and John at the foot of the table. Thomas stood beside John, and they shared a trencher, the hollowed wooden plate that all these people used.

The talk was all between Bates and the Medlycotts, who were thirsty for gossip about Plymouth, and its relations with the new Puritan colony in Massachusetts Bay. John paid this little attention until a question was directed at his end of the table.

"Ezra," Master Medlycott boomed, "tha shut the oxen safe inside, I trust?"

"They are indoors," said Ezra. "And fed and watered."

"I thank you," said Goodman Bates. "Is there fear of Indians at night?"

"Wolves," said Master Medlycott. "My neighbor saw one on his land last week. But it would take a big pack of wolves to bother an ox, I think."

"And a big pack of Indians," said Goodman Bates comfortably.

"No—one arrow would do it." Master Medlycott shook his head. "Satan gave those savages a deadly aim. And now we are selling them guns, heaven preserve us. There'll be a bloodbath one of these days."

"William," said Mistress Medlycott rapidly, "prithee cut some more meat for Goodman Bates. And the children if they need it." And she launched into a description and discussion of the sermon preached in the local meeting-house the previous Sunday, so that there was no more talk of savages.

But when John went to bed that night, on a mattress on the floor of the back room that he was to share with Ezra and Thomas, he took nothing but his nightshirt out of his bundle of possessions. For all the friendliness of this household, he was greatly afraid of what would happen if anyone were to find that his private treasure was an Indian tomahawk.

The next day he watched and waited for a chance to slip away from the house to hide it, and before long he managed to bury it in the ground behind a clump of birch trees edging the yard. There it lay, safely hidden again. Chickens trotted and pecked above it, the roots of wildflowers grew down around it, but nobody knew it was there except John.

The thing he did not yet know was that very close to the Medlycott house, out on the salt marsh, waiting for him, was the place that holds me—the place where my tomahawk was born.

FIVE

Master Medlycott's workshop was a noisy, bustling place, and he employed three general workmen as well as Ezra, Thomas, and John. On John's first morning, two of the workmen had unloaded the enormous tree-trunk logs from Goodman Bates's cart and rolled them to the yard behind the workshop. Other logs from local trees lay here too, waiting to be sawed into chunks and then split length-wise with axes, first into quarters and then eighths, then thinner still. Lengths of wood like this sat weathering in the yard in tall neat stacks—chestnut, red oak, and pine. They would sit there for months or years, until Master Medlycott felt they were ready to become the staves out of which all barrels were made.

I watched all this with fascination. In the life I had lived, our pots and containers were made from bark and skins and clay; we wove baskets from reeds and wood, but we had no need for these massive containers, nor for the great wheels of the carts that had to carry them, nor the great beasts that pulled the carts. The skills of the cooper belonged to a different life, in which the bark of a tree was often thrown away, and all its wood chopped into these prized flat pieces called staves.

John would learn someday to make staves, but he had a long way to go. It took him weeks even to learn the names of Master Medlycott's tools, all of which had come over with him from England. To begin, John was put at the grinding wheel, to learn how to sharpen the blades of planes and spokeshaves and axes. There he sat, in a little cloud of sparks, while he watched the others making casks: bending staves into shape while heating them over a small fire, damping them with water, and whacking iron hoops down over them to hold them together.

They were always busy; there was a great demand for barrels and casks, to carry almost everything the people ate or drank. Many more English families were coming in ships, spreading through this open forest land where my people had hunted and grown crops for so long. Instead of hunting and trapping, they raised animals that ate up everything green, and they were cutting down all the trees. Their buildings were made with deep stone-lined cellars and thick sturdy walls, and once a settlement was built, it did not move. It just grew bigger.

Because of his staves, Master Medlycott had respect for

the trees. He would gaze up in admiration at a tall straight white oak and feel that the casks he made from its wood should be worthy of the splendid tree. But even he treated the tree not as a living creature but as a thing. This was how they thought of our mother the earth, these white men: as a place full of things, put here by their God for them to use.

"Is it not wonderful," Master Medlycott said at dinner one summer day, "the bounty of this land that gives us unlimited timber? My old father would scarce have believed it. He was always scouting about for new wood."

"He'd not believe our stacks of firewood, either," said Mistress Medlycott. "For all the harsh winters, this house is warmer than the last, praise the Lord."

Ezra speared a piece of meat with his knife. "My grand-dad held it was the shipyards ate up the timber. The Queen's ships kept out the Spaniards, he used to say, but every one of 'em used up twenty-five hundred trees."

"And all of oak," Master Medlycott said. "Small wonder it was hard in England to find trees like the one Richard Bates brought us this year. He carries another soon, I believe—we need all we can get, for the tight work." He looked down the table at John, who was sitting dutifully mute with the children, chewing. "Ask me for a sheet of paper and a pen tomorrow, John Wakeley, and tha canst send a letter to thy mother by Goodman Bates."

John stared at him in happy disbelief, and Mistress Medlycott smiled. And the next day, Medlycott set John to cutting staves of white pine to make a simple bucket, so he would be able to write to his mother that he was indeed becoming a cooper.

Sundays, for John, were just as they had been at home: everyone went to the meetinghouse for worship, all day. The minister read from the Bible and preached a long sermon in the morning, and Ezra kicked John if he saw his eyelids droop. Then all the families of the community gathered in another room and ate heartily together, from dishes brought by all the women, and went back to the meetinghouse in the afternoon for the sermon to begin all over again. By this time Ezra's eyes too were in danger of drooping, and John had to resist the temptation to give him even the smallest nudge with a foot.

The meetinghouse and gathering room were much smaller than those in Plymouth, and in summer the air was hot. But it was the only time of the week for people to exchange news and gossip, and often John caught sight of Huldah sitting obediently with the Kelly family. He tried not to look at Master Kelly, though the man was hard to avoid because he was clearly a pillar of the community. Quite often he and Captain Standish were called on to stand up and read from the minister's big Bible.

One summer Sunday, after the meal, John came across Huldah sitting on a boulder at the edge of the common, beside the meetinghouse. She was in charge of two small Kelly children, who were intently watching a row of ants carrying seeds to their nest, and she was wearing a neat dark dress and a little white cap on her head. She looked up and smiled at him.

"Has t'a learned to be a cooper yet?" she said.

John said solemnly, "I have made a bucket of pine, that you can carry vegetables in." He grinned. "But it leaks. I can't do tight coopering yet—that's barrels and such, to hold water."

Huldah said, "Are you happy?"

John blinked. He was not used to direct questions.

"They are good people," he said. "And you?"

Huldah wrinkled her nose.

A man's voice called sharply, "Huldah?"

John looked round and saw Master Kelly striding out of the gathering room onto the grass, looking around him, and he caught Huldah's eye again just for a second before he ducked out of the way and was gone.

He thought of her often, and tried not to imagine the reasons why she was not happy. Perhaps, he hoped, she simply missed her family.

One afternoon in the autumn, before the leaves began to fall, before the Hunter's Moon, Mistress Medlycott asked her husband's permission to send John out into the fields gathering sassafras root for her. The English knew something of using herbs and plants as medicine, especially the women, and those of them who talked to my people were learning more. And Mistress Medlycott had already discovered that her husband's new apprentice was good at gardening; sometimes he even asked if he could help to weed or plant. He recognized as many trees and plants as she did herself.

So John set off, carrying a Pokanoket basket that had come to the family as part of a trade, and he headed in a direction he had never taken before. It was a beautiful calm fall day; the sky was blue and the sun was halfway down the sky.

I watched him.

He threaded his way through the trees behind the house and found himself going downhill, down through the woodland to a small pond. The water was very still, filled with red and gold reflections from the blazing colors of the maples and oaks and ash trees all around it.

John found a stand of small sassafras trees beside the pond, and dug out some roots with his knife. When he had filled the basket, he straightened his back, stretched, and looked around. He had not been here before.

But I had. I had lived here, alone, one winter when I was younger than he was now.

John looked across at the opposite side of the pond—the steep, rocky place where in unthinking rage I had killed a wolf whose only crime was trying to stay alive. I hoped he would not go there. After a moment he turned away, and headed instead to the land beyond the pond, where he could hear a sound like a long, distant sighing. He passed a stand of oak trees—scrubby red oak, not of interest to his master for its timber, but filled with acorns that would attract squirrels and deer.

The trees grew sparse as he went on. Then ahead, suddenly, he saw a great green stretch of salt marsh, broken by three island hummocks of trees. Way out across the marsh, on the horizon, he could see the sea.

High in the sky above him, coasting out from the trees, he saw a red-tailed hawk lying on the wind. He heard its harsh thin cry, and it headed for the nearest of the three islands.

John hesitated. But he had fulfilled his errand and the afternoon was not over yet; he had some time to himself, which was very rare. So he followed the hawk. He walked down into the marsh, careful to tread on hummocks of grass and to hop over the small creeks without filling his shoes with water. Gradually he made his way toward the higher ground of the island, where tall trees rose, cherry and maple, hickory and oak. Somewhere in those trees the red-tailed hawk might be perched high on a branch, watching for small birds or scurrying voles.

Over to his right, hidden behind the mainland trees beyond the marsh, the sun went down. The light was golden now over the marsh. The sky was still blue.

John stepped onto the firm grass of the island, where the trees gradually rose, and ahead of him, in a shadowy gap between two trees, he saw me.

S I X

John caught his breath, and stood very still. At first he was merely surprised, at the sudden sight of an Indian where he was expecting nobody. But then he saw the scar on my face that the wolf had left, the scar that once he had gently touched, and he stared in fear and disbelief.

Very slowly, he put his basket on the ground. He came closer, step by slow step, blue eyes wide just as when he was a little boy.

There I was, looking at him, standing still, bare-chested, undamaged, in breechclout and leggings. But, he now saw, I was not wholly substantial; through me, he could faintly see the trees of the island.

He said, "*Hawk?*"

"John Wakeley," I said. "I greet you. You are older. But I think you are the same."

"You're a ghost," John said. His voice was tight with fear.

"'Ghost' is just a word. I am Little Hawk. The Great Spirit keeps me here, though he has not told me why."

His mind drove out fear as it traveled into the awful memory of our last moment together.

He said, "It was terrible. You came to help, and . . . It was terrible. I have nightmares still."

"I know," I said.

John said, "If I hadn't said your name . . . It was my fault you stayed, it was my fault you were killed."

"No," I said.

Suddenly he was afraid again. "They say ghosts are the work of the Devil. There are fearsome punishments for those who tell of visions. They would say you are an evil spirit."

"Do you think I am?"

"No," he said. "You tried to save my father. You are my friend."

I said, "And you have saved my tomahawk."

"I had to. I had to. Is that why you're here?"

There was a sudden rising chorus of squawks from the trees above us, first one and then others joining it, and after a moment the red-tailed hawk flapped silently up into the sky, pursued by a gaggle of shouting crows.

I didn't know the answer to his question.

I said, "All I know is that something holds me here. To watch, to listen. Perhaps for you I am Manitou."

"Manitou?" he said, puzzled.

One day I would explain that to him, but not now.

"The tomahawk is full of memories," I said. "They are very powerful. If you guard it, take care."

John said, "There are some who turn lies into memories."

He was thinking of Kelly, of course, and Daniel Smith.

"Guard the truth, John Wakeley," I said to him. "Go home to your kind mistress, take her the sassafras roots. Work to become a craftsman. Honor my people, for my sake. If ever you need, you can find me on this island."

"Don't go!" he said.

"Come at this part of the day," I said. "Or at dawn."

The daylight was fading. All at once our time was over, and he could no longer see me.

He ran forward, reaching out his hand, but he could see only the trees.

"Hawk?" he said. "*Hawk!*"

For a moment he looked like the little boy again, but this time desolate, pleading.

Then he grabbed up his basket and hastened away over the salt marsh before darkness swallowed it up, before anyone could guess that he had found anything more than a few roots of a sassafras tree.

Perhaps that meeting changed his life. Perhaps, if he hadn't seen me, he would have been able to bury the horror of seeing me die, and would have merged into his community as a hardworking, God-fearing Puritan in the mold of William Medlycott. Perhaps I would have faded into the background of his memory as a benevolent but heathen savage, which seemed to be the best judgment from an Englishman that any Indian could hope for, even our father Yellow Feather.

Perhaps John would have become a man like all the rest, if he hadn't seen me again. Perhaps. But he didn't.

For a long time after that meeting he was thoughtful and quiet—so quiet that Mistress Medlycott wondered if he was sickening for some ailment, and made him drink dandelion tea. But he worked hard, harder than ever. He filled all his hours with working, pulling weeds out of the garden if he could find nothing else to do in the workshop. He no longer made special times to play with the younger children or to race with Thomas, and they were all very disappointed in him.

He thought and thought about me. He tried to tell himself that he had not seen a ghost, but he knew that he had. In his world, it was a terrible dangerous secret. Though he longed to see me again, he knew he couldn't come near the island unless he was utterly certain nobody could be nearby.

Winter came. Twice John had written to his mother, and she to him. Now a letter came again, delivered by a messenger bringing letters from Plymouth for Master Medlycott, and in it John's mother told him she would be having a baby in the spring. At the bottom of the page was a little note from Mercy, very carefully written. It said, "Dearest Brother, I send you repeckts and I hop you are wel. We miss you. Your sister Mercy."

At first John found tears in his eyes. Then he thought, *Well, at least he couldn't stop her from learning her letters*. Then he wondered what Mercy would have said if she had been free to tell him what their life was like. And when he said his prayers before going to bed that night, as he had done all his life, he added a long particular prayer asking his God to look after his mother.

He rarely had a chance to speak to Huldah Bates, but they exchanged smiles at the meetinghouse on Sundays. The congregation still gathered for food and fellowship between the morning and afternoon sermons, but people did not meet outdoors as the weather grew colder, and Huldah was always out of sight somewhere looking after the youngest Kelly children. There were more people, too, spreading not just from Plymouth but from the bigger Massachusetts Bay settlement to the north, now called Boston.

"On the Sabbath next week, brothers and sisters," said the minister one Sunday, "we shall have an exchange of preachers, if the Lord spare us a snowstorm. I shall preach at our mother church in Plymouth, and this congregation will have the privilege of hearing the learned Plymouth pastor, Roger Williams."

There was a murmur from the congregation, though John couldn't tell whether it was pleasure or disapproval.

"I don't think my father likes Master Williams," Thomas said as they trudged home. His parents and the smaller children had gone ahead by cart. "He says he is too much of a Separatist and that he questions the authority of our magistrates."

"My parents went to live in Holland because they were Separatists," John said. "A place called Leyden. I was born there."

"You never told me that," said Thomas. "Holland! Can you speak Dutch?"

"No. We left when I was four."

"Are Separatists very different from us?"

"I don't think so," John said. "Didn't everyone leave England so they could worship God in their own way, separate from the Church of England?"

Thomas had lost his fleeting interest in religion. "I'll race you to that big pine tree," he said.

"We can't—it's the Sabbath."

"Nobody can see, they're all ahead of us. And Ezra stayed to talk to his cousin."

So they raced, and Thomas won.

By the time they reached home, this cold winter day, their faces were no longer hot and nobody could tell they had been running. In any case, nobody even noticed them, since there was a greater distraction in the yard. Three of my people were there, tall, erect men, each with a bundle at his feet.

Thomas stopped, startled. "Indians!" he said.

I knew one of them: he was Yellow Bear, an elder of the village by the river. He was older than when I knew him, of course, and he was wearing an Englishman's cloth jacket over his deerskin leggings. He was trying to talk to Master Medlycott, who had been helping his wife and children out of the cart.

"No!" said Master Medlycott to Yellow Bear, shaking his head and his tall dark hat. "No! Not today!"

"A trade," said Yellow Bear in English. "A good trade."

He made a sign to one of the other men, who were younger and dressed normally, and the young man flipped open his bundle and displayed a soft, beautifully finished deerskin blanket.

"Good trade," said Yellow Bear, nodding his head firmly. At council meetings he had been one of the most eloquent, persuasive men in our community; it was heartbreaking to see him reduced to a few fumbling words in an unfamiliar language.

"This is the Sabbath! We do not trade on the Sabbath!" Master Medlycott said, loudly, clearly, slowly, as if he were talking to someone deaf or stupid. "No trade!"

The second young man opened his bundle as well, and revealed two smaller child-size blankets, even more beautiful; they were fawn skins, edged with rabbit fur. He thrust them out toward Mistress Medlycott, smiling hopefully.

Mistress Medlycott smiled back, but shook her head and held up her hands. "No," she said.

"Sunday!" boomed Master Medlycott. "It is *Sun-day*! The day of the Lord! No trading!"

Ezra came up behind Yellow Bear; he had just arrived home, catching us up. To the astonishment of everybody in the yard, he said to Yellow Bear in our language, "No trade today."

He was speaking Massachusett, and very badly, but Yellow Bear could understand him. He turned to look at Ezra gratefully.

"This man has traded with the boys before, and these are exceptional skins," he said to Ezra. "Why is he being so unfriendly?"

But he was wasting his time. Ezra too had only a few words of the other's language, and had no idea what Yellow Bear was saying. Fortunately, though, he did have the vital word "day."

"Bad day," he said in Massachusett, staring into Yellow Bear's face as if his eyes could communicate. "Bad day. Go. Come *good* day."

Yellow Bear understood the words, but not of course the reason for them. He shook his head, disappointed. "Very well," he said. He picked up the bundle at his own feet.

"Let us go," he said to the two young men. "These people are very superstitious—it's clearly an unlucky day for trading, for some reason. Their spiritual beliefs are very strange."

John watched and listened, longing to know what he was saying.

The young men folded their skins. Yellow Bear inclined his head formally to Master Medlycott, Mistress Medlycott, to Ezra, John, and Thomas, and turned away, and the three figures walked silently toward the trees and were gone.

"Pah!" said Master Medlycott in exasperation. "These ignorant savages, they have no respect for the Lord's holy Sabbath! What can you do with them?"

"Ezra!" Thomas burst out. "Where did you learn their language?"

"There was an Indian came to services at the meeting-house when I was in Boston," Ezra said. "I was instructed to teach him English, so I picked up some of his words. But only a few."

"Enough to be helpful today," said Mistress Medlycott quietly. "We thank you, Ezra."

"It is a barbarous tongue," said Master Medlycott. His voice was cold.

"It is indeed," Ezra said. "I will take the horses in."

John watched, eyes bright, and I knew I should see him soon again. In his mind I could hear a clear excited determination to come back to my island, and ask me to teach him how to speak the barbarous tongue.

SEVEN

A week went by, with the cooperage so busy that John had no chance to do anything but work, eat, and sleep. Then Roger Williams burst into his life, on the back of a horse.

It was Sunday again, a crisp day with the sun glinting on a thin overnight snowfall that had turned the whole village white. Everyone was arriving at the meetinghouse. William Medlycott greeted Master Kelly, who was bustling about outside the door welcoming people and looking important. John kept out of his way, while peering unsuccessfully for a glimpse of Huldah.

"He should have been here an hour since!" Master Kelly was complaining.

"I hope he has come to no harm," said Master Medlycott. "Wouldst like me to send after him?"

But then a horse came cantering up from the snow-streaked road, ridden by a young man in a long black coat;

he jumped off in a hurry. "Master Kelly!" he cried. "Master Medlycott! Lord be praised, I am not too late!" He offered no explanation, but beamed round at them all; he had a bright, open face and was probably the only man in sight without a beard.

"Welcome, Master Williams," said William Medlycott. "My boy will take your horse."

He reached out his big hand, took the horse's rein, and handed it to John, who was delighted; he was used to horses now, and this was a handsome one.

"Tie him with the others," said Master Medlycott, and turned back to Roger Williams. But Williams had his keen eyes on John.

"Thank you, my boy," he said. "What's thy name?"

"John Wakeley, sir."

"Well, John, tha must lead me to my horse at the end of the day, and I hope our Lord will keep me from sending thee to sleep."

"Yes, sir—*no*, sir," said John, entranced with this unusual preacher, and he led the horse away, rubbed the sweat from it with a handful of hay, let it drink at the horse trough, and tied it with the other patient Sabbath steeds. He slipped into the meetinghouse just in time to hear Roger Williams begin.

The sermon was as unusual as the speaker. He told them his life story. He said that he had been born, raised, and ordained as a minister in the Church of England—which meant, I now saw, the Christian religion as it was practiced in the land from which all John's people came. Their worship was overseen not only by ministers but by bishops over those, and then archbishops, and at the head of all, the country's king. They read and prayed from the book they called their Holy Bible, and from a book of prayers, and no other way of worship was allowed.

But, said Roger Williams, he had come to feel that this system was too severe, and that men should be allowed to worship their God in whatever way they felt best. So he and his young wife—like all here in this room, he said to them—had crossed the great ocean to find a place where they would be free. He described his fifty-six days at sea, and John felt they sounded far nastier than the voyage he and his family took when he was four years old—though he could remember little of that except tossing about in a dark enclosed space full of bad smells.

"Yet though we be in the Promised Land," said Roger Williams, "our brothers and sisters in Boston have failed to take up that promise, and theirs is an unseparated church still in communion with the Church of England. *We should be separate*," he said firmly, and thumped the lectern in front of him, and there was a rumble of agreement in the meetinghouse.

"Aye," said a large man next to John, loudly, and his wife gave him a quick nervous glance.

"Thus I declined the offer to become pastor in the Boston church on my arrival," said Roger Williams, "and said further that I believed the people in this new land should have soul liberty. By this, I mean that religious opinion is one thing and civil authority is another, and the two should be kept apart. Idolatry and false worship are wrong, and so are blasphemy and the breaking of the Sabbath—but they should not be punished by order of a magistrate. The authority of our religious belief belongs not to any magistrate, but to the Lord Jesus Christ."

"Aye," said the man next to John again, and a few others too. But when John glanced at Ezra, he saw that he was frowning.

"As you may know," said Roger Williams, "the good people of Salem, sharing my beliefs, asked me to come and minister to them, but certain of the elders in the Boston church petitioned the governor against my settling there. And then"—he paused, and his face lit up with a smile— "to my great fortune, I was invited instead to the Plymouth colony, whose elders would brook no rule from the governor, feeling like me that church authority is separate. So here my dear wife Mary and I live henceforth amongst you all, and I rejoice to be preaching today in this church of the colony for the first time."

And he went on for a long time with quotations and stories from the Bible, as an encouragement to all these people to live a good life and please their God, so that when they died they might go to Heaven. Before too long, however, he was back to giving them his own opinions on freedom of religion, which seemed to John very different from anything he had heard at the cooperage. He was astonished. Roger Williams didn't even refer to Indians as heathens.

"Brothers and sisters," he said, "we are all the children of God. We are all born with a chance for redemption, in the eyes of the Lord. Let us never forget the cruel divisions that befell our Christian forefathers, in the land from which we all came. The bloody tortures, the men and women burned alive for heresy—and still, the persecution of all freethinkers by the Church of England of today."

He spread his hands to them in appeal.

"Brothers and sisters, let us not follow in their footsteps. *Let us not persecute the people we find here in this new world!* Just as we should pay the Indian for his land, but not steal it, so we should offer him the love and worship of our Lord Jesus Christ, but not force it upon him."

The big man said to Ezra as they left, "A good sermon. And a good man, with proper opinions."

"Some may think so," said Ezra.

Master Medlycott was beside them, but before he could add his own judgment, they were at the door of the meetinghouse, where Roger Williams was bidding his congregation farewell. John was dispatched to fetch his horse.

The young minister swung himself up into the saddle and glanced down at John. Thomas was waiting nearby, though the Medlycott family had gone ahead on its way home.

"Well, John," said Roger Williams, "what's thine opinion?" He was smiling, but it was a serious question.

"I think everything you said was right," said John. He added recklessly, even though Thomas could hear him, "Especially about the Indians."

The bright eyes considered him with interest for a moment. "Good boy," said Roger Williams. "I hope we meet again."

He rode away toward Plymouth, and Thomas and John set off on the rough track to the Medlycott house.

Thomas said, "What was it he said about Indians?"

"Didn't you hear him?" said John.

Thomas grinned at him. "Th'art better at attending to sermons than I am. I like watching people instead. That Huldah girl was looking at thee a lot, John Wakeley, from across the room."

"Was she?" John said.

"She's pretty. But she never smiles."

"I think she's homesick."

"If I worked for Master Kelly," said Thomas, "I wouldn't smile either."

At home, William Medlycott was not pleased with the new minister. "A preacher should preach," he said irritably. "This Master Williams is too fond of expounding his own peculiar ideas."

"He is a good Christian," Mistress Medlycott said mildly.

"And an Indian-lover," said Master Medlycott. "The man's a fool. A savage is a savage until he is converted. And even after."

John listened to them all and said nothing. But he was restless. He thought about the dignified older Indian who came to trade and was turned away. He thought about Roger Williams. He thought about me. Within a few days he woke very early, before anyone else was stirring, before dawn, and slipped outdoors. A half moon was still shining on the snowy yard.

Huddling his jacket round him, John made for the salt marsh—and found it covered by the sea. He had forgotten that the tide came in at times which changed by an hour or so every day. The water had brought little chunks of ice with it, broken from the edges of the little creeks in the marsh that froze on cold low-tide nights.

He stood there, cross with himself, looking out across the icy water. Then he set off round the edge of the marsh to try to get closer to the island, and after much hard scrambling he found that it was not properly an island at all. It was the shape of a pear, with its top facing the land on this side, and the stem of the pear was a low ridge of land emerging from the water now as the tide went down.

The light of dawn was starting to creep into the sky, behind the cold bright moon. John splashed along the ridge to the island, soaking his shoes and hose. And the moment that he reached the first trees, he saw me there, waiting for him.

This time he felt no fear at all.

"Good morning, John Wakeley," I said.

John's thin, intent face broke into a smile. "I knew you'd be here," he said, and then, in a hurry, "Hawk, will you teach me your language? Prithee?"

"Why?"

"I want to be able to talk to your people. I want—I want—" and it all came pouring out: his stored-up horror of the man who had killed me, and of all those around him who talked as if they might do the same to others of my people. Roger Williams had unlocked it. Like Roger Williams, John was in search of tolerance. He talked and he talked, and begged me again to teach him our language.

"How will people ever understand each other without words?" he said. "Master Williams meets with Indians to learn their tongue, Ezra says—though of course Ezra doesn't approve. And how could you and I be talking now, if you hadn't learned English so well?"

I laughed. "I have never learned English, John Wakeley."

He looked at me blankly. "But—" He stopped. I could feel his mind reaching for reason and sliding back again, like a man climbing a muddy slope. Then he gave up, and began to smile again.

"If the Lord hasn't explained to me how it is that I can see a ghost," he said, "I suppose he's not going to explain how I can talk to him either."

I spread my hands. I knew no more than he did.

John shook his head, and I could see him deliberately push the problem out of his mind. "Well," he said firmly, "if I am to speak your language to real people, I need to be taught your words. And your customs, too, and the things you believe. Please, Hawk. Please teach me!"

So I did. I began to teach him our dialect of the Algonquian tongue—then, and often afterward, whenever he could come to me. He had a true gift for language, and he soaked up the words fast, fast. He learned the names of everything we could see on the island: the trees, the water, the rocks, ourselves. Our time was short, as it would always be.

In the last moment before the sun came up, that first day, I taught him to say his first full sentence: "I am the friend of Little Hawk." His smile was an echo of the sunrise.

I pointed him the way he must run, from this part of the island, if he was to get home before trouble greeted him. When he turned back to wave, he could no longer see me.

In the yard of the Medlycott workshop, John found Thomas staring at his tracks in the snow.

"Where have you been?" Thomas demanded.

"I couldn't sleep. I went out to look at the moon."

"You're all wet. Did you fall down?"

"The fire will dry me," John said, and they went indoors for the bowl of cornmeal mush that would fuel them for the morning. John's shoes and hose steamed in the heat from the fire, and Mistress Medlycott scolded him thoroughly for risking an attack of the ague.

But from this day onward, he and I began to use words to shape our mysterious gift of understanding.

E I G H T

The winter wind was howling like an animal. All night long it had been growing stronger, blowing from the sea, across the salt marsh, through the trees. The four winds rule the coast, as they rule the sea itself. The white men knew them even better than my own people did; it was by catching the wind in the sails of their ships that they had come here. But though they were brave in chancing their lives to the sea and the winds, they would never be able to control them.

As the wind grew louder and louder outside the Medlycott house, I could feel its voice driving into John's sleep. He woke, suddenly, like a fish jumping. The dark little room that he shared with Thomas and Ezra was creaking under the force of the gale.

Ezra was snoring, oblivious. Thomas lay silently asleep. The air was very cold. John curled himself into a ball under his rough blanket and tried to go back to sleep, but his body began to tell him that it required him to get up. He ignored it. He curled himself tighter. *Get up!* said his body. *Get up, or I'll have you piss the bed!*

John sighed. He rolled sideways out of the blanket, to sit on the wooden platform that he shared with Thomas, and he reached for the chamber pot that waited in a corner of the room for their nighttime emergencies. It wasn't there. Somebody had taken it away to be emptied, and forgotten to bring it back.

The wind moaned through the chinks in the planked wall of the house. Thomas made a snuffling sound and turned over, taking much of the blanket with him. John sighed again. He pulled on his jerkin, pushed his feet into his shoes, and lifted the bar that held the outside door shut. The wind snatched the door so fast that he was outdoors in an instant, pushing it back, reaching for the bar that would hold it shut from the outside. When it was secure he pushed his way against the wind to the trees at the edge of the yard, where he could relieve his insistent body without the piss blowing back at him.

Buttoning his pants, he looked up at the clouds scudding across the starlit sky—and suddenly froze. Up on the roof of the Medlycott house, sparks were showering out of the log chimney, a long stream of sparks like a blazing fountain. The wind caught them up, whirled them about, dropped them on the roof. As John watched, paralyzed, he saw a flame leap up with the sparks.

And the wind whirled the flame down from the chimney to the thatch, and in an instant the roof was ablaze.

"Fire!" John yelled. "Fire!"

He ran forward to the bucket of water that stood always outside the door, but the water was solid ice.

"Fire!" he yelled again.

There was a banging inside the door in front of him, and he realized that he had shut Ezra and Thomas in. Hastily he pulled up the wooden bar, and they came tumbling out.

"*Never* latch that door with folk inside!" Ezra yelled at him angrily—and then he saw the burning roof, and his voice changed. "Thomas, wake everyone, get them out! John, buckets from the workshop—come with me!"

Thomas dived back to the room and through its inside door, shouting urgently. John ran across the yard with Ezra to the workshop. The wind blew billows of black smoke around them from the burning thatch, and the flames crackled in the chimney-top. Inside the workshop, John groped up at the wall where the buckets hung, and began pulling them down.

"The ladder first!" Ezra shouted to him, and together they hauled a short heavy wooden ladder out into the yard.

William Medlycott came rushing out of the house holding a musket, his jerkin flapping, his hair wild. He headed for the trees.

"Are we attacked?" he called.

"The roof!" John yelled. "It's on fire!"

For a second Medlycott gazed uncertainly into the

darkness, then swung round to where John and Ezra were propping the ladder against the edge of the burning roof. The flames roared in the wind.

Ezra ran back to the workshop, grabbed an axe, and began chopping at the layer of ice on the giant water butts that stood near the well and its pump in the yard. They were kept always filled; it was one of John's regular tasks every evening.

"Buckets, John!" Ezra shouted, and John ran for them.

Medlycott, bigger and stronger than either of them, dropped his gun and came to dip the buckets and swing them down. Turn by turn John and Ezra carried them to the ladder and tried to throw the water up at the flames. Much of it splashed back at them, soaking them, ice-cold. The fire blazed on.

"Stop!" Medlycott yelled. He turned back toward the house, where smoke was starting to drift out of the door. "The house is beyond help, in this wind—come, make sure everyone is out!"

So they ran through the smoky back room and into the kitchen, where Mistress Medlycott and Thomas were herding the children through the front door, grabbing blankets off the beds to wrap round them. The younger boys were seizing pots, clothes, furniture—anything movable that could be saved from the fire. Small Sarah was sobbing. Her mother gave her a quick hug, then looked round, alarmed.

"Matthew! Where's Matthew?"

John was standing beside the ladder that led to the upper

floor; he knew the children slept up there. He stared up, and could see only smoky darkness. Taking a big breath, he clambered up the ladder and into the low room; it was filled with smoke and very hot, and he could see streaks of fire through the planks above him. He crawled all round the space, but found nobody—only two blankets, which he dragged out behind him.

"He's not here!"

Choking in the smoke, he dropped the blankets down the ladder and followed after them. Ezra, waiting, looked wildly round kitchen and bedroom, and saw that a corner of the big bed was still covered by the curtain that these people hung round their beds to keep out the winter cold. He pulled down the curtain and found the little boy hiding terrified behind it, curled into a ball.

"Matthew! Come out!"

John was bent over, coughing. With his free hand Ezra grabbed him by the sleeve and dragged him, along with small Matthew, outside into the air. The yard was full of the snapping of the fire now, and flames were licking up into the sky, blown sideways by the wind. It was not blowing directly at the other buildings, but in the flickering red light of the flames the roof of the workshop looked perilously close.

Medlycott came rushing out of the house with a great armful of metal plates and mugs. "That's the last! Priscilla, no one must go in anymore—the smoke can kill." He stared up at the roof, his face glistening with sweat. "We must wet down the workshop roof, so that the fire will not spread. Ezra, Thomas, come with me. Willie, help thy mother with the little ones. John—are you all right?"

John took a wheezing breath. "Yes," he said hoarsely.

"Run to the farm for help. Though only the good Lord can help us now, I believe."

John was halfway out of the yard when he heard Ezra yell after him, "Be careful of the ice!"

Even so, he slipped and fell twice on the uphill track to the farm of their nearest neighbor. In winter, even the swiftest runners of my own tribe were slowed down by the frozen earth. The track was dark, but he could see his way by the glow from the burning roof. At the farmhouse, John yelled, "Fire! Help! Fire!" at the top of his voice, and because there was a constant danger of fire amongst these people, as amongst my own, the instant the farmers heard him they knew what to do.

In a very short time several men were running back down the hill with John, carrying a cluster of buckets made not from wood but from deer hide, as we make ours, and with long twig-brooms. The farm must have been the community's center for the fighting of fire. Two of the men even pushed a great tub already filled with water, set in a frame with a wheel on either side.

But no men and no water could help the Medlycott house by the time they arrived there. It was fully ablaze, with flames leaping out of its windows, and the voice of the fire was triumphant and loud. Mistress Medlycott and the children had retreated to the barn where the animals were kept, dragging all their saved possessions with them, and that was a good thing, for very soon, with a great *whoompf* sound, the roof of the burning house fell in. Scraps of burning wood flew all over the yard like fiery birds.

The men scattered, but not for long. Within moments they joined the work of wetting the roofs of the other buildings, with a chain of people moving buckets of water from the well, where John and Thomas were taking turns at the pump. And together they saved everything that the Medlycott family owned, except the house in which they had lived. The strong wind that had spread the fire also drove it to burn down very fast, so that the blazing walls shrank lower and lower, and the danger to the workshop shrank with them.

Outside the barn, Mistress Medlycott began to sob as her house disappeared, and the youngest children clustered round her and tried to make comforting noises, as if they were the parents and she the child.

The chain of buckets stilled and the farmer came to the pump to stop Thomas and John. "Well done," he said.

"James Burton, I am greatly in your debt," said Master Medlycott wearily.

Burton put a hand on his shoulder. He was a heavyset man with thick white hair, full of cinders now. "We are all children of the Lord," he said. "And praise God that nobody is hurt. Take heart, William—we shall all help thee rebuild."

Where there had been a fine tall house, there was now a great wide mound of glowing embers, with flames still ruffling to and fro as the wind blew. John could see the stars again now, prickling the dark sky; all the clouds had blown away, and the wind was not so strong as before. Master Burton set two of his men to watch the embers, and the animals in the barn, who had been to leeward of the fire and smoke but made restive by the noise and light. William Medlycott insisted on staying too. John saw that he had his musket with him again.

Burton took everyone else to his farm, where his wife made hot drinks and bundled the children into bed with her own. The others crowded round the wide fireplace, looking with new eyes at the log chimney above it. In all these houses, as in our own, people could only survive the winter cold by keeping a fire banked with dirt overnight, sleeping but alive.

"You must build your new chimney of stone," said Mistress Burton to Mistress Medlycott, "and so should we."

Priscilla Medlycott nodded. She sighed, and sipped her chamomile tea. "Stone was too costly and too slow when first we came," she said. "But if we had not built our chimney out of logs and clay, the house would still be there."

Ezra was sitting on a stool in the shadows, with John and Thomas. "The chimney may not have been at fault," he said. "Perhaps a savage set the fire. They have been known to fire burning arrows at thatched roofs, Master Medlycott said."

"Not here in Marshfield," Mistress Burton said.

"Nor in Plymouth," said John. "And I *saw* our chimney catch fire tonight."

"In other places," Ezra said doggedly.

"I heard that too," said one of Burton's sons. "We kept watch every night against savage attack, when first we built our house."

Ezra said, "We should keep watch still. The heathen is not to be trusted."

John had been feeling friendly toward Ezra for the way he had rescued him from the smoke, but the friendliness suddenly faded. He said, surprised by his own boldness, "In Plymouth I saw a house burn down, but that was the same, a chimney that caught fire at night, and no Indian came shooting burning arrows *ever*."

Ezra turned his head and looked at him with scorn.

"John Wakeley," he said, "you are a child."

NINE

Time went by, and John ceased to be a child.

With the help of all the community, the Medlycotts' home was rebuilt. At their meetinghouse on the Sunday after the fire, they had thanked their God for preserving everyone from death that day, and all of them without exception took on responsibilities for helping to replace the house. Carts creaked their way to the nearest beaches to collect stones the size of a man's head to build the new chimney, and a house rose around it with remarkable speed. For a while John could seldom escape, but he came to talk to me whenever he could. He was full of astonishment.

"Even Ezra is generous," he said in wonder. "They are all warmhearted; they work so hard for us."

"It is a village, a larger family," I said, thinking of my own.

John said, "But they still need warmer hearts for people

outside the family. They need to understand." He grinned at me. "Teach me some more words, Hawk."

So our lessons went on, after the house was finished, and in the years after that, and while John learned words we were each learning the mind and feelings of the other. We were truly friends.

And from this ordained distance that I did not understand, tied to the island and to John Wakeley, I watched my people. My own village, my own family. I could not speak to them, but I watched them with love, and longing, and concern.

My grandmother had taken my death very hard. She knew that One Who Waits valued her greatly as a wise woman in our village, trusting her advice and judgment, but her attachment to this world began to grow thin. I believe she felt that when I had come home after the plague destroyed our village, I had brought her back from the edge of death, and now that I was gone she saw no reason to stay. So before many moons went by, Suncatcher died too, and there was a greater mourning. But hers was a gentle and dignified death, and she traveled quietly into the west, into the mystery that I have yet to solve.

And as the years went by, Quickbird married not Wolfchaser, as I had thought she might, but my friend Leaping Turtle. Though they had grown up like brother and sister, violence and grief had turned them separately into different older people, and it was those two people who came to love and live together.

I watched them, and wished them happiness. But their lives were changing. Thousands more of the white men continued to arrive from over the sea, and their settlements multiplied and spread, as our father Yellow Feather and other sachems sold them the use of land. This selling was not what either side thought it should be.

For my people, the land and the sea belonged to the Great Spirit, and all that could be bought or sold, attacked or defended, was a share in its use. For the white man, the land itself could be owned, as a man owns his hand or his foot, and therefore they now believed themselves owners of the land on which we used freely to live and plant, fish and hunt.

So gradually my people moved south, or west, away from the new houses and farms—and away from the greed of the great hogs that the white men released into the forest, who would gobble up not only the acorns that were food for the deer, but often the crops that we were growing too.

This I watched. So did John.

Most of his time was spent in the house, the workshop, and the meetinghouse. William Medlycott worked hard, and expected the same from them all. Gradually, steadily, John was becoming a cooper. He had gone from making simple pails and tubs to the much more complicated art of making casks, and even shaping his own staves.

He had grown stronger too. He was taller than Thomas now, and his shoulders were broad, his hands big enough to keep tight hold of the stave he was shaping at the draw bench. Mistress Medlycott, who felt her life's work was to nourish the young, gave him second helpings at every meal.

Whenever he could get away at dawn or twilight, he made his way to the island and to me. He took great care that nobody should see or follow him. Each time I taught him more of my people's language, and he grew more and more fluent. But while he lived at the cooperage, this was a dangerous secret—for there was no living person who could have taught him. And he could hardly explain that he had learned from a ghost. The white men believed that only witches could speak to ghosts, and in the land they came from, witches were tortured and killed.

He made a mistake only once.

When he was in the workshop one morning splitting hickory poles, to make the hoops that would hold a cask together, he heard voices raised outside. Two were the deep voices of Medlycott's English workmen, accented and familiar, but with them was a lighter, questioning voice, using what sounded like a word of Pokanoket.

"Please," he heard. "Please . . ."

John put down his drawknife and went outside.

Large, bearded Edward and Isaac had paused in loading a cart with oak staves and were trying to understand a young Indian, neat in deerskin tunic and leggings, who had emerged from the trees edging the yard. He had something in his hand, holding it out hopefully, but he had very few words of English.

"Borkid," he was saying. "Need borkid."

"Thinks we're a farm, does he?" said Edward amiably. He said very loudly to the Indian, "No! Not here!"

"Down the road!" boomed Isaac, pointing to the gate.

"Borkid!" said the Indian insistently. His face lit up as he saw Ezra emerging from the kitchen with a bucket in each hand, and he pointed. "Yes!" he said. And added, in Pokanoket, "I want to trade for a bucket, if you will allow me."

John opened his mouth, and quickly shut it again.

"He knows you, Ezra!" Edward said in relief. "Ask him what he wants."

Ezra's few words of my language had made him the house translator, in spite of his low opinion of my people. He looked with distaste at the young Indian and said in Massachusett, "Want trade?"

The young man's face lit up. "Yes, please," he said. "I have more to carry than I expected. I should be grateful for a bucket."

Ezra looked at him blankly. He said again, "Want trade?"

The young Indian's smile faded. "Borkid," he said again in his attempt at English, and reached helpfully for one of the buckets in Ezra's hands.

Ezra angrily jerked it away from him.

Isaac said mildly, "Perhaps he is asking to buy a bucket."

"To steal one, more like," Ezra said. He gave the young Indian a sour look and said again, "*Trade.*"

"Of course," said the young man politely in Pokanoket.

"I'm afraid I have only what I was wearing, because this was unexpected, but here it is."

He held out his opened palm, and on it was a necklace, a string of beautiful small fish carved from bone. Stepping forward to peer over Ezra's shoulder, John caught his breath in admiration.

But Ezra snorted in disdain and shook his head violently. "These heathens think only of vanity," he said. "Is that his idea of a fair exchange? A bauble for a craftsman's bucket? Amongst devout God-fearing folk?"

"'Tis a pretty thing," said big Isaac unexpectedly.

Ezra ignored him. He was full of righteous indignation, his tufty yellow beard jutting. "No!" he said to the young Indian.

"But it's all I have with me," said the young man. "It's very valuable. I had it from my grandmother, and if she knew I were offering it for trade, she would eat me alive."

Ezra understood none of this; he heard only argument and threat. He dropped one of his buckets and pointed imperiously at the trees. "No!" he shouted. "No trade! Go!"

The young man blinked at him.

"Get rid of him!" Ezra snapped at Edward and Isaac. He picked up the bucket and stalked off into the workshop.

The big workmen loomed over the young Indian, but he was already turning away, his back very straight. Uncomprehending and dignified, he stalked away into the woodland from which he had come. Edward shrugged at Isaac, and they went back to loading their cart.

And John, distressed, darted back into the workshop, seized a bucket he had made the week before, and ran across the yard and into the trees.

He was at once on one of the old paths made by my people, leading to the lake, but it was a while before he caught up with the young Pokanoket. He found him with a girl, both of them staring at him in alarm.

In an instant John was babbling in Pokanoket, without thinking. "Forgive me, I had to follow you to apologize for the rudeness of my fellow. I know he sounded hostile, but he did not understand what you were saying."

The young man was so astounded at this fluency that he didn't think to question it. "I meant no harm," he said. "I simply wanted a container. I came with my sister to help her gather cattails; we filled our baskets and Small Dove was so excited, she wanted to carry more."

"See how many there are!" said Small Dove to John happily. She was very young, he saw now, with gleaming black hair down her back. He saw too that cattails stood in a great fringe at the end of the pond, round which he and Thomas annually gathered willow shoots for Mistress Medlycott.

"Grandmother sent us to this pond," said Small Dove. "She knew of it from when she was a girl. She will be so pleased!" A heap of cattail heads lay at her feet, beside two grass-woven baskets brimming with the long rushes.

John said, "That's an excellent harvest."

"I knew the barrel-maker lived nearby," said the brother,

"so I thought I could get something for her. But—" He shrugged.

John held out his bucket to Small Dove. "Here. For you. For your cattails."

Delighted, the girl reached out a hand; then she paused and looked up at her brother. "Fast Cloud?" she said.

Fast Cloud reached up to his neck, and John saw that the string of intricate little carvings was back around it. The young man started to pull it over his head.

"No," John said. "This is a gift. An apology."

"We must trade," Fast Cloud said, trying to maneuver the necklace over his scalp lock.

John said, "I have sisters too. Please."

They looked at each other, and I could feel Fast Cloud noticing, as once I had, the honest appeal in John Wakeley's blue eyes. There was a moment's tension, and then the young Indian smiled, let the necklace drop back, and held out his hand. John took it.

"We thank you," Fast Cloud said.

"Go well," said John.

Small Dove happily took the bucket, and they all inclined their heads to one another. Then John went back along the faint trail through the trees. He reflected as he went that the grandmother of the two Indians had lived in a different time. Today that pond was considered to belong to Master Medlycott, as part of the land granted him by the Plymouth Court.

When he emerged into the Medlycott yard, Ezra was

waiting for him. He confronted John, furious, his bearded chin thrust out like a weapon.

"You went after the Indian, didn't you? Did you trade that bucket with him?"

"It was my bucket," John said. "I made it."

"Have you no shame? To trade for a decoration! Do you pay no attention to the preacher? The Lord requires modesty of apparel, with shamefacedness and sobriety, the Bible says. Not *necklaces*!"

John said patiently, "I listen very carefully to the preacher, Ezra, but his care is my immortal soul, not the rules of trading. In any case I didn't trade for the bucket. I gave it to him."

"*What?*" Ezra said.

Isaac and Edward paused in their loading, and looked at John with astonishment.

John said, "It was a gift."

"To the heathen," Ezra said, dangerously quiet now. "I send away a begging heathen boy, and you deliberately reverse that decision. And go after him with a gift."

John's patience was starting to fray. "He wasn't begging, he was trying to trade. You were too hard on him. He needed a bucket, and the necklace just happened to be all he had with him to offer you."

Ezra said, "*And how do you know that?*"

And to this, John suddenly realized, he could give no answer. No answer that might not lead to his being hanged as a witch.

There was a long pause.

John took a deep breath, and he said, "I'm sorry, Ezra. I suppose I was guessing. I behaved foolishly. I'm sure you were right. I beg your pardon."

So Edward and Isaac went back to moving the pile of staves, and the incident faded from their minds very soon. But in Ezra's tight, pious mind, John was confirmed as a soft young man on the slippery path to becoming, like Roger Williams, an Indian-lover.

Sometimes, in the warmer half of the year, John was able to talk to Huldah Bates at the meetinghouse. She too was growing taller, and she was prettier than ever; she looked like a woman, and because they liked each other, they were awkward in talking together. He did learn that although she was fond of the children who were her charge, and of Mistress Kelly, she was made miserable by Master Kelly, who was a bullying, demanding man.

And one magical day, John was able to spend more time with her.

"John," said Mistress Medlycott early one morning, "wouldst like to visit thy family today?"

He stared at her in wonder. She smiled.

"Goodman Bates will come this morning with a load of timber," she said. "He'll take Master Medlycott back to Plymouth with him for a day and night, for business—and you shall go too. Thy mother needs to see how her boy is becoming a man."

John knew this must be her doing; Master Medlycott had released him to see his mother and sisters only a very few times in the last four years. "Thank you," he said. "Oh, thank you!"

"Goodman Bates will be carrying his niece, too," Mistress Medlycott added, deliberately casual.

"Huldah Bates?" John said. He was trying very hard to sound casual too, as his spirits leapt like a deer in spring.

"The very same," said Mistress Medlycott, and she went off to feed the hens, smiling to herself.

It was a sunny day in late summer, before the fall of the leaves; the trees overhead glowed red and orange among the green. John and Huldah shared the back of Goodman Bates's cart with a dozen small barrels called firkins, sent from the cooperage to a Plymouth customer, and they talked and talked, and laughed, and enjoyed being together. Even William Medlycott, when Goodman Bates paused to water the oxen, chatted amiably with them as they all ate their bread and cheese. He talked about England, something John had never heard him do before.

"The autumn leaves are gaudier here than where I grew up, that's for certain," he said, the rich, rounded accent more marked in his voice than usual. "But you should see the bluebells in the spring, back there. Blue as the sea, all over the ground, like nothing you'll see here. A Devon spring is beautiful, and after that it's never so hot as here, and never so cold, though we have our storms, oh dear me yes, roaring in off the Atlantic."

"You sound homesick, Master Medlycott," said Huldah, who had been born in England but couldn't remember it.

"Not I," said Medlycott. "I left an ungodly land to have freedom to worship with the Saints, and to live without rule of bishops or fear of a monarch—and so shall my children and their children, by the grace of God."

"With more chance to thrive," said Goodman Bates, getting to his feet and brushing off crumbs. "As shall we this day, if we set off again now."

And the cooper and the carter discussed business the rest of the way to Plymouth, while John and Huldah sat together among the barrels, talking their way into a relationship that would last as long as they lived.

Plymouth was far bigger and busier than they remembered. They could see a bristle of ships' masts in the harbor. John climbed down from the cart at his family's house, and his mother wept happily at the sight of him. Her three-year-old son Samuel was afraid of him and hid his face in her skirt. There was another new baby too, a girl, whimpering in a cradle that was being rocked by John's youngest sister, Patience. Patience jumped up to greet him, and for a moment he did not recognize her, because she was no longer the little girl he knew.

Now she was thirteen years old, and her older sister Mercy was sixteen—and living on the other side of town, caring for a sick neighbor. John wouldn't be able to see her this time. He begged paper from his mother and wrote a note for Patience to carry to Mercy later. Then Daniel

Smith came home from work, covered in sawdust as usual, and was not pleased to find paper used for so frivolous a reason. He gave John a cool welcome and warned him that he would sleep that night on a wooden shelf in the storage room behind the kitchen.

When Daniel had washed, he reported to the family that there was excellent news in the town today: Roger Williams had been called for reprimand by the General Court in Boston.

John said impulsively, "But he is a good man!"

"Indeed? Have you met him?" Daniel enquired loftily.

"Yes, I have. He came to preach in Marshfield when he was pastor here in Plymouth."

"Then you should know better," Daniel said. "He has dangerous ideas, and is a peril to the young. All through his two years here he was consorting with the savages as if they were Christians—and now he is attacking King Charles's charter for presuming to grant us their land! Governor Bradford sent him back from Plymouth to Salem because of his strange opinions, and clearly he has grown worse."

"His thinking is very advanced," said John's mother unhappily.

"Advanced!" said Daniel. "It's ridiculous!"

John swallowed down the angry words that wanted to spill out of his mouth. He said, "What else has he said?"

Daniel made a noise like a snort. "He questions the very basis of our government! All God-fearing men swear allegiance to the colony, but Roger Williams holds it is not proper for them to use the words 'So help me God.' Nor should the magistrates enforce our rules to keep the Sabbath Day holy, he says—or even to worship!"

It was like listening to the spluttering of Master Medlycott. I was constantly amazed by the heat with which Englishmen talked of their religion.

John said, "This is what he called the separation of church and state, is it not?"

Daniel scowled. He said curtly, "The court has called his opinions erroneous and very dangerous, and they are right! They may well banish him."

"Where would he go?" said John.

"I neither know nor care," Daniel said. Then he led them all in the family evening prayers, and took even longer than he did before.

Huldah's visit to her family, John discovered the next morning on their way home, had been no better than his own. They sat together once more in the back of Goodman Bates's cart, which was loaded now with timber for Master Medlycott's cooperage. Huldah told John she had hoped that she would come home after her five years with the Kelly family, but clearly there would be no room in the house. She too felt that she no longer belonged. She was sad and muted, and John ached for her. Without any thought for the Puritan rules of propriety, he put his arm round her shoulders.

"Thy mother still loves thee," he said.

Huldah said, "I know."

"And my mother's affection for me is no less, but time changes all our lives. She has had two more children since I left. We can't go back, we have to go forward."

"Yes," said Huldah. She sniffed.

John took a deep breath, and said something he had said often in his mind, half-dreaming, on his way into sleep.

"Huldah," he said bravely, "when I am a journeyman, will you marry me?"

Huldah said nothing, and his heart dropped. He wondered gloomily if she was appalled.

"That's three years from now," he said in a smaller voice.

Huldah said, "You may change your mind, in all that time."

"I shan't," John said.

"Nor shall I," said Huldah.

She turned her face up to him, smiling, and in a whirl of happiness John kissed her gently on the mouth. It was a moment neither of them would ever forget. And they sat there together, his arm around her, her head on his shoulder, until the voices of Goodman Bates and Master Medlycott above their heads rose in some minor argument, reminding them where they were.

John removed his arm, and he and Huldah looked at each other and smiled. Under cover of a fold of her skirt, they held hands.

But soon they were at the Kelly homestead, and because Goodman Bates had a package to deliver here as well as his niece, he drove the cart into the yard, all the way up to the house. It was a handsome house; it seemed bigger than before. Mistress Kelly was in her herb garden with two small girls; the children ran out calling in delight when they saw Huldah.

John got to his feet to help Huldah down from the cart and handed her bundle down after her. She looked up at him for one last moment, and he locked it into his memory.

In the next moment, Master Kelly came out of the house in his shirtsleeves. He called crossly to Huldah, "And long past time! Get into the house, girl—little Abby is sick, and Dorothy has been needing thy help all day!"

Goodman Bates clambered down as Huldah hurried into the house, and he handed Mistress Kelly her package. "We made as good time as we could," he said mildly. "Good day, Mistress."

"Good day, and very many thanks to you," said Mistress Kelly, an ample, patient lady. "We missed your niece only because she is a treasure." She smiled up at Master Medlycott. "Good day, William."

"William!" Master Kelly called. "I need four barrels by Thursday, if you haven't sold everything to Plymouth. Slack stock, for tobacco."

His voice was imperious, and the linen of his shirt was of better quality than those of the other men; there were clearly degrees of rank even in this society that prized equality.

"You shall have them," said Master Medlycott in his deep, untroubled rumble. "John here is becoming a good hand at a slack cask, and even my Thomas, too."

Master Kelly looked at John, who was standing tall among the logs and lumber on the oxcart. The eyes narrowed a little in his foxy face. "Th'art John Wakeley?" he said.

Master Medlycott laughed. "Double the size, is he not? My Priscilla feeds up our young men."

John said suddenly, "Master Kelly?" His voice came out louder than he had intended, from nervousness.

"Well?" said Master Kelly.

"With your permission—and Master Medlycott's," John said, stumbling, "if there is a day whenever—when Huldah has an hour to herself—may I call on her?"

Master Kelly said instantly, "No."

The word was so sudden and obdurate that it seemed to cause a ripple in the air.

Mistress Kelly said gently, "Walter—"

"He is an apprentice," said Master Kelly. "He is not a freeman, to make such a request. He may speak to her at the meetinghouse, as is fitting, as all our brothers and sisters in Christ may speak to each other. But that is all." He looked up at Master Medlycott. "How long does his apprenticeship have to run, William?"

"Three years, I believe," said Master Medlycott.

Kelly's eyes shifted to John. "Perhaps we will consider the matter in three years' time," he said.

———

And he gave a sharp quick nod of his head, as if stressing the proper authority of his decision. But John knew, and I knew, that there was far more behind it than that.

I could feel John's distress filling his mind and all his waking thoughts. Very soon, at dawn, before the sun rose over the salt marsh and turned it gold, he made his way to see me again, on the island where my tomahawk was born, the one place where we could meet. There was nobody else to whom he could speak openly about Master Kelly.

"He is the man who killed you!" John said to me. "He is wicked! You should be haunting him!"

"Haunting?"

"Appearing to him, terrifying him, rousing his guilt!"

"Is that what you believe the dead can do? Is that written in your Holy Bible?"

John paused. "I don't know. I don't think so. Well, the Witch of Endor called up the ghost of Samuel for Saul."

"What did that ghost say?"

"He warned Saul of trouble, just as he had when he was alive."

I said, "That doesn't sound terrifying."

"No," said John thoughtfully. "But people are always terrified of ghosts. Everyone says so."

"Perhaps that's because none of them has seen one," I said. "Except you."

He said, "What is your word for ghost, Little Hawk?"

"We have none," I said.

Then the sun rose huge and red over the salt marsh, bringing color into the world, and I was gone from John's sight.

Winter came, and John's chances of speaking to Huldah almost disappeared. They had to be content with looking at each other across the meetinghouse, except on the rare occasions when Master Kelly was away and his kindly wife allowed them to speak. So they smiled when possible, and listened to the other members of the congregation exchanging news. The talk that washed around them was often concerned with Roger Williams, who was clearly still angering the Puritans of Boston by questioning their rules.

Ezra's opinions, which John also heard at some length every day at home, were very much like those of Daniel Smith. There was a great deal of indignant talk about Roger Williams in the Medlycott house, and the more John heard, the better he liked Roger Williams.

"Does it not seem," he said hesitantly to Master Medlycott and Ezra, as they all took a breath in the workshop one day, "that we all came here to escape authority, but are imposing an authority of our own?"

"There must be order," said Ezra. "Without order, we have chaos. Look at the three of us here, we are the master cooper, the journeyman, and the apprentice. In order. We are a little world."

Master Medlycott laughed. "Th'art a philosopher, Ezra," he said, and took a great swig from a jug of water.

"But this is a little world of work," John said. "It is governed by the knowledge of the craft. When you are a master cooper, you will be the same as Master Medlycott."

"Not the same," Ezra said. "He will still have more experience."

"And more customers," said Master Medlycott, who was not a philosopher. He chuckled.

Ezra was deadly serious, however; he shook his head, frowning. "Order comes from above, John Wakeley," he said. "This is something you seem to have difficulty in understanding. We are the children of the Lord God, put here to obey his laws—and so we must obey those he puts in office above us."

"Not if they interpret those laws wrongly," John said.

"And who are you to judge?" snapped Ezra. He looked at John coldly, as if he were a hostile stranger. "Our Lord said, 'If you love me, keep my commandments.'"

John said, "But there's no commandment about taking land away from the Indians. Those in office—"

Master Medlycott held up his hand. "Enough," he said. "Back to work. The opinions of Roger Williams have no place in this workshop."

And at the meetinghouse some weeks later, they all learned that the Boston court had banished Roger Williams, and ordered him to be put on a ship back to England.

"And they say," said their informant, a merchant visiting from Plymouth, "that the General Court sent to Salem to arrest him, but found he had run away, leaving his wife behind with their two children. One of whom is a babe in arms."

Ezra stared, scandalized. "Do they know where he went?"

"They say he has gone south," said the merchant, "and taken refuge with his Indian friends."

Master Medlycott gave a snort of disgust. "At least his children have been spared from a life with the heathen."

"Oh no," said the merchant, who was the focus now of a small attentive group, and enjoying it. "He has sent for his family, and they have gone already—his wife would not be persuaded otherwise."

"The magistrates should have restrained her," said Master Medlycott.

The merchant spread his hands. "He is outside the bounds of Plymouth Colony. They could do nothing. It is thought that he wishes to establish a settlement of his own."

Ezra said, "It will not be a place for proper God-fearing men."

John said slowly, "And our colony's laws do not hold beyond its borders, I suppose."

"They do not, John Wakeley—that way lies wilderness!" said Master Medlycott. He shook his head. "Give thanks to the good Lord that tha'rt living safely here in the civilized world."

But John was thinking no such thing, nor was he giving thanks—except to Roger Williams, for opening a door in his mind. A perilous door, through which he intended to go.

T E N

Two winters had passed, and it was spring. At the meeting-house every Sunday, John and Huldah managed at least to smile at each other, and at the best of times to sit and talk for a few moments. These moments were often quietly engineered by Mistress Medlycott or Mistress Kelly, both kind-hearted women who could sense the emotions involved.

But one day there was a meeting full of unexpected turmoil. When everyone was seated, waiting for worship to begin, the minister unexpectedly introduced Miles Standish, the military leader of the Plymouth Colony, who lived nearby in Duxbury.

"Captain Standish has some events of importance to us all to report," he said. "And Master Kelly, too."

Standish came to the lectern; he was a short, muscular man, wearing the padded jacket of the militia, and his red-dish hair and beard were flecked with grey. Kelly followed and stood nearby; since he too was short, stocky, and in uniform, they looked almost like brothers. John had not seen Master Kelly in the meetinghouse for some weeks—which had greatly helped his chances of speaking to Huldah.

"By the providence of our Lord, brothers and sisters, we have had a great victory," Standish said. His voice was clear and forceful, and carried round the room, over the attentive heads. "As you know, our brother Walter Kelly here and others have been helping to defend the Connecticut colonists against the warlike Pequots of that coast. The Pequots are among the boldest and bloodiest of the savage tribes, and have sought to ally the Narragansetts with them to drive all Englishmen out of this land."

He paused, eyes roving over his silent audience.

"But the Narragansett Indians and the Mohegans, having had many past quarrels with the Pequots, chose to join with the English. And in this latest assault, God gave us such good fortune that these Pequots are almost totally destroyed!"

Voices murmured through the room. There were a few calls of "Amen!"

Standish said, slowly and with ceremony, "Master Kelly is but newly returned from the battle, and will relate all to you."

The congregation murmured again and then hushed, as Kelly stood up at the front. He was less eloquent than Captain Standish but no less self-confident.

"Our company under Captain John Underhill being

arrived to join our Connecticut brothers," he said, "the hasty Narragansetts directed us to surprise the Pequots before dawn, in a village where many of the tribe lay sleeping. And so we did, creeping up silently on their fortifications. Then our men attacked with great speed and courage. Those Pequots who fought, we slew with the sword. The rest died by fire. The Connecticut captain John Mason had us set fire to their wigwams."

John was sitting behind Mistress Medlycott. He saw her shift uneasily on her bench, and she bowed her head.

"The flames spread fast through the whole village, and the savage devils screamed long as they died," said Master Kelly with satisfaction. "We were all around the wall, waiting to stab any who ran outside. And the Narragansetts were there to kill them too, though they did little except to jeer at the Pequots as they burned. Thus the God of Battles gave us triumph over those who would murder good Christian men and women! In this and other attacks it is thought that seven hundred Indians died. The good Lord be praised!"

There was a rumble of agreement in the room.

John clenched his fists in an effort to stay silent, and felt his fingernails cut into his palms.

"Where were the other attacks, Master Kelly?" called out Master Medlycott, sitting beside John.

"I was present only at one of them," said Master Kelly, "when we drove the people of a smaller Indian settlement into a swamp. There we beset them all day and all night.

We killed many, but so miraculously did the Lord preserve us that their arrows wounded none of our men. I had an arrow through my sleeve with not so much as a scratch."

"God be praised," said a woman's voice from among the listeners.

"Amen," said some others.

"Those Pequots who survived from the swamp, we took prisoner," Master Kelly said. "The women and the maid children were disposed about in the towns. All the male children have been set on a ship to Bermuda, for the plantations there."

John could bear this no longer. He spoke up, suddenly, his voice shaking.

"Master Kelly," he said, "may I ask a question?"

Walter Kelly heard his voice but did not recognize him, out there in the audience. "Of course," he said.

John stood up. He said, this time loudly, clearly, "Were there not innocent women and children in the village of people that you burned alive?"

There was a long silence in the meetinghouse. Some heads turned.

John sat down again, but not before Kelly had recognized him.

"Yes, John Wakeley," he said coldly. "There were many. You call them innocent? As our captain has said, they belonged to a people grown to a height of blood and sin against God and man. And do you think the Indians would have spared English women and children from death?"

The minister was on his feet at once, headed for the lectern. "Brothers and sisters," he cried, "let us give thanks for Master Kelly and Captain Standish and all our brave soldiers, and praise God for our triumph over the murderous heathen! In the words of the Bible, the Lord was pleased to smite our enemies, and to give us their land for an inheritance. Let the whole earth be filled with his glory!"

So they were launched into the long customary pattern of worship for the day, with a break between the two sermons for eating and talking—from which John deliberately kept away, taking a long time to check on the welfare of their horses. And Master Medlycott said not a word to John until they were all back at home, away from the congregation, when he erupted in furious rage.

"Shame on you!" he shouted. "Shame on you for slandering a brave man who defends our safety! And in public! And bringing shame to this house, as my apprentice!"

"I did but ask a question," John said coldly.

"A question—it was an accusation! Who are you to question the actions of your betters, of a good devout Christian?" He was on the brink of striking at John. "Ezra warned me of thy foolishness, I should have listened! Out of here! Away with thee! I'll have you no more in my workshop or my home!"

"William—" said Mistress Medlycott.

"Out!" bellowed Medlycott, his face scarlet. The children had crept away outdoors, frightened by his anger, and Ezra was drifting toward the back room.

But cosy Mistress Medlycott, never known to raise her voice in anything except merriment, was standing four-square in the middle of the room facing her husband, beside John, like a mountain lion defending her cub. And though she was a good Puritan wife, she was shouting right back at him.

"William! What is this rage? Tha know'st this boy—he has been part of this family for five years and more!"

"He is a fool!" roared Medlycott.

"He is no fool, but a good devout Christian too! Can you not recall the nature of the question he asked?"

Medlycott paused, for a crucial second. He was so taken aback at the fury bursting out of his tranquil wife that he actually found himself hearing what she said.

Mistress Medlycott pressed on. "He asked us to consider that our soldiers burned alive hundreds of women and children! *Burned them alive!* Children like your own! Not fighting men, our enemies, but innocent children! Have you ever heard of Indians doing that to us?"

"Indians have killed white women," Medlycott said. "And children too. And tortured them, they say."

"Then is this the way of a Christian, to behave like a savage but a hundred times worse?"

John dared not open his mouth, but he was full of wonder at hearing her say everything that was in his own mind.

Mistress Medlycott said with total proud conviction, "My husband would never have been party to such a slaughter of the innocents."

There was a very long pause, and then Master Medlycott said quietly, "No, I would not."

John said nervously, "Forgive me, Master Medlycott—I should have said nothing in public without your permission. I spoke from my heart and not my wit."

Master Medlycott stood looking at him for a moment. John had grown so tall that they were almost eye to eye. Then Medlycott sighed, and put a hand briefly on John's shoulder.

"Tha'll be a good cooper, John," he said, with the rounder English accent that came into his voice at certain moments. "But perhaps the best place for you will not be in this colony."

"Yes," John said. "I have thought about that."

He came to see me one day a little while later. It was one of his visits early in the day, in the first glimmering of dawn. The salt marsh and its islands were less isolated than once they had been. More of the bordering woodland had been cleared for farming, and in season, the farmers cut salt marsh hay to feed their multiplying livestock. Men paused briefly on my island once in a while, though most avoided it because of the tangles of vines among its trees, which brought up fearsome blisters on their English skin.

The tide was low; only meandering little creeks remained in the marsh. John came along the stony ridge that I called the stem of the pear-shaped island, and I was there waiting for him.

"You asked the right question in the meetinghouse, John Wakeley," I said.

He smiled a little. His gaze, as always, was a little indirect; all this time we had never looked each other straight in the eye. I felt he could see me only at the edge of his vision.

He said, "Do you know every single thing I say and do?"

"Not everything. I sense your thoughts. Some of them."

"Do you guide them?"

"Oh no. You are your own man."

"And full of horror at the massacre of the Pequots," he said. "How can men listen to the screaming of children in agony, and have no pity?"

Some questions have no answer. In this world, one small thing leads to another small thing, and they twine within time to cause events, both good and terrible. We see this pattern only when we look back at the past, and though we talk of learning from history, we do not learn. And even a ghost cannot explain to the living why this should be so.

I said to John, "It is an endless river of conflict, that was set in motion by the first white man to set his foot on this land. And before that. By the first of my people to fire an arrow at another man, by the first Englishman to shoot a gun."

"We should never have come here," John said.

"There was conflict here between our tribes before you ever came."

"But did any Indians ever cause a village of men and women and children to burn alive?"

"I think not."

Grey light was washing into the sky above the sea, above the marsh, as the sunrise came close.

"I shall leave here as soon as I am done with my apprenticeship," John said. "I shall go to join Roger Williams, who works against conflict."

I had only a few moments left, to make a request.

"Will you do something for me, before that time comes?"

"I shall see you often before then," he said. "But of course. Anything."

"To remember something that has happened in a place," I said, "my people make a memory hole in the ground. Two hands wide, two hands deep, lined with stones. It lies always beside a track, and is kept open by the generations after, and it holds . . . memories."

"I'll make one here," John said eagerly. "Right here where I am standing."

And as he was smiling at me, the edge of the sun flamed up over the sea, the first light of the new day, and I was gone from his sight, almost for the last time.

He came back to the island one afternoon, with a bucket of stones he had collected from the edge of the river that flows through the salt marsh. They were small, water-rounded stones, older than his people or mine. He had brought a short iron spade too. He would not be able to see me at this time of the day, he knew, but that was not why he had come.

At the beginning of the island, the place where the stem-ridge joins the top of the pear, he dug a memory hole. As he dug out the soil he tossed it into the marsh, where it disappeared among the grasses. The sides of the hole did not crumble, or collapse, because he was digging not into marsh mud but into solid sandy ground.

He lined the hole with his small stones, pressing them firmly into the sides. He gave it a stony rim as well. It looked beautiful. Watching him, I was suddenly back with Leaping Turtle, in our second village, digging the storage pit to keep corn for the winter. I wondered what had become of the pit and of the village, but I chose not to know. They too were almost certainly ghosts by then, replaced by an Englishman's farm.

John stood back and admired his memory hole. A branch from a clump of scrubby oak put it in shadow; nobody would notice it.

"This is for you, Little Hawk," he said to the air, and then looked up suddenly, as something out over the marsh caught his eye.

It was an osprey, broad wings lying on the breeze, coasting out toward the sea. He could just hear its strange, thin call.

Perhaps it was my Manitou. He is with me often, now as then.

John went back, along the ridge and across a field, and joined one of my people's old tracks, now a white man's road. Coming toward him he saw Thomas.

"There you are!" Thomas said. "I was looking for you—where did you go?"

John said, thinking fast, "I thought I'd pick blueberries. But it's too early; they're all still green." He indicated his empty bucket, and hoped Thomas would not think to enquire about the spade.

Thomas didn't. Like John, he was now a young man, but he still had his cheerful, uncomplicated disposition. "Th'art a solitary fellow, John. I shouldn't do nearly so well without company. I used to wonder why you would creep away so early in the mornings sometimes, long before sunup."

John blinked at him. He had always taken such care to be sure nobody noticed his visits to the island, so that nobody would follow him.

"But then I realized," said Thomas amiably, "that you just wanted some time to be on your own. After all, you are never alone even in sleep, with Ezra snoring next to your ear."

Ezra's snores were legendary between them. He was not a large man, but the sounds that issued from his throat every night were like the grunts of an ox.

John grinned. "If Ezra marries," he said, "I hope he finds a young woman whose hearing is dull."

"Ezra is too much in love with casks to marry," Thomas said. "Casks and the meetinghouse. I think he will be my father's journeyman for the rest of his life. But you and I will not."

They were walking back along the rutted track toward the workshop, since the two hours of freedom William Medlycott had granted them (at his wife's request—it was her birthday) were almost up.

"We have a year of apprenticeship yet," John said. When he had first arrived, Thomas was already working for his father, but Medlycott had soon put them both on the same level. He had said Thomas always treated cooperage as a chore until he saw John so clearly enjoying it.

"And then you will marry Huldah Bates and fly away," Thomas said. "And perhaps I shall fly after you."

John looked at him in surprise. His feelings for Huldah were no secret in the house, but he had never heard Thomas talk of leaving before.

"Surely your father hopes you will take over from him one day," he said.

"My father is a cautious man," Thomas said cheerfully. "That's why he has made Willie apprentice—he wants to feel there will still be a Medlycott cooper if I don't fulfill his hopes."

Of the six Medlycott children, Willie was the third son; a chubby thirteen-year-old often to be seen sitting at the workshop's grindstone, solemn and intent, sharpening the cooper's tools. He was a helpful, hardworking boy, though slower-witted than his big brother. Thomas often teased him, but gently.

"But of course you'll fulfill his hopes," said John, as they turned past the field where the four new Medlycott cows were grazing. He looked at Thomas a little uncertainly. Did he not really want to be a cooper?

Thomas said, as if reading his mind, "It's not that I don't want to be a cooper, but I have a mind to do it on board ship."

"On a *ship*?" said John in horror.

Thomas snorted with laughter. "Tha looks as the minister would, if I said I coveted his wife! What's wrong with a ship?"

"You can't swim, for one thing."

"I should be inside the ship, not towing it. That sea captain who came after casks the other day, he said the bigger vessels have their own cooper aboard. Think of it, John! Voyages to other countries! Maybe the West Indies! Adventure!"

"And a very uncomfortable death!" said John. He made a deep gurgling sound, and punched Thomas in the ribs.

Thomas punched him back, still laughing—and then added in a hasty whisper, as they came to the workshop door. "It's a secret! Remember! Don't tell!"

"Not I," John said. It was a very small secret to keep, he thought, compared to the risk of being hanged for the Devil's work of communicating with a ghost.

ELEVEN

The seven years were up and John was a journeyman cooper, skilled at making not only pails and tubs but every size of cask, with their quirky names: pin, firkin, kilderkin, barrel, hogshead, puncheon—even the enormous 108-gallon butt. From the beginning he had loved this occupation: the cooper's craft of making circles. He was more skilled than Thomas, but they could both now call themselves coopers.

Master Medlycott and Ezra told them horror stories of their own graduation from apprenticeship, in large cooperages back in England.

"Very rough and rude it was," said Ezra. "With all my fellows pulling off my clothes and rolling me down the bank into the river. In winter."

"Praise the Lord there is no river by our workshop," said Thomas.

Ezra said gravely, "But the pond is not far away."

"They stuffed me naked into a great butt," said Master Medlycott, "and poured more nasty kinds of liquid on me than I care to remember. The smell was in my hair for weeks."

John and Thomas became nervous after this, and kept a cautious eye on Ezra and Master Medlycott at the start of every day. But in the end there was no ritual, just a family dinner in their honor, and Master Medlycott presented each of them with a signed letter called a Certificate of Craft. The children cheered—particularly Willie, who had by now realized, to his dismay, what a vast amount an apprentice had to learn to become a journeyman.

The community had grown, with its center still the meetinghouse, and I could sense that the elders who were its most important people did not admire John. He was known as a skilled craftsman, but they still remembered his challenging question to Walter Kelly—who had now become an elder himself, much given to expressing firm moral pronouncements on the behavior of his neighbors. It was felt by the elders that John Wakeley, by some accident of nature, shared some of the disturbing opinions of Roger Williams. Nobody would have been surprised or grieved if he were to leave to join the new community that Master Williams was said to have founded—along with a trading post—some seventy miles to the south.

This was exactly what John had in mind. He had written

a letter to Roger Williams, sending it by a Marshfield merchant who was headed for the trading post, but he had no idea whether it ever arrived. Also he had no intention of leaving alone; he wanted to marry Huldah and take her with him. He confided this to Mistress Medlycott—choosing a day when her husband was away, since they both knew Medlycott's mistrust of Roger Williams's ideas.

It was late summer, and Mistress Medlycott was sitting on her porch in the sunshine, shucking beans. John sat on the edge of the porch, his long legs dangling.

"I know Master Medlycott will let me go," he said. "But asking for Huldah is not so easy."

Mistress Medlycott said, smiling, "Will she have you?"

"Yes, she will," John said. "I'm very fortunate." He smiled too, but then worry took over again. "But Master Kelly will never agree to it. He refused ever to let me visit her, as you know."

Mistress Medlycott had already discussed this possibility with Mistress Kelly while sewing a quilt, though she wasn't going to admit that. "Huldah is twenty years old, John," she said. "A good age to know her own mind. And she is not an indentured servant—the arrangement between the two families was informal, I believe. I think you should be bold, and at Sunday meeting ask the Kellys for a chance to discuss this with them."

She nodded her head firmly. She knew—though John did not—that Master Kelly was away for a week or more on business for the militia.

So it was Mistress Kelly to whom John nervously spoke after the sermon on Sunday morning, with Huldah hovering in earshot, and to his amazed delight she instantly gave them both her blessing.

"You must both go to Plymouth and ask permission of Huldah's family, of course," she said. "And you of yours, John Wakeley, though I know your mother will be pleased. I shall miss you sorely, Huldah, but out of affection, not need—the girls are of an age now to do all the chores for which you came. And so they should, to learn to be good, accomplished wives when they too leave home."

And before long the Kelly daughters, now ages nine and twelve, were abuzz with excitement at the prospect of Huldah being married—though among these sober Puritan people, a wedding was a quiet civil matter and not a cause for a festive or even religious celebration.

And so John came to see me.

He told me everything that had been happening to him, as he always did. Even though he knew that I could sense his mind and his heart and every moment of his life, the telling was important to him. And to me. It was the way things might have been between our peoples, if they had not been so aware of difference.

We talked for a long time, for the last time, until it was almost the moment for the sun to rise beyond the salt marsh.

He said to me, "There's no help for it—I have to leave

this colony. I can't live with the way they treat your people. Will you come with me?"

It was hard to explain to him.

"This is the only place where you may see me," I said, "but still, wherever you go, I shall see you. I shall be with you. We are friends."

John said, "I can tell nobody about you. Even Huldah would think me mad, or a witch. Why in the name of God are you still here, to be my friend?"

He spoke Pokanoket to me deliberately all the time now, even though he knew we could understand each other whatever language we used. He spoke it as if he had known it since childhood.

He put out a hand toward me, beseeching, something he had never done before in all this time, but there was no substance that he could touch.

And I had no answer for him, or for myself.

I said, "It is mystery."

That afternoon, John found Goodman Bates sitting in the Medlycott living room with a mug of beer; he still spent the night there whenever he made a delivery. Mistress Medlycott was sitting at the table beside him, shelling beans.

The settlement had grown so much that Goodman Bates carried goods and people to and from Plymouth every week now. He had a grander wagon, covered in canvas over metal hoops, though it was still drawn by slow, sturdy oxen. Other drivers carried passengers much faster in carts and carriages drawn by horses, but they were also more expensive.

Goodman Bates raised his mug in salute. He had a great private disdain for the severer members of the colony, and was as genial to John as he had always been.

"Congratulations, free man," he said. "I have just come from Duxbury, and I leave for Plymouth in the morning. I shall be glad to carry you and my niece with me at no charge, if that would please you. It is my gift to you both."

John gazed at him, startled. He saw Mistress Medlycott smiling at her beans, and began to feel, rightly, that he was the object of a benevolent plot.

"I am most grateful," he said. "But is not tomorrow very short notice for Huldah and Mistress Kelly?"

"Not at all," said Goodman Bates. "Mistress Kelly said her girls were all cock-a-hoop at the thought of a wedding."

He took a long draft of beer.

"Master Kelly is still away with the militia," he added blandly, "but she said she was sure he would agree. We shall leave before dawn."

Mistress Medlycott caught John's eye, smiled a little, and looked away again.

John was thinking rapidly, and trying not to shout with delight. He was overjoyed at the thought of leaving with Huldah, but there were things he would now have to do in a hurry. He said, "Thank you again, Goodman Bates. If you will excuse me for a while—I have some work to finish."

"Tell them all I require them within the hour," Mistress Medlycott said, turning the spit over her fire. "This meat will be spoiled if it cooks too long."

"I will," John said.

And he left the old friends to their gossip, heading not for the noisy workshop, but for the barn. He checked Goodman Bates's oxen, contentedly eating in their stalls beside the Medlycott horses, and then he took a spade and made his way through the trees to a clump of birch trees that he knew very well.

It was a grey, misty afternoon and a fine rain was falling. John cleared away a layer of dead leaves and dug the spade into the ground behind the birches. The soil came out easily, because he had dug here every few months for the past seven years. Once more he uncovered the familiar sight of my tomahawk, still intact, its blade still tightly embedded in the wood of the bitternut hickory tree. For the last few years it had been folded inside an old piece of leather for protection.

John took out the tomahawk, carefully, and wiped off a little dirt. But this time it was only the piece of leather that he dropped back into the hole.

He filled in the soil and put back the layer of dead leaves. Nobody would know that anything had ever been buried here. He put the handle of the axe through his belt so that it was hidden under his jacket. Then, quietly, he went back to the barn and left the spade. He looked round carefully to make sure nobody was watching him and he ran out of the house, down the track, down toward the salt marsh and the sea.

He had always felt that when he left this place he should take the tomahawk back to me. But now the leaving was almost upon him, and in the light of the day I would not be there to tell him what to do with it. He knew only, as he ran, that he wanted somehow to say a farewell.

He reached the low ridge at the head of the salt marsh, and walked along it to the island. He could see the footprints of deer disappearing into the trees, through the fringe of scrub oak. Beyond the island the salt marsh was half-covered with silver water as the tide crept in, and he could just make out an osprey wheeling toward the sea, a brief dark silhouette against the grey-white sky.

John took the tomahawk out of his belt and looked down at it, perplexed. Then, beside the track, barely visible through the leaves, he saw the memory hole he had made for me.

He thought, *Of course.*

He knelt down. Nobody was in sight anywhere, on this damp grey day. Using the blade of the tomahawk, he scraped out all the carefully laid small stones from the bottom of the memory hole, and set them aside. Then he dug out enough soil to leave a space for the tomahawk, and laid it gently down in there.

He looked down at it for a moment, remembering many things. Then he covered it with soil and set the small stones firmly back on top, so that the memory hole was just as it had been before.

He stood up, brushing the dirt from his britches, and he looked up at the island, into the shadowy trees.

He said aloud, "Good-bye, my friend Little Hawk. Thank you. Remember me. I shall always remember you."

He was speaking Pokanoket.

Very early the next morning, John bundled up all his belongings and steeled himself to make his farewells. Goodman Bates sat up on his wagon, waiting; they would go from here to the Kelly house to pick up Huldah. Everyone was gathered in the yard of the house. The children cried. Willie shook John's hand. So did Ezra, and clapped him on the shoulder. Mistress Medlycott hugged him as she had when he first arrived, though now John was taller and broader than she was, and gave her a warm, grateful embrace of his own.

To John's surprise, Master Medlycott hugged him too. "Th'art a good craftsman in spite of thy perilous ideas, John," he said, the old accent strong again for a moment, "and I wish thee well, wherever it may be. Here are the tools you cut your teeth on, as is our tradition." And he gave John a large handsome bundle that held all a cooper's tools that could be carried, fitted into a folded leather carrying case.

"Thank you, Master," said John. "I thank you with all my heart. For this and for much, much more."

"One other thing," said Master Medlycott. "It was a thought of Priscilla's, of which I heartily approved. We have two young replacements for Aaron, as you know, but he has some hearty years in him yet. He is an early marriage gift."

He whistled, and out of the barn came Thomas leading Aaron, who was a horse: a sturdy, handsome, broad-backed horse who had patiently carried panniers of casks to customers for years, or sometimes both Thomas and John at the same time.

John opened and shut his mouth, but no sound came out. This was an astounding gift, particularly for a young couple faced with the prospect of walking seventy miles to Roger Williams's trading post.

Thomas grinned. "And tha can shovel up after him," he said.

Huldah and John rode to Plymouth sitting high on the bench seat of the wagon next to Goodman Bates. The horse Aaron plodded behind, his bridle tied securely to the back of the wagon. Goodman Bates devoted himself to giving his rural passengers the ominous news from England, where, he said, the arrogant King Charles had ruled with no Parliament for ten years now.

"No wonder so many good Englishmen sell their lands and goods to bring their families to our colony," he said. "Plymouth grows apace, you will scarce recognize it."

John said, "Have you heard news of Master Roger Williams since he left the colony?"

"Oh yes," said Goodman Bates amiably. "Your hero is the governor's ear to the Indian tribes south of here, they say. He was always a great talker, as you recall, and he talks in the savage languages too. But he has a good head on his shoulders—there is much trade established with his new settlement. Some younger men have joined him in his town of New Providence. They say a fair piece of land is to be had there for thirty shillings."

On the bench, Huldah's hand crept toward John's and squeezed it. He gave hers a squeeze in return, though he had no idea how they could acquire thirty shillings.

In Plymouth there were more streets than before, more horses and carts, more storefronts, more noise—and they saw Indians here and there among the English faces. Most of these were from my people. Our sachem Yellow Feather had forged a stronger relationship with the colony in the past few years, selling them land in exchange for cloth, metal tools, and other goods from overseas. But even though the whites now bought the land instead of simply taking it, it was they who set the price, and each sale was registered by their court.

Cattle grazed on the common, and the crowing of roosters punctuated the day. Plymouth sounded and smelled like a farmyard. Down by the harbor there was the smell of the sea instead, but John and Huldah's families lived inland, at different ends of the main street. In their snatched talks over the years, the two of them had come to realize that their parents all knew each other from the days of their first arrival, and that as a small boy John must have played with Huldah's eldest brother Edmund.

It was at the Bates house that Huldah's uncle Goodman Bates first stopped; it was set back a little way from the road, behind the workshop of Huldah's father, who was a carpenter. Huldah jumped down and ran into the workshop, and John slowly followed, finding her clasped in the arms of a big bearded man who, to John's great relief, held out a hand to him even before letting his daughter go.

"So this is the man who would steal my beloved daughter," said Master Bates, shaking John's hand. "Welcome to our family, John Wakeley."

And so it went, as everyone at this warmhearted house welcomed John, from six-year-old Dauntless, who looked startlingly like Huldah, to his former playmate Edmund, now a journeyman blacksmith as big as his father. John left Huldah to spend the night with her family, and set off eagerly for his own home. Goodman Bates had taken Aaron away to be stabled with his own horses overnight. Tomorrow John would fetch Huldah to meet his mother. He and Margaret had exchanged letters, but he hadn't been home for almost a year and he ached to see her.

He strode happily along the wide Plymouth street, still marveling at the way the town had grown during his seven-year absence; even in late afternoon it was bustling with people, horses, carts. Ahead, a large group of people came walking toward him, and he saw with surprise that they were Pokanokets, formally dressed; there were feathers on a few of the heads.

He gazed at them, thinking of me.

A wagon drawn by four horses came rattling toward him on the other side of the street—and suddenly John saw a very small boy run into its path from the group of Indians, in pursuit of a lumpy leather ball. Instinctively he dived forward to grab the child, and caught him just in time. The wagon rattled past, with an angry shout from the driver.

John rolled in the dust and scrambled to his feet, clutching the child, who was whimpering softly. "It's all right," he said to the boy in Pokanoket, "it's all right, don't be afraid, everything's all right. . . ."

He was still soothing him as the child's mother reached him, taking the boy from his arms, scolding. She was young and pretty, dressed in soft deerskin, and very upset. "You must never do that," she babbled to the boy, "never, in this busy town—"

"He's not hurt, I think, just frightened," John said.

"Thank you," she said. "Thank you so much. You saved his life."

"Be more careful with that ball, little man," John said to the boy.

The girl was still too shocked to smile. "You are very kind," she said.

They were both speaking Pokanoket without thinking about it, and a deeper voice broke in, this time speaking English.

"Thank you, my friend. I thank you for my foolish son."

It was an older man, much older than the girl. He was the center of the group, and clearly a person of importance.

He had lines painted on his strong-boned face, as did several of the other men, and two splendid red-tipped eagle feathers in his hair.

"You are welcome," John said. "Children do these things."

"Who taught you to speak my language so well?" said the man.

John smiled. "A good friend," he said.

The man hesitated; he was curious, but could sense that John was eager to be on his way. "I am in your debt," he said, "and I thank you again."

They gave each other a little bow and went in their separate directions. John strode the last few yards to his mother's house, and the group of Pokanokets made its measured way along the street. They were headed for a visit with Edward Winslow, a former governor of Plymouth Colony, who had a farm in Marshfield not far from the Medlycotts but was often in Plymouth to help his successor, Governor Bradford. Two or three of them looked back from time to time at John.

And I was caught in amazement at what I had just seen. Although John did not yet know the man he had just met, I was filled with wonder at my first sight of the great sachem of my people, our father Yellow Feather.

When John arrived home he was dusty but happy, and even happier to find that Daniel Smith was away for a few days with Walter Kelly. Both were trusted lieutenants in Captain Standish's militia, and Standish had taken them to

Boston for a meeting with the Massachusetts Bay General Court.

As John walked through the door, his mother looked up from her baby's cradle, stared at him, and burst into tears. She held out her arms, and whispered into his collar, "You look so like . . . for a moment I thought you were Benjamin back from the dead."

Both John's sisters had left home to marry. The baby in the cradle was the third child his mother had had with Daniel; their first son, Samuel, had died of a fever when he was four years old, and there was a daughter, Rebecca, who was now three. John played with his half-sister Rebecca, and after a first bashful half hour she was fascinated by the big brother she didn't remember having seen before, and kissed him good night before she went to bed.

John and Margaret sat up late, talking by firelight.

"I remember Huldah Bates as a child, she was a sweet little girl," Margaret said. "God be praised that you have found each other. And you are a true trained cooper now, John. I am so proud of you. Master Hawthorne is the only cooper in Plymouth, down by the harbor—there is more than enough work for another. Or perhaps you think of working for him?"

John looked into the fire, then took a deep breath and told her of their plans to travel to New Providence and join Roger Williams.

Margaret was silent for a moment. Then she reached out and took his hand.

"You must follow your conscience, my dear," she said. "Sometimes indeed the Lord tells us to do things we might not have chosen ourselves. But I hope you and Huldah will first marry in Plymouth—yes?"

"Of course," John said. He smiled. "Otherwise I fear you and Mistress Bates would never speak to us again."

But the next morning, things changed.

He had slept in the back room that had been added as a workshop; he had been out to pump some water for his mother; he was sitting at breakfast with her and Rebecca. The door of the house opened abruptly, and there silhouetted against the morning light was Daniel Smith, carrying his musket, with Walter Kelly close behind him.

John got to his feet, still chewing a piece of bread. His mother jumped up as well. Rebecca remained contentedly seated.

"Father!" she said. "Look, my brother John is here!"

"So I see," said Daniel Smith.

"Welcome back, husband," said Margaret. "Master Kelly! Will you break your fast with us?"

"We have eaten. I thank you," Kelly said.

John stood there. He had swallowed his bread, but he couldn't speak. His mother knew nothing of his confrontation with Walter Kelly in the Marshfield meetinghouse. And the sudden sight of these two men together had rushed him back through the years, to the terrible moment of their first encounter.

"John has finished his apprenticeship!" Margaret said

proudly. "He is a journeyman cooper, out in the world. And he is to be married!" She pulled out the bench beside the table. "Pray you, come and sit down."

Daniel came in, leaned his musket against the wall, and gave a fatherly pat to Rebecca's small bonneted head, but Kelly remained in the doorway, looking at John. He stood tense, holding his musket; his face was flushed.

"And who do you intend to marry, John Wakeley?" he said.

John said, "Now that she too is out in the world, by courtesy of Mistress Kelly and yourself—Huldah Bates."

"Never!" Kelly spat the word out like a gunshot.

Margaret looked from one to the other of them in alarm.

"You are not worthy of that good God-fearing girl!" Kelly said loudly.

John stood up tall, trying desperately to be calm.

"Begging your pardon, Master Kelly," he said. "Huldah is a free member of this colony, able to choose who she shall wed, and her family approves of the match."

"Huldah is part of my household!" Kelly shouted.

The baby woke up and began to cry. Margaret went to the cradle.

Daniel looked at John, frowning. He said, "If you wish to be a craftsman in this community, do not offend one of its most respected elders."

John said, "But Huldah is no longer living in Master Kelly's house. She was not an indentured servant, it was a private agreement between families. She is twenty years old, and she is here in Plymouth, and she and I are to be married."

"You'll not marry here!" snapped Kelly, furious. He stalked out of the door. Daniel went after him.

John turned to his mother and kissed her on the cheek, then reached for his bundle of tools.

"Good-bye, mother," he said. "God bless you."

And he was out of the door after them, leaving Margaret unhappily rocking a screaming baby.

Kelly was marching down the street, with Daniel hurrying after him. "Master Kelly!" Daniel called.

Kelly paused, and swung round toward John. "There is a price to pay for attacking your betters!" he said. "Marshfield wouldn't have you, and no more will Plymouth! I'll take good care of that!"

Now John was losing his temper too. "And you'll do us no harm," he said, his voice rising, "for we are bound for New Providence and Master Williams's tolerance!"

"Art mad?" cried Daniel. "That troublemaker? He lives with the Indians! Do you want to raise savages?"

"Of course he does!" said Kelly violently. "They are all idolators! They care more for the heathen than for the chosen people of God!"

Something in John's brain snapped.

"And did the Lord God ordain one of his chosen people to shoot an innocent man?" he shouted. People passing by were staring at them. "To kill one who was trying to save a life?"

"Hold your tongue!" Daniel said in panic. His eyes darted around the street, as if looking for escape.

John shouted, "And then to hide the body so that none should see?" Anger was flooding through him, bursting out of its long suppression. "If you had been honest men, you would have confessed your mistake openly to all, and asked forgiveness of God!"

Now people were pausing, curious, alarmed.

Daniel grabbed him, pinning his arms to his sides. "Stop!"

John stopped. He stood still; he took a deep breath. He looked hopelessly at his stepfather, a God-fearing, bigoted man who happened to be in the wrong place at the wrong time nine years before.

"It was an innocent mistake," Daniel said. His eyes held John's for a moment, and perhaps there was a hint of a plea in them. But it was too late.

Kelly stood facing John, quietly now, but his quietness was more ominous than his rage. Though he was a head shorter, he had an icy confidence.

"You ignorant young fool," he said softly. "Get out of this colony! You know nothing of the intentions of the Lord for his Saints, nor the treachery of the savage peoples. Go to New Providence and be damned. And an Indian shall wear the scalps of your children at his belt!"

TWELVE

So John and Huldah left Plymouth, riding their gentle, sturdy horse. John did not visit his sisters, and he did not see his mother again. Huldah's family put them on their way, with tears and loving wishes, and with as many tools and as much food as would fit into the panniers across Aaron's broad back. Walter Kelly was a powerful member of the Governor's Council, and there was danger in his ill will.

John and Huldah rode for a long time along the road southwest from Plymouth, an English road made from one of my people's old tracks. Late in the day John worried that the weight was too much even for Aaron, so he dismounted and led the horse. Huldah sat above him, side-saddle, swaying uncertainly. Her only experience of horses at Master Kelly's house had been to sit behind one in a wagon.

They had a little money, and they used some of it to

spend their first night on the road at a trading post that had a few extra rooms to rent out to travelers. On they went the next day, early, southward on the road. By afternoon they had almost despaired of finding a place to stay, until they came to a farm whose owner was working hastily to bring in his crop of corn. He was alone and overburdened, so John pulled out his work knife and joined him in the field while Huldah rode Aaron—very nervously, her first time alone with the horse—to the house.

She found the farmer's wife, very pregnant, trying simultaneously to shell peas, light a cooking fire, and chase twin two-year-old boys. Very soon they too were working together, exchanging life stories, and John and Huldah ended up spending not just that night at this farm but two more days and nights as well. They became fast friends with Adam and Prudence, who had sailed from England only four years ago with more money than some, but much less experience of planting and building. They were struggling but hopeful. Like several nearby friends, they had settled within the outer bounds of Roger Williams's New Providence.

Reluctantly they all separated on the third day. Prudence held the two-year-olds out of harm's way, as Adam helped John and then Huldah up on to Aaron's patient back.

"The road is good, but grows narrower, and in five miles or so you will find it divides," Adam said. "Both forks meet again eventually—but the last time I was that way, the left was a clearer track."

When John and Huldah reached this point, however, they found that since Adam was last there a great deal of rain must have fallen. They took the left fork in the road, but very soon their way was barred by a flooded stream, with trees so dense on either side that Aaron could not push through.

They retraced their steps and took the right fork, but soon it too divided, into two tracks that were not much more than paths. They were lost.

"Which way shall we go?" said Huldah. They were both down from the horse now, standing together, baffled.

"I don't know," John said.

They both stared at the divided track. Aaron twitched his long tail. The woodland was very quiet, but for the birds singing. Then they heard a very faint rhythmic rustle, like the sound of running feet.

Both their heads went up. John put his finger to his lips.

Round the corner of one path came a young Pokanoket, running in the long-distance lope that I knew so well. He checked in midstride as he saw them, and I could feel his instinctive impulse to melt away into the trees. But his curiosity was greater than his caution. He paused, eyeing them warily.

John called out in our language, "Greetings! Can you show us the way to the coast?"

Huldah gazed at him in amazement. She had no idea what he was saying. She had felt she knew everything about John that there was to know, but he had not told her that he could speak the Indians' tongue. And certainly not who he learned it from, and how they met.

"Greetings," said the young man, surprised. He came closer, and then his expression changed. He paused, respectful.

He said, "You are the man from Plymouth, are you not? The Speaker!"

"Well . . . yes, I'm from Plymouth," John said.

"Who saved little Trouble. The boy with the ball. I was there."

John grinned. "Is that what they call him—Trouble? They are right!"

"The youngest son of the Massasoit," said the young man. Massasoit was the formal title of our father Yellow Feather, though all the Englishmen thought it was his name. All except John, who had learned better from me. He stood staring for a moment, thinking back to the distinguished Pokanoket in the Plymouth street.

"That was the Massasoit?" he said, amazed. "That was your great leader Yellow Feather?"

"Of course. Did you not know?"

Huldah said plaintively, "John? What's happening?"

"I'm sorry," John said. "He's a Pokanoket and I think he's going to help us." He turned. "This is Huldah Bates, who is going to be my wife."

The young man inclined his head to Huldah, with courtesy but no real interest. "I am Stardancer," he said.

"He says his name is Stardancer," John told Huldah.

"It is a beautiful name," said Huldah, still baffled.

Stardancer said to John, "Speaker, where are you going?"

"To New Providence," John said.

"You cannot reach it before night. The house of our father Yellow Feather is not far from here, I know he would wish to offer you hospitality. May I take you?"

John said to Huldah, "We are offered shelter for the night. I promise you it's safe. May I accept?"

Huldah swallowed nervously, but she trusted him. "Of course," she said.

I could sense John's excitement, and of course I shared it.

"Thank you," he said to the young man. "That would be most kind."

So Stardancer—a runner who had been sent to carry a message to an English trading post, but who knew this new task would be considered more important—led John, Huldah, and Aaron to the house of our father Yellow Feather. The house to which, years before, Leaping Turtle and I had once been headed, but to which only Leaping Turtle had come.

John and Huldah walked in wonder through the Pokanoket town, whose inhabitants glanced at them with mild interest and sometimes an amiable nod; English visitors were not infrequent here. Stardancer summoned a boy who led Aaron away to be fed and stabled, horses now being familiar to my people. Then they arrived at the house, and he asked John and Huldah to pause while he announced them.

The door flaps were open wide, this summer day. They heard a murmur of voices, and suddenly, there was Yellow Feather: tall, bare-chested, in fringed deerskin pants, his hands out in welcome.

He said to John in Pokanoket, "There is no one to whom I owe more, or whom I would more gladly entertain."

And seeing the incomprehension in Huldah's face, he instantly switched to English. "Please enter my home," he said. "You are most welcome."

It was like all the sturdy winter houses of our people, but bigger and more handsome, its walls bright with beaded hangings and soft deerskins. It was, after all, the house of a man whom the first English settlers described as a king. There were two smoke holes in its lofty roof, two fireplaces beneath them, though only the farther fire was alight, for cooking. Sleeping platforms mounded with rugs and pillows surrounded the walls, and there were even a couple of English-style chairs.

Three women and a girl of about eleven were busy preparing a meal; one of them was the young mother of the boy John rescued from the wheels of the cart. She too came forward to greet them, smiling.

"Welcome to our house," she said to Huldah in faltering English. Then to John, in Pokanoket, "Speaker, I am so glad to be able to offer you some small gratitude for your saving our son."

She pointed: the boy was asleep in a corner of the house, curled up on a pillow, taking a nap.

"There is Trouble," said John, smiling.

Yellow Feather laughed. "His other name is Metacom," he said.

It was a warm, companionable evening of a kind I had never seen in my lifetime between my people and the English. But our father Yellow Feather had been enabling such meetings ever since he took a large group to feast with the first white arrivals in Plymouth, at a thankful celebration of harvest and survival. His friendship toward them had increased after one of their leaders, Edward Winslow, came to help him recover from an attack of a fever that could kill.

And I saw now that his tolerance had not grown less. When the strict Puritans of Massachusetts Bay had banished Roger Williams, it was Yellow Feather who had first given him shelter, and the chance to buy land to found a settlement of his own. For twenty years or more, by shrewdness and diplomacy, Yellow Feather had been juggling relationships between the whites and the other tribes to maintain a state of peace within this land.

Gradually the house filled with people eager for a sight of the white man who had saved Yellow Feather's son. They all called John "Speaker" because word had spread that he could speak their language better even than Master Williams.

There was much eating and drinking before the evening was done, with children far more in evidence than John and Huldah were accustomed to. Small Metacom even seated himself for a few moments on John's knee before he wriggled off to some other distraction. Most of the talk was in Pokanoket, but Yellow Feather and any others who spoke any English were careful not to make Huldah feel an outsider.

At length the house began to empty, though Yellow Feather, his eldest son Wamsutta, and two of his advisers were still deep in conversation with John. At the request of Yellow Feather's wife, Huldah went with her to spend the night in the women's house, where they might be of help in the impending birth of a baby.

"I've done it three times before," she said cheerfully to John, "so perhaps I can be useful—though I'm quite sure they don't need me. I hear tell that Indian women have far fewer problems than we do."

"Good night, my dear," John said. "It seems likely that neither one of us will find much sleep."

And he was right. He had been discussing Roger Williams's banishment with Yellow Feather, who regarded Williams as a close friend, and he had begun to feel that the mind of his host was like a limitless sponge. Like all careful negotiators, Yellow Feather was an insatiable collector of reports and opinions.

"Roger Williams has taught the colony that they may not take our land without paying a price," he said, "and it seems to me that his disagreements now with them—and yours too—deal only with your own laws."

"That's true," John said, and he began describing the

Puritan insistence on government imposing the rules of how a man might worship. But Yellow Feather held up his hand.

"Conflicts within a people are for their own argument," he said. "The need is for peace *between* peoples. Your people have things that we find useful"—he touched the knife at his belt, and pointed to an iron pot beside the fire—"and we have the land you want. So we trade. If we trust our exchange, there is no conflict, and no war."

Shadows flickered round the house; it was lit now only by the fire. Wamsutta was the last one left with them. He was a handsome young man of about eighteen, like a younger copy of his father, but more distant, more wary; John was not sure what to make of him. He was frowning into the fire.

"I think you are more trusting than I am, my father," he said.

"I do what is necessary," Yellow Feather said. "Our ties to the colony keep us safe. Without their balance we would be wholly subject to the Narragansetts."

"The white men will support you only as long as you sell them land," Wamsutta said.

Yellow Feather laughed softly. "There is much land," he said. He leaned forward and tapped his son on the knee, one tap for each word. "*I want peace for my people*. I will do what I must, for that. And if some of John's people distrust what I do, and some of my own people question what I do, still there is a broad way in the middle that we can all tread. In prosperity, and safety, and in peace."

Wamsutta sighed. Then he got up abruptly and turned to the door. "It is late."

"Sleep here." His father waved at the platforms further up the house, where several bodies lay peacefully asleep.

Wamsutta shook his head. "I salute you both." He bowed his head, and he was gone.

John yawned, covering his face apologetically. But Yellow Feather had not finished with him yet.

"Speaker," he said. "John Wakeley. I wish to know who taught you to speak our language so remarkably well."

"A good friend," John said.

"So you said before. What friend?"

John looked at the strong, confident face under the greased scalp lock, a leader like none he had ever met before, and I could feel the sudden leap of trust in his mind.

He said, "His name is Little Hawk."

Yellow Feather paused, expressionless. He said after a moment, "When did he teach you?"

"Often, these past years," John said.

Another pause. Yellow Feather said, "My people have been much diminished by plague, and again by the small-pox. There are few clan names I do not know. Our only grown warrior named Little Hawk was secretly murdered by an Englishman a long time ago."

"Yes," John said. "I was there. I was ten years old. I shall never forget."

"His friend said that there was a boy," Yellow Feather

said softly. "A desperate boy who screamed for help. And Little Hawk went to give it."

John said, "It was because I called his name that Little Hawk tried to help me. And they killed him, because they thought his help was an attack. I had met him once before, when I was the age of your little Trouble."

"A name is very powerful," Yellow Feather said. "And telling your name is a gift, freely given."

John hesitated. He said, "I . . . see him."

He was waiting for disbelief, but Yellow Feather was listening, untroubled, expectant, so the words came tumbling out. "I have seen him often, often, these past years, and we are true friends. Perhaps I shall see him no longer, because it was always in one place. An island, in a salt marsh. We must have spoken in our minds at first, because somehow we each understood what the other said."

Yellow Feather said, "You are a fortunate man."

"Then I asked him to teach me to speak your language. And he did."

"He knew you would use it well," Yellow Feather said.

John said in English, suddenly hoarse, "God rest his soul."

If I had still been alive, I might have wept.

"Ah," Yellow Feather said. "He will have rest when it is time." He sat quietly for a moment. "Tomorrow my people will take you to Roger Williams," he said. "I hope you will come back and talk to me again."

"I will," John said. "I will indeed."

Yellow Feather stood up, and touched him on the shoulder. "Let us sleep now."

So they fell onto sleeping platforms on either side of the room, and slept till sunrise. And the next day Stardancer and three others mounted horses and escorted John and Huldah to the place where Roger Williams lived. As they left, Yellow Feather and his council stood ceremonially in the central square of the Pokanoket town to wish them a safe journey. I could feel John's excitement as he rode. Huldah rode behind him, her arms about his waist, and she too was excited, though full of uncertainty.

And among the families watching them ride by, I saw some who had once lived in my village, but had now moved here. Two of them were my friend Leaping Turtle and my sister Quickbird.

They were older, but they were the same. I saw that they were husband and wife now; they had two children, a girl holding Quickbird's hand, and a smaller boy in Leaping Turtle's arms. His father was holding him up high so that he might see John, the Speaker of their language, the white man who had saved the life of the little boy's friend Metacom.

Leaping Turtle had no idea that he had seen John before. But in a wonderful instant, I found that the years had not made him forget me.

"Do you see the Speaker?" said Leaping Turtle to his son. "Do you see him, Running Hawk?"

PART THREE

BURNING MOON

ONE

Jedediah and John rolled the last of six barrels down to John's jetty, where Roger Williams was waiting in his biggest canoe. Williams scrambled out to help them angle it to the edge, and into the arms of the three Narrangansett Indians who would help him paddle the load to his trading post at Wickford.

"You are ready?" said one of the Indians. They were sturdy men; over the years since John and Huldah had come here, I had seen many of their tribe working with, and for, the independent-minded people of this settlement.

Roger Williams said in the Narragansett dialect, "Almost ready. I must bid farewell to the children."

I felt John's mind storing away the words; he was still endlessly fascinated by the connections between the Pokanoket he had learned from me and the tongues of other tribes. He had heard several of those by now. This was his fourteenth year in Providence Plantation, and of course Huldah's, and it was their three children to whom Roger Williams wanted to say farewell.

The three Englishmen walked back up the hill. In the field above them, one of John's two new cows lowed, a deep, mournful sound.

Williams glanced up at the field. He said, "Resolved Scott lost a calf to wolves three days since."

"So I heard," John said. "These two are shut in the barn every night."

"That's the third attack this year, and it won't be the last," said Jedediah. "Have you penned your sheep, Roger?"

"I have, for now. We have a mind to ship them over to the island where we keep the goats. Soon, before the ewes get closer to lambing."

"Wolves can swim," Jedediah said.

"Not that far," said John. "The Lord is on Roger's side. He gave wolves legs, not fins."

They headed over the rough grass to the workshop, the piles of cut staves, then the house. Jedediah Watkins was John's partner, a burly, amiable man who had been called in to witness John and Huldah's wedding in Roger Williams's living room the day after they had arrived. Williams often claimed cheerfully that he had given John two marriages that day.

John and Jedediah were the master coopers of New Providence, and they divided their time between two workshops: Jedediah's, in the center of the fast-growing settlement, and John's, here on the other side of the river. John had wanted to be able to supply people by boat, in this watery countryside. He and Huldah had also wanted more land; as he grew older, he found that he loved farming and fishing as much as making barrels.

Roger Williams looked back at the cows again. "There's no help for it," he said. "The community must begin paying a bounty for the head of a wolf. If we do that, the Narragansetts will be glad to help, I believe."

"And Benjamin will be pestering me again for a gun of his own," said John. "I beg you to set a limit on the age of bounty hunters."

"Ten years," said Williams.

John said, "Twelve."

Roger Williams smiled. "Agreed," he said.

The Wakeley children came running out from the door of the house—a shingled house, built around a massive brick hearth and chimney. There were three of them—Benjamin, Samuel, and Katharine—and they were rapidly growing. Benjamin had passed the height of his father's shoulder.

Katharine reached up for one of Jedediah's enormous hands. He had four sons and no daughter, and was always indulgent with her. "We have finished our lessons, and I learned a psalm," she said.

"Very good," said Jedediah. "Which psalm was that?"

Katharine said very fast, "O praise the Lord, all ye nations, praise him all ye people." She paused. "Um . . . ," she said.

"For his merciful kindness is great toward us," said Samuel, with the confidence of his nine winters, "and the truth of the Lord endureth forever. Praise ye the Lord."

"Yes," said Katharine.

Benjamin patted his small sister on the head. "Mother said she chose the shortest psalm there is, so Katharine would remember it."

Jedediah said, "Number one hundred and seventeen."

John chuckled. "A good Baptist memory," he said.

Katharine let go of Jedediah's hand, to escape psalms, and moved to Roger Williams. She said in a loud whisper, "Mother made bread and she has some for Aunt Mary."

They went into the kitchen. Three loaves of corn bread sat on the scrubbed wooden table, and Huldah was wrapping a fourth in a cloth. She held it up to show Williams.

"Keep it dry in thy boat," she said. "And kiss Mary for me. Do you preach for us in town on Sunday?"

"The trading post needs me for some days, I fear," Roger Williams said. He gave Huldah a curious look. "Th'art worshipping with Jedediah still?"

John sat on the edge of the table. He said amiably, "And Benjamin too. Every Sunday, over the river they go to Baptist meeting. I admire the dedication, even if I do not share it."

Huldah put her hand on his, gratefully. "It is a sensible church, with no threats and punishments. I love the freedom of worship, that they call the priesthood of all believers."

"Keep away from Boston, then," said Roger Williams. "That's precisely what they condemn. They would arrest you for unlawful beliefs."

"They grow more severe by the month, it seems," Jedediah said. "There are far more whippings and brandings in Boston than in Plymouth. Is it true they burned thy book, for preaching freedom of religion?"

"That was in England," Roger Williams said. "In Boston they merely call me heretic." He smiled. "They would banish me, but they did that long since."

"They call us all heretic," John said.

"I despair of them, these self-righteous men," Roger Williams said. He shook his head despondently. "All these years, and they have learned nothing from their own history. Nothing. They have escaped repression in order to repress others—not just Indians, but good Christian folk. There is a line my father used to quote, of which they would heartily disapprove because he heard it in a playhouse. I think of it often now. *'Lord, what fools these mortals be!'*"

"They be indeed," said John.

The children were standing in a group, quiet, listening.

"In a playhouse?" said Katharine to Roger Williams. She had heard of plays, and secretly wished she could see one some day.

"Hush," said Huldah, but Roger Williams was smiling at Katharine's small, wide-eyed face.

"We lived in London, in Holborn," he said. "My father was a merchant tailor. Across the river was a playhouse called the Globe where they played the works of William Shakespeare."

"I have heard of him!" said Samuel. "I think."

"One night in particular my father never forgot," Williams said, his face creasing in affectionate memory. "He would tell it over and over when I was a little boy. It was before I was born—a performance of Shakespeare's play 'A Midsummer Night's Dream.' Attended secretly by Queen Elizabeth, my father claimed. And he remembered a sprightly boy actor saying that line, playing Robin Goodfellow, making fun of a bunch of folk like us. 'Lord, what fools these mortals be!'"

He laughed ruefully.

"Dangerous fools, I fear," Jedediah said.

"The danger of the wolves is closer to us," said Roger Williams. "They eat our calves and our lambs. Let us defend ourselves from the wolves, and hope that the Lord will defend us from the men."

One Sunday Huldah came home flushed and agitated from attending the Baptist meeting with Benjamin. It was summer; John was sitting in the house with the door open, reading the Bible to Samuel and Katharine and his journeyman, Peter. He looked up in concern.

Huldah flopped into a chair, and Benjamin fanned her with his hat.

"Mother and I have been having an argument," he said rather guiltily. "About something I want to do, and she thinks I shouldn't."

Huldah sighed. She said to John, "Do you remember Roger's friend Peregrine Barrett, who was the other witness at our wedding?"

"Of course," John said. "A kind, happy man, I haven't seen him for a long time. The Barretts went to settle Aquidneck Island, did they not?" He grinned at her. "More of your Baptists, I believe."

Huldah said bleakly, "He grew old, his wife died, he lost his sight. He sold his house and had to go live with his daughter in Boston. So he is cut off from his own way of worship and I am very sorry for him—" Suddenly her voice rose, and she thumped the arm of her chair. "But I do *not* think Benjamin should be concerned in this—he is far too young and it is dangerous!"

"Benjamin?" said John, bewildered. He looked at his son.

Benjamin looked down at his hat. "Jedediah is going to visit Master Barrett in Boston and worship with him, and I want to go too," he said. "Master Barrett is a poor blind old man with no Baptist friends and I think it is a shame."

There was a pause.

"Well," said John, "perhaps you may go."

Benjamin's head jerked up, and Huldah stared at John reproachfully. John stood up and came to put a hand on her shoulder.

"Jedediah and I are *both* going to Boston," he said. "Next week. We have had word that our shipment of iron will be arriving. So Jedediah is not making a Baptist pilgrimage to save old Peregrine from isolation—first of all, it is a journey for work."

Huldah relaxed a little. "He didn't mention that," she said.

"Well, he was speaking to Baptists and not coopers. But however warmly Jedediah may feel toward a lonely old man, he wouldn't make so long a trip just to say a prayer."

"That would be a great risk," Huldah said.

"I would be willing to take Benjamin with us," John said. "He would be an extra pair of hands."

"I would!" said Benjamin eagerly.

"And we will make time to visit Peregrine, of course. Poor soul."

Huldah said uneasily, "Please be careful. Please."

John said, as a sudden realization blazed into both his consciousness and mine, "We might visit the Medlycotts, too, on the way."

And so we were able to see each other, he and I, just once more.

Their long journey took them first to Plymouth, where Jedediah took a boat to Boston. John's mother had been dead for some years, but he and Benjamin paused to visit his sister, and then they took the wide, busy road to Marshfield. The Medlycott house was still wrapped in its farmland and trees, though there were more farms nearby now, and it was still a busy cooperage, bustling and noisy. John led his horse through a working yard far more crowded than before, with Benjamin following, and at last found himself facing the outstretched arms of Thomas Medlycott, a big man so like his father that John thought he had gone back in time.

Master Medlycott was dead, but Mistress Medlycott wept with the pleasure of seeing John, and Benjamin was swept up by Thomas's sons. Ezra was no longer there; he had become so rigorous a Puritan, they told John, that he had a government post now in Boston. They all talked deep into the night until weariness forced them to stop.

And in the early morning, when everyone else was still asleep, the moon gone, the sky still dark, the stars not quite yet beginning to fade, John went out walking down to the salt marsh and its faint ocean horizon.

The tide was low; nothing stood in his way. He walked along the stony ridge until he reached the island. Somewhere nearby was the memory hole he had made for me long before, with my tomahawk buried beneath it. Lacking any care, the memory hole had silted over, but he knew it hadn't gone.

Nor had the memories.

He crossed the island, through the scrub oaks and the black cherry trees and the great tangles of brier and poison ivy, until he was on its far slope, facing the eastern marsh and the sea.

He turned back toward the trees.

"Hawk?" he said. "Are you there?"

Very faintly, a glimmer of light was coming into the dark

sky. There I was, looking at him, just as he had seen me when he was young.

"I am very glad you came, John Wakeley," I said.

John let out a breath, and smiled. "Hawk," he said. "Little Hawk."

"I told you. Even though this place holds me, I told you I should always be at your side."

"I know you are. I feel you, often. But it's not as good as talking to you." He stood gazing at me for a moment, that off-center gaze that was the only way to see me, and then he sat down suddenly on a rock.

"Oh, Hawk," he said, "what is to be done? Do you see all that happens? The fury that killed you was bad enough, but it never goes away—it grows worse."

I said, "I see much. And I wonder why I am left here to see, with no power at all to help the good or hinder the ill."

"And can you always tell one from the other?" John said. "Sweet Thomas Medlycott over there, he gave us so warm a welcome, we were so close as boys—there is no malice in him. But when he took me to my bed at night, he showed me the gun that was close to hand, against attack from the savages. No, he said, they had never been attacked yet, but no savage could be trusted."

I said, "My people do not always trust each other. Our father Yellow Feather has had to strive always not just to pacify the colonists with land, but to keep peace between the tribes."

John thought about this for a moment, but then he shook

his head. "I think I fear my own people more," he said. "Sometimes I fear this journey I am making with my son. When we stopped in Plymouth, I went to see my sister Mercy. She is married to a man as devout as my stepfather, Daniel, and she has children the same ages as my own. Benjamin was out in the garden with them while Mercy and I talked. And within an hour we heard a terrible shouting outside the door, and there was Benjamin with the biggest boy, Jonas, rolling on the ground, fighting. They wouldn't stop, I had to separate them. Ben's face was covered in blood."

He paused. "He is a peaceable boy," he said. "But he said Jonas had called me a heretic and an Indian-lover, and said I would go to Hell. And Jonas shouted that these things were true because his father had said them, and I could see from my sister's face that this was true."

He shook his head unhappily. "My own sister's son," he said. "I wonder what it will be like in Boston. I wonder if we are walking into danger."

"I wish I could tell you," I said.

"These people, they have no charity either for the Indians or for Christians who do not follow their own harsh rules. They talk about the word of the Lord, but they do not listen to it. Shall we all destroy each other, in the end?"

I knew no more of the answer to that question than he did.

"Change is made by the voice of one person at a time," I said. "Like our great sachem Yellow Feather. Like your friend Roger Williams. Like you."

John said bleakly, "You think that will be enough?"

"It's all we have," I said.

Light was growing in the sky.

John said, "This is a blessing. I needed to see you."

"Here I am. Older and younger than you. With the scar on my face that tells you who I am."

"The wolf scar," John said.

"The wolf I had to kill in order to stay alive, even though he was only trying to do the same thing."

"But you had no choice. We too kill wolves, to keep them from eating the animals that we want to eat. We *choose* to do it. We have choices all the time, and so often we make the wrong ones."

I said, "I have not seen you make a wrong choice yet."

"Except calling you for help, that day."

"Who is to tell whether that was wrong?"

"Yes, all is mystery," John said. "That's what you always say, in the end. But you are my Manitou, Little Hawk. Guide me."

"Treasure your uncertainty, then," I said. "Wrong choices come out of strong convictions that will not bend. You have always known that by instinct, on your way through this beautiful, dangerous world. You are a good man, John Wakeley. Follow your instincts."

"As my friend Hawk followed his," John said. He looked at me with a wry smile, and got to his feet.

Behind him, dawn was bringing color into the sky, a faint blue, streaked below with red and pink and gold.

"I would do it again," I said. I put my arm up to the sky. "Look. Look at the beauty."

John turned his head, and as he looked, on the horizon a sliver of scarlet light blazed out of the sea and the sun came up. And when he looked back, I was gone.

T W O

John, Benjamin, and Jedediah spent two days in the busy harbor of Boston, where Benjamin gazed in wonder at the ships that plied the Atlantic or sailed down to Bermuda or more faraway islands. Watching, I felt wonder of my own, at the size and bustle of this growing town. Our land was being changed into a new and different world.

John and Jedediah found the agent from whom they were buying their iron, and they hired a ship to take it, and them, back down the coast toward home in a few days' time. Then they set out to find the house of Jedediah's blind old friend, which was across the Charles River and its marshes, in an area called New Town.

Confused by the streets that masked the way to the river, Jedediah stopped to intercept two men walking toward them.

"By your leave, friends—"

The men paused. The taller of the two was in the uniform of the militia; the other was muffled in a cloak, even though the day was warm.

"If you please, we seek the crossing for New Town," Jedediah said politely, but the smaller man stepped past him, staring at John.

"John Wakeley!" he said.

It was a moment before John recognized the narrow, foxy face and the intent eyes, but the years had changed them very little.

"Ezra!" he said warmly. "I was speaking of you just the other day, with Mistress Medlycott and Thomas! How do you? My son Benjamin, my partner Jedediah Watkins—Master Ezra Clark."

Ezra nodded to them briefly. "I do well," he said.

John said to Benjamin, "Master Clark was journeyman in Marshfield when I was first an apprentice—he taught me many things." He turned back to Ezra. "But you have changed your calling, I hear."

"I assist at the governor's office," Ezra said with a touch of self-importance. His face was more lined, his hair more grey than yellow; he smiled no more than he ever had. He was looking carefully at John. He said, "Are you not still a member of Roger Williams's colony? In Providence Plantation?"

The militiaman turned his head to look at John.

"Yes indeed!" John said. "We have the cooperage for New Providence—we are in Boston for a shipment of iron hoops."

"I hear that you people have great dealings with the Indians," Ezra said.

There was a moment's pause.

John gave him a broad smile. "So must your governor, indeed, and with such good result—the praying villages multiply wonderfully!"

Ezra sniffed. His gaze flickered over Jedediah and Benjamin, then back to John. "What do you seek in New Town?"

"Garden Street, if you please," Jedediah said.

Ezra kept his eyes on John. He raised an eyebrow.

"We are visiting a friend," John said.

"You are in luck," Ezra said. "Garden Street is close by the new meetinghouse, you may hear Pastor Mitchel preach, a most devout and learned man."

"Ah," said John. "We will be sure to attend."

"And who is the friend you visit?" Ezra said.

His voice was casual, but the persistence made John uneasy. Before he could answer, Jedediah said, "Mistress Wilton is her name."

The militiaman turned his head again. He said to Ezra, "The widow Wilton. You recall?"

"I do," Ezra said. "Her father has come to live with her of late, from the Providence Plantation."

He paused, deliberately, and John knew this required a reply. He said, still smiling, "Yes indeed—Peregrine Barrett, a good friend. He was a witness at my wedding to Huldah, long ago."

"I hear he is a Baptist," Ezra said.

The words hung in the air, cold as icicles.

Jedediah said, "He is an old man, and not well."

"Baptists deny the whole structure of our colony's church. I hope you are not infected with those same heretical thoughts," Ezra said, his voice rising a little.

John's smile began to fade, but he still spoke civilly.

"We are infected with thoughts as Christian as your own, I can assure you, my friend," he said. "And should be very grateful for directions, if you please."

So Ezra gave them directions and a cool farewell, and he and the militiaman strode away.

And John, Jedediah, and Benjamin found their way to Peregrine Barrett, who was so pleased to hear their voices that he wept. He was a melancholy, bent old man, very fragile, with a widowed daughter who looked almost as old herself, but tended him with close devotion and had food and three beds carefully prepared for their visitors. They ate a soup of peas and onions, of which Benjamin had three helpings, and they drank cider that had been made from last year's apples, gathered by Mistress Wilton from the two trees in the house's little garden.

Then they prayed, and Jedediah preached a little, and old Peregrine was so moved and grateful that he shed a few more tears. His daughter's eyes were moist as well.

"May God bless you all," she said to John afterwards. "We go to the meetings on Sundays, of course, else we would face a whipping. But my father is Baptist in his heart and soul, and he has been so starved of his church's company. However long he has left to him, now he will go to the Lord a happy man."

John and Jedediah found this so touching that they took Peregrine's Bible, made a selection of readings, and decided that next morning, before they left, they would give him a short service just as if it had been a Sunday. In freethinking Providence, members of the Baptist church apparently did this often in their own homes, with no need for a minister.

"I'll turn thee Baptist yet," said Jedediah to John cheerfully.

John smiled at him. "Never!" he said. "But I believe in freedom of worship. Like Roger. And like our Lord."

So they all praised their God together the next morning—six of them in all, since Mistress Wilton's neighbor had once been a Baptist and had asked if she might join them. They stood in a group in the little living room and Benjamin read from the Bible. But as I could see, and could not tell them, there were two men in the street outside, who had been peering in at the window the day before and were back again this day. When Jedediah was reading a last long prayer, the door of the house was suddenly flung open and the two men burst in, shouting, "Shame! Shame!"

They were carrying heavy sticks, with which they thumped the walls and the floor, looking as if they would prefer to be thumping the people. They were the constables of New Town, they said, and they arrested John and Jedediah for conducting a religious service in a private house, without being ministers of the colony's church, and for preaching heretical beliefs.

"Did Ezra Clark send thee?" John said.

"Silence!" shouted one of the constables, and he banged his stick on the floor again. He glared at Mistress Wilton and her father. "And shame on thee too! Shame!"

Old Peregrine groped for John's hand. "These are good Christian men," he said tremulously to the constables.

"They would lead thee to Hell, old man," said the second constable. He reached into his big pocket and produced two lengths of rope.

Then they tied John and Jedediah's hands behind their backs, and took them to jail.

Mistress Wilton looked after Benjamin, who was both frightened and indignant. Two days later John and Jedediah were taken before the Boston magistrate and fined thirty pounds each, in English money. This seemed to be a huge sum, more than the cooperage earned in a year. I could sense John's anger; it was a kind of cold fury, deep and passionate, and I had never felt it in him before.

"I will not pay it!" he said.

Jedediah said heavily, "We must. The alternative is a whipping, and you know what that does to a man's body. My friends will raise the money, we can repay them over time."

"No!" John said. "They must pay for thee, certainly— one of us must be able to work. But I will not bow to them,

I will not! Trust me, Jedediah—I have reasons of my own. I will not submit to these men, who come to this land in the name of freedom and impose their own rules. Trust me. Let me do what I must do."

And though Jedediah pleaded, and Benjamin, and blind Peregrine begged him to accept money for the fine, John would not change his mind. Jedediah's fine was paid, and he was released. He was able to arrange for the shipment of their iron, but he was powerless to reach the only man who might have been able to intervene for John, Roger Williams, because Williams had gone to England seeking a charter for their colony and might not be back for a year.

A few days later John was taken before the governor at the General Court, and he was sentenced, with no opportunity for any defense, to thirty lashes of a whip.

John stared at the governor's icy face and did not say a word.

They took him to the whipping post in the center of Boston one fine morning, stripped him to the waist, and tied his hands to the top of the post. A crowd of the good people of Boston came to watch. Whippings seemed to be fairly common among these English, for the breaking of one rule or another, and there were always people who would flock to see another being punished.

Among my people, our sachem administered punishments, but this colony had one man whose particular job it was to whip, or to brand faces with a hot iron, or to cut off ears, or to kill. They called him the executioner. He was, Mistress Wilton said bitterly to Jedediah, a devout Christian who went to church at every opportunity and prayed more loudly than anyone around him.

The executioner's whip had a heavy handle and three very long thin strips of leather, each knotted at the end. He took it in both hands, raised it over his head, and lashed the three whips at John's back with all his might. He did this very slowly, pausing between each lash to collect his strength.

After the first few lashes John's back began to bleed. By the end it was a dreadful, bloody mess, but the executioner had not been able to make John so much as whimper.

I could feel John's pain, and over it all his absolute determination not to utter a sound. And I knew that this was his answer to all of them: his refusal to be vanquished not just by the executioner, but by Ezra Clark, by Daniel Smith, by all those who harmed others in the name of their God, and above all by that devout man Walter Kelly, who had killed his friend.

I do not know how the news of John Wakeley's cruel punishment reached the ears of my people. Nor did Jedediah, Benjamin, and the group of friends who carried him to Mistress Wilton's house, for the one day that they were allowed to wash his wounds before taking him into banishment. They knew only that when they reached the outskirts of Boston the next morning, carrying John out of the Massachusetts Bay Colony in a cart over bumpy, potholed roads, they were met by a large group of Pokanokets carrying a litter. One of them was Stardancer.

He reached out to Benjamin, whom he had known since he was a baby, and put his hands on the boy's shoulders. He had a little English, these days. He said, "The Massasoit sends us to help you fetch the Speaker home."

Benjamin looked at him with his eyes full of tears, and nodded, because he was too grateful to speak.

Their litter looked to me very much like the one on which Leaping Turtle and I and our fellows had carried Suncatcher out of our old dead village and into a new life. This one, however, was carried by eight men spaced round its four sides, and it was skillfully designed to give support to the body of a man able only to lie facedown, or propped on his hands and knees.

Very slowly and gently, they took John out of the cart and put him on the litter. The friends from Boston took their leave of Benjamin and Jedediah, and turned back. And at a slow, smooth pace, the Pokanokets carried John all the way to Sowams and beyond, to his own house and family. One of them was the son of a medicine man, and tended his back and gave him the juice of certain plants to drink, to help the pain.

The journey took three days.

Huldah was distraught, but she understood what John had done. She would not let Benjamin or Jedediah say a word of self-reproach.

"He went there for Peregrine," she said. "But the rebellion was his own. Refusing to pay their fine was his blow against their arrogance. He was fighting for freedom of belief." She looked at Benjamin's grim face, and at Samuel and Katharine. "Remember that," she said.

And as Stardancer and his companions prepared to leave, in trying to express her gratitude she told him that they had acted with true and wonderful compassion, as her Lord would have done.

Stardancer smiled, and made his farewells. He made no comment, but I could see in his face the puzzlement that I still share. How could all these people have a religion that valued compassion and respect so highly, and yet so often treat each other with neither of those things?

THREE

Slowly, John's back healed. Huldah gave birth to their fourth child, a boy whom they named Roger. The work of the coopers grew, as the town grew. John's journeyman, Peter, moved south to Aquidneck Island to start a cooperage in Portsmouth, but Benjamin would soon be done with his apprenticeship and take Peter's place. Samuel was apprenticed too. The family divided its time between farming and the making of casks, once in a while even fishing from a canoe, almost as Leaping Turtle and I had done.

Roger Williams came back from England with his charter, and was named president of Providence Plantation. More English families were arriving every year, and in all the existing towns around Plymouth and Massachusetts Bay, a new generation of white men was taking over from the first. Like Benjamin, like my people, they were born here; they had never known any other home. But unlike my people, they were not born with the deep inherited sense of connection to this land, and the life lived upon it for centuries. Land, for most of them, was property, opportunity, and a source of wealth. And once my people too had begun treating the land as property to be sold, or exchanged for the white man's goods, it was too late to stop.

Our father Yellow Feather had kept the peace by selling land, for a long time. He and Wamsutta even sold the land round their own village, to a group of the Plymouth leaders, and moved a little way south to Mount Hope, overlooking the bay. As the years went by, Yellow Feather, grown older and wearier, retired fifty miles northward to live a quiet life among the Quabaugs of the Nipmuck tribe. There he died, and Wamsutta became sachem of the Pokanokets as his father had been for so long.

The people from my village had long drifted in this direction, as the English settlements spread out from Plymouth and Boston to cover the land where once we hunted and fished and farmed. Leaping Turtle and Quickbird and their children were among those who had joined the groups moving nearer to Mount Hope, away from the "praying villages" in which the Indians had turned Christian, and they kept to the old ways. I watched them, and I watched as their children grew up, but I was bound more closely to watching John.

He spoke to me often, if he was alone in the woods or the fields. Whether or not he still believed that I could hear him, he spoke to me. He would tell me what he and

Huldah and his children were doing, as he would have told a living friend. I think he could sense my presence, and he still missed talking to me, as I missed talking to him.

Our leader Wamsutta was not so intent on peaceful dealings with the English as his father had been, but he did his best. He even requested that he and his younger brother Metacom should henceforth be known by the English names of Alexander and Philip. But though the colony's diplomatic governor Edward Winslow had been a good friend of Yellow Feather, his son Josiah Winslow was a very different man. He was now leader of the Plymouth militia. One dark day he came with ten armed men to confront Wamsutta, now Alexander, for having twice sold land not to Plymouth, but to the people of Providence Plantation.

Josiah Winslow arrested Alexander, our sachem, at gunpoint. After being held for a night at Winslow's house in Marshfield, Alexander became ill, and a few days later he died. Many of my people believed he must have been poisoned, including his brother Philip, who succeeded him as leader of the Pokanokets.

I watched tensions rising between the multiplying English and the Indians, over the years that followed. Neither side was seeking war, but one incident after another brought the danger of it closer. When three Pokanokets were hanged by the English for a murder that some thought they had not committed, the tension rose to a peak.

I watched, and I ached for my people. And for John's people too.

Philip, once Metacom, did not remember the day when John Wakeley rescued little Trouble from the trampling hooves of an English horse. He had been told about it, of course, but had forgotten it long since, and he had never really known John, the friend of his father's once called the Speaker because he had a gift for speaking our language. That gift was no longer remarkable. Many Indians now spoke at least some English, and an English minister had even translated their Bible into the Massachusetts dialect of our language.

The problem between our peoples was rooted not in language but in many things that Philip could not control, on either side: greed, resentment, arrogance, pride. Along with the new generation of colony-born Englishmen there was a new generation of Pokanokets, younger, driven by the same high emotions. I saw many of them begin to collect around Mount Hope, and I saw the colonists in Providence Plantation begin to feel fear.

A meeting was called at the Wakeleys' house, because everyone knew that John had had more dealings with Indians in his lifetime than anyone but Roger Williams. His four closest neighbors were there; they were gathered on benches outside the house, because it was summer, and two had brought their wives. Jedediah was there too. They were anxious to make a plan in case of an emergency; there was talk that Philip might declare war on the English, and Philip's village was only a few miles away.

"He is an intelligent leader in a very difficult position," John said, "and I don't think he wants war. But I hardly know Philip—not as I knew his father."

Jedediah sighed. "Plymouth planted the seed of this when they forced him to sign that treaty. Asking a sachem to become their subject—and to give up all his tribe's muskets, which their own people had sold him!"

"He has been replacing them through land sales ever since," said a grey-haired farmer, bent but still brisk.

"Of course," said Jedediah.

A younger man said, "And these executions of Indians for murder—it was a bad business. I heard tell Josiah Winslow made their trial uncommon swift."

"Plymouth has a lot to answer for," John said.

Standing behind him, Benjamin glanced down. Inside John's shirt collar he could see the edge of the long-healed scars. "And so does Boston," he said.

The grey-haired farmer said, "Blaming does us no good. What are we to do if we are attacked?"

"We have muskets, and a good supply of powder and shot," said the young man.

"If your farm is surrounded," said the grey-hair, "that supply may not last long."

"We shall all be scalped!" said one of the wives, and she started to cry.

Huldah came across and put an arm round her. I could feel the warmth in her that always reminded me of Quickbird.

"We shall not be scalped, nor killed," she said. "We shall

trust in the Lord, and devise the best way we can of warning each other in case of attack. So that if one family is in trouble, all the rest can come to its aid."

The young farmer said, "A bonfire in each yard, ready to be lit. To send up a smoke signal, as they say the Indians used to do."

"There is a garrison at Bourne," said another. "The best thing if attacked would be to flee there, on horses. The Indians will likely be on foot."

"Bourne is too far," said the grey-hair. "My house is the largest here—perhaps we should fortify it into a garrison."

Jedediah said, "A town is safer than a garrison. Perhaps you should all consider moving to Providence town."

"Roger Williams has said the same," John said. "He feels that we should all be prepared to leave now, in case things grow suddenly worse."

The others all stared at them.

"But this is our land," the young farmer said.

In an oak tree beside the house, a mockingbird was singing its loud double, triple song. On and on it went, a new phrase each time and yet on and on, on and on.

Among all the Pokanokets gathered at Mount Hope, I saw now the start of something I had never seen in life. They began the war dance, to the beating of drums, that goes on and on for days and weeks to bring courage and fierceness to a peak before an attack is launched. In the summer heat the young men danced, sweating, angry, aching for action.

There were calls to attack the English. There were prophecies that no war would succeed unless the English attacked first. Dust swirled round the moving feet as the dance and the drumming went on.

My sister's children were grown men and women, and their parents were dead. The oldest son, named for me, was a strong, tall warrior, respected by his fellows. He was there among the dancers, stamping, swaying. He knew nothing of John Wakeley; he knew nothing of me, except that long ago I had been killed by an Englishman. Like his brothers and all the men of his generation, Running Hawk was part of the force that began this war.

I watched, and I listened, with dread.

The English knew that the drums were beating, and they continued to fortify their largest homes into garrisons, where people might take shelter with soldiers to defend them. But they did nothing in attack.

An Indian messenger came to Roger Williams in Providence.

"Your people have driven us too far," he said. "You must know that you yourself will never be harmed. But be warned that peace can no longer be maintained."

Roger Williams sent at once for John and Huldah, and some other friends in outlying farms, begging them urgently to come at once and take refuge in his house. One of his sons thundered up to the Wakeleys' door on horseback, shouted his message to Huldah when she ran out, and then cantered off again to the next farm.

John and Benjamin were halfway through putting the head on a large cask. They dropped their tools and ran to hitch the horses to their two carts, which already waited near the house. In a flurry of packing and loading, the family seized clothes, food, supplies, anything of value that could be moved, and piled boxes and bundles onto the carts. Samuel saddled the riding horses. Roger drove his mother's best chickens, all indignantly squawking, into a carrying coop.

"And the cows?" he shouted to John. "They're in the far field!"

"Leave them."

"The Indians will kill them!"

"Sooner the cows than us!"

So the Wakeleys, like all their neighbors, fled from their home toward the town.

The war dance went on, for days and days.

Perhaps Philip promised his army of impatient young men that they might raid unoccupied houses, with no killing except of animals, in order to enrage the English and force an attack. Perhaps. I saw only that there came a point, on a Sunday when the English were all at worship in their meetinghouses, when finally a group of Pokanokets erupted northward from Mount Hope.

They ran swiftly across their own territory toward the English farmlands, near a garrison where a force of English soldiers had been gathering. The families from the nearby farms had already taken refuge inside the garrison, just as the Wakeleys had gone to Providence.

Philip's angry young warriors looted the farms, and slaughtered the cattle and pigs that for years had been trampling the corn in neighboring Pokanoket fields. Because now they had muskets as well as their bows and arrows, this was not hard. They killed no people, only the animals, which they cooked and ate that night with noisy pleasure.

These attacks on English property went on at intervals: a provocation, though never a threat to any human life. Not until one morning when two Englishmen, a farmer and his son, came out from the garrison to check their own farm and found Indians looting it. The son had a musket.

"Stop them!" shouted the father, furious. "Shoot!"

So the son aimed at an Indian and fired. The man fell, but stumbled up again and fled with the others. The farmer and his son rescued as many belongings as they could carry, and went back triumphant to the garrison.

The next morning, a trio of Pokanokets who spoke some English went openly to the garrison and asked to speak to the commander. One of them was Running Hawk.

"We have killed nobody," he said, "yet this boy shot one of our people. We wish to know why."

"Is your fellow dead?" said the commander.

"Yes," Running Hawk said. "He is dead."

The commander looked at the boy, a loutish fifteen-year-old who had been bragging endlessly about his shot.

The boy shrugged. "What of it?" he said. "He was a thieving Indian. It was no matter."

"Fool," said the commander. He turned to look at Running Hawk's icy face, and he said in apology, "This is the word of an idle lad."

"It gives us our answer," Running Hawk said.

He swung round abruptly, and the three men walked away.

Early the next morning, before news of this had reached Providence, Huldah was helping Mary Williams prepare breakfast when Benjamin came clattering through the kitchen, pulling on his coat.

"Where are you going?" she said in astonishment.

"To the house, very quickly, with Father. He says he is going mad without his tools, he wants to fetch them."

"Jedediah has tools, for goodness' sake!" said Huldah. Jedediah's cooperage was near the Williams's house, and they were all working there now.

Benjamin kissed her on the cheek and made for the door. "It's not the same—I know what he means. I'd like to get mine too."

Huldah followed him. John was outside with the horses.

"Don't worry," he said to her, "we shall be there and back very fast. The Indians are stealing cows now and then, they say, but not up here, and there's been no violence yet."

"Please be careful," Huldah said.

"Of course." He swung himself onto his horse. "Is there anything you want us to bring?"

"My cloak from the press, perhaps. Just come back as quick as you can. God bless you both."

John blew her a kiss as they rode away. "All will be well!" he called.

But the Pokanokets were fanning further out over the countryside that morning, seeking more farms, seizing more cattle, angry over the death of their fellow the day before. Running Hawk and two others, riding in search of plunder, came upon the Wakeley farm.

They saw two horses tethered outside the workshop. Horses were as valuable a prize as guns.

Benjamin was in the house, pulling out the cloak Huldah had asked for. John was in the workshop, collecting his tools. He looked out the window, and he caught his breath as he saw the three Pokanokets riding up. He knew he had to get to them as fast as he could, to tell them who he was, to reason with them.

Running Hawk reined in his horse at the gate, and kept guard as the other two dismounted to take the white man's horses. He cocked his gun and held it to his shoulder, tense, watchful, in case of an angry shot from anyone inside.

John came running out of the workshop, still with a cooper's tool in his hand. It was his best drawknife, in a long canvas case.

But to Running Hawk it looked like a musket.

Instantly he swung his gun toward John and he shot him. In the moment between the pressure of his finger on the trigger and the sound of the explosion, he heard John shout in Pokanoket, "Stop!"

It was too late to stop.

John dropped to the ground. The horses reared at the noise of the shot; the Pokanokets tried to calm them. Running Hawk jumped down and ran to John.

He was lying on his back, a great stain on his chest, with blood coming out. He looked up, and he said in Pokanoket, "I beg you not to harm my son."

He had no idea who it was that he was talking to.

He thought for an instant of me, as the years dissolved, as he went out of time, and he said, "I am the friend of Little Hawk."

Then he died, the blue eyes still open.

"Come!" shouted one of the others urgently to Running Hawk. They were mounted again, leading the horses away. Running Hawk looked down once more at John, amazed and bewildered, and then he turned and ran back to his own horse, and followed them.

From a window of the house, Benjamin shot at him. But his musket misfired and there was only a small clicking sound, that nobody else heard.

Except me.

FOUR

King Philip's War, a terrible, bloody business with much brutality on both sides, blazed through what is now called New England for more than a year. Many English settlements, including Providence, were burned to the ground, and more than six hundred English were killed—though not Roger and Mary Williams, nor Huldah and her family.

Running Hawk died, and all his family. So did more than three thousand of my people, and those who survived the war retained only tiny amounts of land. Philip's head was cut off by the English and stuck up on a pole above the fort in Plymouth, where their Captain Miles Standish had put the head of Wituwamet half a century before. Hundreds of "Praying Indians" from our villages that had embraced Christianity died after being shipped to an internment camp on Deer Island, in Boston Harbor, and almost a thousand of my people were shipped by the English to Europe or the West Indies as slaves, including Philip's wife and son.

I watched all this, as I have watched the fate of my tribe and all the others in the long years since.

My people still live in some parts of this New England, a few thousand of them, on tribal reservation lands. They keep alive our traditions and our spirit; they struggle to revive language in places where it has faded away; they fight for the rights of the tribes under the nation's law. They are the soul of the land to which we belong, where once we roamed free. But now they share that freedom with others, in the new nation to which they too belong. They are Americans.

I have been watching it all so long, like a bird trapped in this house of sky and sea and land. Here I have stayed, on the salt marsh island where my tomahawk was born, and where it has rested for so long in the memory hole that John made for me. I have told my story, but even now I am not released. Somewhere, beyond our knowledge, is the long home to which we are all freed to go, in the end.

I want to go home.

I want to go home.

PART FOUR

RIPENING MOON

There is a dog on my island now, where in all the centuries there has never been a dog before. He looks like a wolf. His name is Pan.

It is high summer; the salt marsh is green, the sea deep blue. As time went by, the English farmers began to harvest hay for their animals from the marsh, and they dug drainage ditches among the creeks where my people had come in canoes to hunt and to fish. But after two centuries or so, in 1898 a great hurricane broke through the coast and gave the river a new estuary, out through the marsh, so that salt water now came flooding round the islands at high tides. This is the way of things.

The only grass that will grow in a marsh that is salt has no value for haying, so the farmers went away. The islands bear the names of their forefathers. Today, on the first island only the wild creatures live; but on the second there are a dozen or so houses, some occupied all the year, some only in summer.

On the third salt marsh island, where John and I talked so often, there has been for a hundred years or so a small house occupied only in summer. In winter, nobody has been there but the birds, the animals, and the trees, many of them overgrown with huge thickets of the vine called poison ivy, the plant we were careful to avoid. It is high summer now, and in places the poison ivy's leaves are turning the brilliant red that overtakes them in the fall.

A little while ago the summer home began to fall down, and now a new person has come and replaced it with a sturdier house. It is a woman, in her middle years. She has dark eyes and hair, and her name is Rachel. She is a painter. She appears to live alone.

I watch her, and think sometimes that she looks as my grandmother Suncatcher may have looked at that age. She is tall and lean, and works often on the land, planting only the trees and bushes that belong here. "Natives," she calls them. The dog who looks like a wolf lives here with her.

It is August, the time of the Green Corn Moon. Rachel is digging, pulling out a network of greenbrier roots. She keeps well clear of the poison ivy, but she has a helper, a big sunburned man called Gabe, who must be one of those who are not poisoned by it—he has spent much of this day hacking down its twining trunks and hauling up its roots. The sun is low in the sky now, but he is still pulling poison ivy out of the cherry trees, compulsive, unharmed.

"The tide's coming in, Gabe," Rachel says. "Better go home, or you'll be stuck here for hours."

"I'm going," he says. "But look, here are the trees I brought from the nursery. On sale—and all native."

He leads Rachel to his truck, and the group of little trees he has unloaded from it, all in pots. The wolflike dog, who has been lying in the shade, gets to its feet and pads after them.

"Two crab apples," Gabe says, "two more junipers, a river birch, another arrowwood. And a little orphan guy, there's not much demand for them—a bitternut hickory."

"Great," Rachel says.

"Oh, and there's this," Gabe says.

He reaches in through the front window of his truck. "My guys found it this afternoon when they were edging the driveway, just where your land starts. They thought you should have it."

And he hands her the head of my tomahawk.

I did not expect this. For a moment I am lost in a sound like the sigh of the wind, the breath of the sea.

Beside Rachel, the wolflike dog barks suddenly, loudly.

"Shut up, Pan," Rachel says.

"Looks like an Indian axe head," Gabe says. "Should go to their museum, I guess, if it's some sort of sacred object."

"You're right," Rachel says. "Thank you."

She holds the axe head as he drives away, running her fingers over it. The dog watches her warily.

Rachel goes back to the place where she was digging

and sits down on a log, looking out at the salt marsh as the water is driven across it by the rising tide. The outer island is already surrounded by water, out there. Every tree along its edge stands out, in the clear light of the dying day. The dog lies down at Rachel's feet and goes to sleep.

With the axe head in her hand, she sits there for a long time, thinking. She does this often, in this same place. Sometimes I think she is talking to the land in her mind.

Behind her the sun goes down. The water darkens, but for a little while the last rays of the sun linger on the outer island, and its trees are golden. Then the color dies and the sun has truly set.

As she turns back toward the west, she sees me, a figure through whom she can also see the trees and the sunset sky. She catches her breath, and is still.

It is only for a moment. My instinct at first is to hide myself. I am gone again.

Rachel blinks, breathes again, peers at the place where I was. There is nothing.

The sleeping dog beside her gives a great sigh.

"All right, Pan," she says, and they get up and head for the house. Rachel puts the glimpse of me out of her mind as a trick of the light, and she walks to the house. But she looks back once more before she goes in.

The bottom half of the house is full of canvasses and paints, with two easels, and some of the pictures that Rachel has painted, here and elsewhere. They show the salt marsh in every mood and weather. Some include birds, and other creatures, though very few of them include people. She is a good painter.

She does not sleep well that night. Dreams flicker in and out of her mind, dreams of snow and summer, of a bow and a tomahawk, of deer and of a wolf like her dog Pan; dreams of a frozen pond and a slithering eel, a swaying cart and a crowded unpaved street.

She dreams of blood, and severed heads. Twice she wakes abruptly, her heart racing, certain that there is the sound of a gunshot in her ears—but each time Pan is sleeping peacefully on the floor beside her bed.

I am not giving her these dreams, but I can sense them, and I am sorry.

After the second waking, she lies there restless, and at length gets out of bed. It is early morning but still dark. There are no curtains at the windows of this house, and she looks out of the window at the stars.

Suddenly she sees a shooting star streak across the northern sky. Then another. Rachel knows the stars, and now she remembers the summer meteor shower.

"The Perseids," she says to herself.

The dog gets to his feet, stretches, and makes an enquiring noise.

"All right, Pan," she says, and she pulls on some clothes and goes downstairs and outdoors, with the dog following. As she passes the table beside her door, she picks up the axe head that has been lying there all night.

There is a wooden picnic table on the grass between

the house and the trees. Rachel hoists herself onto this table and lies there on her back, looking up. She sees the dark sky flicker with shooting stars, one after the other, darting across the sky like sparks blown out of a fire by the wind.

"Look," my father said, that first time, holding me in his arms and pointing upward. "They are your ancestors, Little Hawk. Every year at this time they leap, they dance. It is Manitou. They are saying to us, 'Look, we are still here. We are watching over you. We dance for you, in our beautiful home.'"

Rachel watches the meteors for a long time. Sometimes she sees one only from the corner of her eye, but still she sees. The axe head is still in her hands, warm from her skin.

She watches until the sky begins to brighten with the beginnings of dawn, and the meteors can no longer be seen, and then she sits up and swings her legs over the side of the table.

And she sees me standing there, looking at her.

She sees a bare-chested American Indian, in deerskin pants and moccasins, his hair greased up into a scalp lock—but the body has no substance, and through it the trees are still faintly visible.

The dog Pan sees me too. He gives a whimper that is like the start of a howl, a sound Rachel has never heard him make before, and he creeps under the table and lies there on his belly.

Rachel is afraid—I can feel her fear—but she doesn't run, she doesn't move. She sits there gazing back at me with the axe head in her hands, for a long time. Her knuckles are white, she is gripping the axe so hard.

But very gradually the hands relax, the fear loses its hold.

Then she takes a deep breath and lets it slowly out again, and she says, "Who are you?"

"I am Little Hawk. Of the Pokanoket tribe, of the Wampanoag Nation."

"The People of the First Light," Rachel says. "Of course."

Since she can understand me, it does not occur to her that I am not speaking her own language, nor she mine. She is talking to a ghost, without fear now and without question; she is astonishing.

She says, half to herself, "I knew—I knew there was something. . . ."

Then she says to me, "You should be out there with the shooting stars, Little Hawk."

"I wish I were."

"What holds you?" she says.

She is a wise woman, even though she is not old. Before I can say anything, the memory of her dreams puts a shadow into her mind, and she shakes her head, as if to shake it away.

"Yes," I say. "Those things, perhaps."

She says, "You gave me those dreams?"

"You dream my memories, I believe."

She holds up the axe head. "And this?" she says. "Does this belong to you?"

"It was mine. It belonged to my father, and to his father before him. It was buried on this land, in a place that we called a memory hole."

"A long time ago," she says. "When it still had a handle."

"Of course. The day I was born, my father came to this island and tied twin stems of a bitternut hickory tree around that axe, to grow together as one and become its handle. And so they did, and it was my tomahawk, as it had been for my father's father."

Rachel sighs. "And used in war, to fight the invaders."

"Not by me."

But as I say that, I know that it would have been, if I had lived. Unless I had become someone like John.

"Was this your land?"

"The land belongs to no one. The land *is*."

"Ah," says Rachel ruefully, "that's where we went wrong from the start, isn't it."

She slides down off the table. Pan still cowers beneath it, silent. "My dog is afraid of you," she says.

"But you're not afraid. Not now."

"You don't seem frightening. You seem sad. And . . . tired."

Oh, I am tired beyond belief. Tired of the memories.

"You will see me only until the sun comes up," I say, as much to the dog as to her.

Rachel glances out at the marsh. "So . . . the times between night and day, the times between tides. The Celts knew about those too. The hesitations in time, when it doesn't rule everything. Like the moments that we paint."

She looks down at the axe head, and runs her fingers over it again.

She says, "I'm trying to take care of this piece of land, Little Hawk. I'll do my best."

Something about the tilt of her head reminds me of Suncatcher again.

I say suddenly, "Are you Wampanoag?"

She shrugs. She says, "There are all kinds of tribes in me, most of them from across the ocean. And I don't belong to any of them. If human beings weren't so big on belonging to groups, I don't believe they'd fight wars."

"But you would fight for this piece of land, if someone tried to take it away from you."

Rachel smiles at me. "Like you said, the land belongs to no one. The land *is*."

It's like Leaping Turtle throwing a ball back to me, when we were boys. I smile back at her.

The sky is growing brighter.

Rachel sits there for a long moment, looking at the axe head. Suddenly she puts it down on the table and strides over to the group of trees in pots, left by Gabe. She comes back with a small tree in one hand and a spade in the other.

She looks at me. "Is this axe head a sacred object?" she says.

"No. It is my tomahawk."

"I think we should give your tomahawk back to the land, Little Hawk," she says.

"It has been buried for a long time," I say.

"But this time we free it from the memories," Rachel says. "We plant a tree with it, to grow for tomorrow. This tree."

It is the bitternut hickory.

As the first blaze of the sun comes up out of the sea, the first light out of the east, she slams the spade into the ground and begins to dig.

In the end, all it takes is one small action, by one person. One at a time.

Time breaks open around me, and all at once there is more light than a hundred suns, more light than I have ever seen.

From somewhere out over the salt marsh there is the faint cry of an osprey, the fish hawk.

Rachel looks for me, but I am no longer there.

She says softly, "Fly in peace, Little Hawk."

And I am gone to my long home at last, set free, flying high, high beyond the world. High, high, into mystery.

TIMELINE

When the English and the Europeans first came to North America, there were more than a thousand tribes of proud, deep-rooted, and sometimes warring indigenous people all over the continent. On the east coast the white settlers multiplied, and started to push the Native Americans to the west. Complicated battles were fought for land, involving the French as well as the English and the tribes, until the wars of 1776 and 1812 separated the white settlers of this land from Britain forever, as Americans. After that, the conflicts over land use were between these new Americans and the indigenous Americans whom they called Indians.

In 1804 Congress passed an act allowing President Thomas Jefferson to exchange any Indian lands east of the Mississippi for land west of the river.

In 1807 Jefferson wrote to his secretary of war, "If ever

we are constrained to lift the hatchet against any tribe, we will never lay it down til that tribe is exterminated, or driven beyond the Mississippi."

In 1814 the Creeks were defeated in Alabama by Andrew Jackson, and the Americans acquired more than 20 million acres of Creek land.

Andrew Jackson wrote to President James Monroe in 1817, "I have long viewed treaties with the Indians an absurdity not to be reconciled to the principles of our government."

In 1825 President Madison told Congress that removing Indian tribes from all the states was "of very high importance to our union" because ". . . it is impossible to incorporate them, in such masses, in any form whatever, into our system. . . ."

In 1830, urged by Jackson (now president), Congress passed the Indian Removal Act, authorizing the forced removal of the Cherokee, Choctaw, Creek, Chickasaw, and Seminole tribes to "Indian Territory" west of the Mississippi River.

The designated Indian Territory stretched from the north of Texas to the north of Nebraska.

In 1838, on the "Trail of Tears," the Cherokee were forced by 7,000 US troops to leave their homes and belongings and walk to northeast Oklahoma. Out of 15,000, more than 4,000 died of exposure and famine on the march.

The other tribes listed in the Act were also forced to leave, but the Seminoles refused, and for seven years they fought a US army that outnumbered them ten to one. Many were killed on both sides. No peace treaty was ever signed, and though some Seminoles went west, others fled into the Florida Everglades and stayed there.

During Jackson's presidency, more than 45,000 Indians were relocated to the west, and the US acquired 100 million acres of Indian land.

The treaty ending the Mexican-American War in 1848 gave the United States New Mexico and Arizona, whose boundaries included the ancestral lands of the Navajo. In 1864 about 9,000 Navajo were forced into "The Long Walk" of 300 miles to a 40-square-mile reservation called the Bosque Redondo. The survivors were allowed to return four years later to an area one-tenth the size of their former land.

In 1862 President Abraham Lincoln approved the Minnesota hanging of 38 Dakota Indians summarily convicted of murder and rape, after a bloody war sparked by the government's failure to honor the terms of a land-sale treaty. Lincoln had reduced the total of death sentences from 303, but it was still the biggest mass hanging in the history of the United States. All Dakotas were forced to leave their homes in the state.

In 1875, 1,500 Apache and Yavapai were made to walk 180 miles, in winter, from the Rio Verde Indian reserve to internment on the San Carlos reservation; many died on the way. When 200 returned 25 years later, they found their land occupied by white settlers.

In 1887 Congress passed the Dawes Severalty Act, under which every Native American family was offered ownership of 160 acres of tribal land to farm or—after 25 years—to sell. It was intended to Americanize the Indians, and it made their traditional way of life impossible.

In 1889 the western Indian Territory was reduced to an area the size of present-day Oklahoma. A year later it lost half its land when the Oklahoma Territory was formed, and in 1907 it was incorporated into the State of Oklahoma, and disappeared.

The whites' hunger for land reached the Plains Indians, between the Mississippi and the Rockies, through gold prospectors, buffalo hunters, and the spread of the railways. The Sioux were forced into reservations, in spite of a victory over General Custer and the US cavalry at Little Bighorn, and US troops massacred hundreds of Sioux, including women and children, at Wounded Knee in 1890.

In 1911 a "wild man" emerged from the countryside near Oroville, California: thin, frightened, and naked but for a piece of canvas round his shoulders. He was the last living member of the Yahi, the only California tribe to have escaped total extermination by the whites, and the anthropologists who became his friends called him Ishi, which in his language means "man." He had been living much as all indigenous Americans lived before the whites came. Until he died in 1916, he lived and worked in the University of California's Museum of Anthropology in San Francisco, where you may still hear his recorded voice telling a story. He was the last "wild" Indian in North America.

In 1924 the US gave all Native Americans the right to citizenship and a vote (54 years after African Americans, four years after women of any race). Since this right was still governed by state law, however, many could not vote until 1948.

By the time the Dawes Act was repealed in 1934, Native Americans had higher rates of alcoholism, illiteracy, poverty, and suicide than any other ethnic group in the US. Generations of children had been forced to speak only English in government schools, and today tribes are fighting for immersion programs to keep their languages alive. By the 2010 Census, the nation's population of "American Indians and Alaska Natives, including those of more than one race," made up 1.7 percent of the total population.

The *Mayflower* brought its 102 white passengers to the land of the Native Americans on November 11, 1620.

A U T H O R ' S   N O T E

I look out from my study window across a salt marsh, at the mouth of a Massachusetts river. This land must have looked much the same since the end of the last Ice Age. In winter the salt marsh is brown-white and the creeks fill with tiny icebergs; in spring there's the first hint of green, and the egrets come back, and a pair of ospreys. For years, kayaking through the creeks, I have been haunted by the thought of the first Americans, who saw these things too; who for thousands of years hunted over this land without ever changing it.

Out of that haunting I wrote this book. It is a work of the imagination, set within a framework of historical events. Little Hawk and John Wakeley are fictional, as are their connections with Roger Williams and Yellow Feather (Ousamequin, known to his English contemporaries by his title as grand sachem of the Wampanoag Nation,

Massasoit.) The latter two were of course real people, and after much research into all the contemporary sources, I have tried, with respect, to put words into their mouths that they might have said.

The tribes of the northeast of America left us no record of the early seventeenth century, because their languages had not yet been written down. Pilgrims like William Bradford and Edward Winslow wrote their own accounts, some of which you can find in a collection called *The Mayflower Papers*, edited by Nathaniel and Thomas Philbrick. And the Library of Congress has put all 456 pages of Roger Williams's long-winded but fascinating letters at archive.org.

Of the many books written about America's early history, I owe most to Nathaniel Philbrick's marvelously vivid *Mayflower: A Story of Courage, Community, and War*.

I've taken just one intentional liberty with history by copying for John Wakeley the whipping inflicted by the Massachusetts Bay Colony on the Baptist Obadiah Holmes in 1651. The Colony also whipped several other Baptists of whom they disapproved, and some years later they hanged three Quakers.

What did Little Hawk's language sound like? In the seventeenth century, all the tribes of southern New England spoke closely related languages of what is called "the Eastern Algonquian subfamily." For the sound of the words, you can find some help in the Aquidneck Intertribal Indian Council's *Cultural History of the Native Peoples of Southern New England*, put together by Dr. Frank Waabu

O'Brien (Moondancer) and Julianne Jennings (Strong Woman), or in Anne Makepeace's excellent film *We Still Live Here: Âs Nutayuneân*, which tells the story of the Wampanoag linguist Jessie Little Doe Baird and her determination to revive her tribe's lost language. If it's not in your library, you can find it at MakepeaceProductions.com, and the language project itself at wlrp.org.

The Pokanoket tribal website is at pokanoket.us and the most detailed Wampanoag site is at mashpeewampanoagtribe.com. Plimoth Plantation, with its astonishing reproductions of early American life—and of the *Mayflower*—is at plimoth.org.

And if you reached my timeline, and were caught by a mention of "the last wild Indian in North America," you can read about him in *Ishi in Two Worlds* by Theodora Kroeber (University of California Press, 1961). Ms. Kroeber was married to Ishi's anthropologist friend Professor Alfred Kroeber, and we owe them both a huge extra debt. They were the parents of Ursula K. Le Guin.

A READING GROUP GUIDE TO

GHOST HAWK

BY SUSAN COOPER

ABOUT THE BOOK

Little Hawk is eleven years old when he is sent into the wilderness alone in what his tribe calls his "proving time." His only tools are a bow and arrow, a knife, and a tomahawk that his father crafted on the day of Little Hawk's birth. During the three moons that he is away, he survives an encounter with a lone wolf and treacherous weather conditions. Upon his return he finds that his entire village has been wiped out by the "white man's plague." Not too far away in the Plymouth Colony, ten-year-old John Wakeley is about to begin his own journey to manhood. Though his people are prejudiced against the native peoples, John realizes that he cannot live with such hatred and must follow his heart to a new territory. The two boys become men in very different ways, but their lives are intertwined forever.

Read aloud the passages from Roger Williams and Woody Guthrie at the beginning of the novel. Discuss the relationship between the two passages and what they have to say about American history.

DISCUSSION QUESTIONS

1. Explain why Little Hawk is considered an omniscient narrator. How does the element of surprise at the end of Part One explain the title of the novel?

2. Contrast the role of women and men in the Native American culture. Compare these gender roles to those of the Pilgrim culture in the Plymouth Colony.

3. The "proving time" is a survival time in the wilderness when eleven-year-old boys prove that they are men. How do Little Hawk's parents prepare him for his proving time? Discuss Little Hawk's journey. At what point does he realize that he will survive? Explain the moment he realizes why this proving time is so important to his people. How does he know when it is time to return to his village? Discuss how his manhood is further tested when he returns.

4. Foreshadowing is a literary device that hints of events that come later in the story. Suncatcher, Little Hawk's grandmother, says, "You will see me first when you return, Little Hawk." How does this statement foreshadow what Little Hawk finds in his village when he returns from his proving time?

5. Morning Star allows Suncatcher and Quickbird to believe that the other is dead. Justify his lie. Why does Suncatcher call it a "half a lie?" Discuss what John Wakeley means when he says, "There are some who turn lies into memories." What other lies are told in the novel?

6. Little Hawk says of his Manitou, "I never expected it to come as a comfort for shame." Why does he feel shame? How do his emotions reflect the beliefs of his culture? Explain why he is comforted by his Manitou.

7. Little Hawk makes several references to loneliness. How does his Manitou relieve his feelings of loneliness? Why is it necessary for Little Hawk to take his road to manhood alone? What other characters in the novel suffer from loneliness?

8. Fear is another emotion that Little Hawk experiences. Discuss the purpose of the sweathouse. How does Little Hawk overcome his fears? How does John Wakeley deal with fear?

9. Contrast the way the Native Americans view the land and nature to the way the white men view it. Cite evidence from the novel to support the claim.

10. Trust and mistrust are themes in the novel. How do Little Hawk and John Wakeley trust one another? What is the basis of Leaping Turtle's mistrust of all white men? How does Yellow Feather represent trust?

11. Explain the views of the Puritans. John recognizes Master Kelly as the man who killed Little Hawk. How does this recognition cause John to question the religious views of the Puritans? Why are the Puritans uncomfortable with Roger Williams? Discuss the attitude of the elders of the meetinghouse toward John. How does this explain why John admires and follows Roger Williams?

12. Compare and contrast John's relationship with his stepfather to Thomas Medlycott's relationship with his father.

13. John experiences several life-changing moments in the novel. What are the most significant changes? How do these events make him a man? Contrast his journey to manhood with that of Little Hawk.

14. What does Little Hawk's tomahawk symbolize? How is it significant to the plot of the novel? Discuss how burying

the tomahawk helps John come to terms with Little Hawk's death? How does Rachel free Little Hawk?

15. Discuss the tensions that develop between Little Hawk and John's people. Little Hawk says that "greed, resentment, arrogance, and pride" are the root of the problem. What evidence from the text supports Little Hawk's observation?

ACTIVITIES

1. The novel is divided into four parts: Freezing Moon, Planting Moon, Burning Moon, and Ripening Moon. Find a quote from each section that best explains the title of each section.

2. Explain the following simile: "I could feel his mind reaching for reason and sliding back again, like a man climbing a muddy slope." Write a simile that describes Little Hawk's thoughts when he returns to his devastated village.

3. Like simile and metaphor, personification is a literary device that creates certain images in the reader's mind. What is the difference between personification and simile? Discuss the following example of personification: "It was the voice of the sea, whose anger would last much longer than the storm that had stirred it into life." Identify other

examples of personification in the novel. Write a sentence that uses personification to describe the moment Rachel buries the tomahawk.

4. The "white man's plague" killed everyone in Little Hawk's village except Suncatcher. Make a list of the symptoms of the plague from those given in the book. Use books or the Internet to identify the specific disease, when a cure for the disease was discovered, and the scientists responsible for the discovery.

5. Read about the basic beliefs of the Pokanoket tribe of the Wampanoag Nation on the following website: pokanoket.us. Discuss how Yellow Feather upholds these beliefs.

6. Read more about one of the following characters: Roger Williams, Squanto, Miles Standish, Governor William Bradford, or Edward Winslow. Write an acrostic poem that reveals the man's contribution to the Massachusetts Bay Colony.

7. Discuss the following question: "How could all these people have a religion that values compassion and respect so highly, and yet so often treat each other with neither of those things?" Use specific examples from the novel to make your points.

8. A Boston court banished Roger Williams and ordered him to return to England. Instead he escaped to the Rhode

Island territory. Stage a drama of the courtroom trial of Williams. Include a judge, jury, and people to speak against and for Williams.

9. Research the Pokanoket tribe of the Wampanoag Nation today. Little Hawk says, "I can see past, present, though not future." Assume that Little Hawk can see the future and write an essay regarding the current state of the Wampanoag Nation from Little Hawk's point of view.

Guide written in 2013 by Pat Scales, a retired middle and high school librarian who is currently a children's and young adult literature consultant and specializes in curriculum and free speech issues.

This guide, written to align with the Common Core State Standards (corestandards.org) has been provided by Simon & Schuster for classroom, library, and reading group use. It may be reproduced in its entirety or excerpted for these purposes.

Turn the page for a look
at the first book in
The Dark Is Rising sequence,

OVER SEA,
UNDER STONE

by Susan Cooper

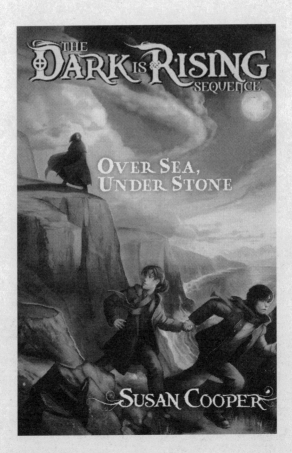

WHERE IS HE?"

Barney hopped from one foot to the other as he clambered down from the train, peering in vain through the white-faced crowds flooding eagerly to the St. Austell ticket barrier. "Oh, I can't see him. Is he there?"

"Of course he's there," Simon said, struggling to clutch the long canvas bundle of his father's fishing rods. "He said he'd meet us. With a car."

Behind them, the big diesel locomotive hooted like a giant owl, and the train began to move out.

"Stay where you are a minute," Father said, from a barricade of suitcases. "Merry won't vanish. Let people get clear."

Jane sniffed ecstatically. "I can smell the sea!"

"We're miles from the sea," Simon said loftily.

"I don't care. I can smell it."

"Trewissick's five miles from St. Austell, Great-Uncle Merry said."

"Oh, where *is* he?" Barney still jigged impatiently on the dusty grey platform, glaring at the disappearing backs that masked his view. Then suddenly he stood still, gazing downwards. "Hey—look."

They looked. He was staring at a large black suitcase among the forest of shuffling legs.

"What's so marvellous about that?" Jane said.

Then they saw that the suitcase had two brown pricked ears and a long waving brown tail. Its owner picked it up and moved away, and the dog which had been behind it was left standing there alone, looking up and down the platform. He was a long, rangy, lean dog, and where the sunlight shafted down on his coat it gleamed dark red.

Barney whistled, and held out his hand.

"Darling, no," said his mother plaintively, clutching at the bunch of paint-brushes that sprouted from her pocket like a tuft of celery.

But even before Barney whistled, the dog had begun trotting in their direction, swift and determined, as if he were recognizing old friends. He loped round them in a circle, raising his long red muzzle to each in turn, then stopped beside Jane, and licked her hand.

"Isn't he gorgeous?" Jane crouched beside him, and ruffled the long silky fur of his neck.

"Darling, be careful," Mother said. "He'll get left behind. He must belong to someone over there."

"I wish he belonged to us."

"So does he," Barney said. "Look."

He scratched the red head, and the dog gave a throaty half-bark of pleasure.

"*No,*" Father said.

The crowds were thinning now, and through the barrier

they could see clear blue sky out over the station yard.

"His name's on his collar," Jane said, still down beside the dog's neck. She fumbled with the silver tab on the heavy strap. "It says Rufus. And something else . . . Trewissick. Hey, he comes from the village!"

But as she looked up, suddenly the others were not there. She jumped to her feet and ran after them into the sunshine, seeing in an instant what they had seen: the towering familiar figure of Great-Uncle Merry, out in the yard, waiting for them.

They clustered round him, chattering like squirrels round the base of a tree. "Ah, there you are," he said casually, looking down at them from beneath his bristling white eyebrows with a slight smile.

"Cornwall's wonderful," Barney said, bubbling.

"You haven't seen it yet," said Great-Uncle Merry. "How are you, Ellen, my dear?" He bent and aimed a brief peck at Mother's cheek. He treated her always as though he had forgotten that she had grown up. Although he was not her real uncle, but only a friend of her father, he had been close to the family for so many years that it never occurred to them to wonder where he had come from in the first place.

Nobody knew very much about Great-Uncle Merry, and nobody ever quite dared to ask. He did not look in the least like his name. He was tall, and straight, with a lot of very thick, wild, white hair. In his grim brown face the nose curved fiercely, like a bent bow, and the eyes were deep-set and dark.

How old he was, nobody knew. "Old as the hills," Father said, and they felt, deep down, that this was probably right. There was something about Great-Uncle Merry that was like the hills, or the sea, or the sky; something ancient, but without age or end.

Always, wherever he was, unusual things seemed to happen. He would often disappear for a long time, and then suddenly come through the Drews' front door as if he had never been away, announcing that he had found a lost valley in South America, a Roman fortress in France, or a burned Viking ship buried on the English coast. The newspapers would publish enthusiastic stories of what he had done. But by the time the reporters came knocking at the door, Great-Uncle Merry would be gone, back to the dusty peace of the university where he taught. They would wake up one morning, go to call him for breakfast, and find that he was not there. And then they would hear no more of him until the next time, perhaps months later, that he appeared at the door. It hardly seemed possible that this summer, in the house he had rented for them in Trewissick, they would be with him in one place for four whole weeks.

The sunlight glinting on his white hair, Great-Uncle Merry scooped up their two biggest suitcases, one under each arm, and strode across the yard to a car.

"What d'you think of that?" he demanded proudly.

Following, they looked. It was a vast, battered estate car, with rusting mudguards and peeling paint, and mud caked on the hubs of the wheels. A wisp of steam curled up from the radiator.

"Smashing!" said Simon.

"Hmmmmmm," Mother said.

"Well, Merry," Father said cheerfully, "I hope you're well insured."

Great-Uncle Merry snorted. "Nonsense. Splendid vehicle. I hired her from a farmer. She'll hold us all, anyway. In you get."

Jane glanced regretfully back at the station entrance as she clambered in after the rest. The red-haired dog was standing on the pavement watching them, long pink tongue dangling over white teeth.

Great-Uncle Merry called: "Come on, Rufus."

"Oh!" Barney said in delight, as a flurry of long legs and wet muzzle shot through the door and knocked him sideways. "Does he belong to you?"

"Heaven forbid," Great-Uncle Merry said. "But I suppose he'll belong to you three for the next month. The captain couldn't take him abroad, so Rufus goes with the Grey House." He folded himself into the driving seat.

"The Grey House?" Simon said. "Is that what it's called? Why?"

"Wait and see."

The engine gave a hiccup and a roar, and then they were away. Through the streets and out of the town they thundered in the lurching car, until hedges took the place of houses; thick, wild hedges growing high and green as the road wound uphill, and behind them the grass sweeping up to the sky. And against the sky they saw nothing but lonely trees, stunted and bowed by the wind that blew from the sea, and yellow-grey outcrops of rock.

"There you are," Great-Uncle Merry shouted, over the noise. He turned his head and waved one arm away from the steering-wheel, so that Father moaned softly and hid his eyes. "Now you're in Cornwall. The real Cornwall. Logres is before you."

The clatter was too loud for anyone to call back.

"What's he mean, Logres?" demanded Jane.

Simon shook his head, and the dog licked his ear.

"He means the land of the West," Barney said unexpectedly, pushing back the forelock of fair hair that always tumbled over his eyes. "It's the old name for Cornwall. King Arthur's name."

Simon groaned. "I might have known."

Ever since he had learned to read, Barney's greatest heroes had been King Arthur and his knights. In his dreams he fought imaginary battles as a member of the Round Table, rescuing fair ladies and slaying false knights. He had been longing to come to the West Country; it gave him a strange feeling that he would in some way be coming home. He said, resentfully: "You wait. Great-Uncle Merry knows."

And then, after what seemed a long time, the hills gave way to the long blue line of the sea, and the village was before them.

Trewissick seemed to be sleeping beneath its grey, slate-tiled roofs, along the narrow winding streets down the hill. Silent behind their lace-curtained windows, the little square houses let the roar of the car bounce back from their white-washed walls. Then Great-Uncle Merry swung the wheel round, and suddenly they were driving along the edge of the harbour, past water rippling and flashing golden in the afternoon sun. Sailing-dinghies bobbed at their moorings along the quay, and a whole row of the Cornish fishing boats that they had seen only in pictures painted by their mother years before: stocky workmanlike boats, each with a stubby mast and a small square engine-house in the stern.

Nets hung dark over the harbour walls, and a few fishermen, hefty, brown-faced men in long boots that reached their thighs, glanced up idly as the car passed. Two or three grinned at Great-Uncle Merry, and waved.

"Do they know you?" Simon said curiously.

But Great-Uncle Merry, who could become very deaf when he chose not to answer a question, only roared on along the road that curved up the hill, high over the other side of the harbour, and suddenly stopped. "Here we are," he said.

In the abrupt silence, their ears still numb from the thundering engine, they all turned from the sea to look at the other side of the road.

They saw a terrace of houses sloping sideways up the steep hill; and in the middle of them, rising up like a tower, one tall narrow house with three rows of windows and a gabled roof. A sombre house, painted dark-grey, with the door and windowframes shining white. The roof was slate-tiled, a high blue-grey arch facing out across the harbour to the sea.

"The Grey House," Great-Uncle Merry said.

They could smell a strangeness in the breeze that blew faintly on their faces down the hill; a beckoning smell of salt and seaweed and excitement.

As they unloaded suitcases from the car, with Rufus darting in excited frenzy through everyone's legs, Simon suddenly clutched Jane by the arm. "Gosh—*look!*"

He was looking out to sea, beyond the harbour mouth. Along his pointed finger, Jane saw the tall graceful triangle of a yacht under full sail, moving lazily in towards Trewissick.

"Pretty," she said, with only mild enthusiasm. She did not share Simon's passion for boats.

"She's a beauty. I wonder whose she is?" Simon stood

watching, entranced. The yacht crept nearer, her sails beginning to flap; and then the tall white mainsail crumpled and dropped. They heard the rattle of rigging, very faint across the water, and the throaty cough of an engine.

"Mother says we can go down and look at the harbour before supper," Barney said, behind them. "Coming?"

"Course. Will Great-Uncle Merry come?"

"He's going to put the car away."

They set off down the road leading to the quay, beside a low grey wall with tufts of grass and pink valerian growing between its stones. In a few paces Jane found she had forgotten her handkerchief, and she ran back to retrieve it from the car. Scrabbling on the floor by the back seat, she glanced up and stared for a moment through the windscreen, surprised.

Great-Uncle Merry, coming back towards the car from the Grey House, had suddenly stopped in his tracks in the middle of the road. He was gazing down at the sea; and she realised that he had caught sight of the yacht. What startled her was the expression on his face. Standing there like a craggy towering statue, he was frowning, fierce and intense, almost as if he were looking and listening with senses other than his eyes and ears. He could never look frightened, she thought, but this was the nearest thing to it that she had ever seen. Cautious, startled, alarmed . . . what was the matter with him? Was there something strange about the yacht?

Then he turned and went quickly back into the house, and Jane emerged thoughtfully from the car to follow the boys down the hill.